THE NIGHT OF THE WOLF

First world edition published in Great Britain and the USA in 2023
by Severn House, an imprint of Canongate Books Ltd,
14 High Street, Edinburgh EH1 1TE.

severnhouse.com

British Library Cataloguing-in-Publication Data
A CIP catalogue record for this title is available from the British Library.

ISBN-13: 978-1-4483-0666-4 (cased)
ISBN-13: 978-1-4483-0671-8 (e-book)

All Severn House titles are printed on acid-free paper.

Typeset by Palimpsest Book Production Ltd.,
Falkirk, Stirlingshire, Scotland.
Printed and bound in Great Britain by
TJ Books, Padstow, Cornwall.

About the author

Cassandra Clark is an award-winning scriptwriter for theatre, radio and television. She is the author of the highly-acclaimed Hildegard of Meaux medieval mysteries, as well as this series featuring Brother Rodric Chandler.

www.cassandraclark.co.uk

BOOK ONE

clutched in her hands. Reaching out he prised the package from between her fingers and she stifled a gasp.

'That hurt!'

'I told you I could be strict.'

'You can tell me what it is . . .' She sidled against him. 'Dearest Rodric – please be kind to me. You've no idea how dreadful my life is with that horrible old man—'

'You must not do this, Evelyn. Go back to your bed. Where is your husband?'

'Sleeping. Dreaming of money and sheep.'

'If he did not dream of money and sheep you would be living in poverty. Go back to him.'

Even as he spoke he could feel her heat as she pressed the length of her body against his with greater urgency. Her shift was no more substantial than gossamer and was already rucked above her waist.

As she caressed him she was careful to avoid his wounds but not careful about anything else. 'He's too old for me,' she whispered, lips tickling his ear.

He felt her tongue flicker along his jaw to search for his lips, darting small kisses until she found them. It had been an age since he had held Matilda in his arms and now she was far away, in safety as he hoped, somewhere away from London maybe, perhaps in Guelderland, or still on the ship, or travelling in safety in a char with the others through the countryside around Dieppe. With Adam.

The name entered his head and like a speck of grit would not be dislodged even as Evelyn pressed her lips against his and her tongue continued its teasing entry between his teeth.

He could push her aside in anger now. Say a prayer. Keep vows made to St Serapion as a boy, pretend he did not want her – more honestly 'it': the sin, a double sin to break faith with his saint and with her husband.

He could be a saint himself, resist temptation, if only she would not . . .

He heard her exclaim with pleasure as if there was no going back as she slid beneath him.

'I think you'd better leave.' He rolled aside and pushed the coverlet back.

Archbishop Arundel and the recent self-crowned king, Henry IV, Bolingbroke, the Duke of Lancaster of ill-fame. This duo of usurpers had decided to invent a law to allow them to burn alive any person who happened to hold views differing from their own. Censorship rose to the top of their list of things to do when they seized power.

It so happened that after the bowmen had snatched him from the stake, Master Chaucer's scrivener, Adam Pinkhurst, had quickly pushed a small package of some banned booklets into his hands as he fled. 'Keep them safe! Take them out of London! It's the only copy of the master's *Canterbury Tales*!'

This young woman, Evelyn, the wife of a wool merchant who had chanced upon an attempted ambush not far from here, had found the books when she had tended his wounds afterwards.

He hoped she had not realized the importance of what she had found under his pillow, that she would keep her mouth shut as, surely, as an adulteress, she was bound to do?

The men employed by his host, a merchant prominent in the sheep trade between Wales and London, were lounging about the yard and from their knowing glances when the merchant's wife appeared halfway through the morning, he guessed she shared her favours lavishly among them. It made him wonder about her husband. He liked him. Not only because he and his men had saved him from the attack of a gang of ruffians, but for his steadiness and unassuming good sense and ultimately for his kindness to a stranger.

They had sounded each other out as soon as Chandler regained consciousness after the attack. Glancing round and wondering where he was after being hit over the head, he had taken in the orderly and well-kept chamber in which he was lying and then noticed the worried face hovering above his own.

The man had moved back with a look of relief when he saw Chandler come round.

'Don't try to move. You must be in pain. Could be worse though. Our leech woman has staunched your blood and cleansed your wounds. She left some salve with instructions to my wife to keep you lying in bed until she returns later on.'

'I won't ask where I am,' Chandler murmured through bruised lips as he tried to force a smile.

'You may. And I'll tell you. You are in my house in the middle of a town called Chester.'

Chandler struggled to form a few words in reply. 'All I remember is riding along a greenway . . . in the sunlight . . . then sudden shouting . . . and men appearing from nowhere . . .' It came back to him in a sudden swamping of images. Strangers bursting out of the bushes on both sides of the track. 'Four or five . . . mounted . . . well-armed—'

'We're plagued by outlaws in the woods all round here. After the destruction wrought in Cheshire by Bolingbroke on his way to meet King Richard when he landed in Wales last summer, many families were dispossessed . . . many men outlawed and forced to escape to the woods. Any traveller is fair game now, the men and their families being in such straits.' He grimaced. 'This so-called king, Henry, does not like Cheshire archers. Too much in favour of King Richard and the late prince, his father.'

Chandler stared at the man in astonishment at such open speech. In London he would have been thrown into Saltwood Castle and tortured, talking like this about Henry. *So-called king?*

He looked at him anew.

Unaware of Chandler's thoughts he condemned himself further by saying, 'The Cheshire archers objected to being called out to help a man take the crown from his cousin for no reason other than ambition and rank greed. They showed their disapproval by withholding their fealty. And Henry showed his disapproval by crying havoc on the county, as I'm sure you heard.'

He gave Chandler a quizzical glance then, glancing over his shoulder he lowered his voice. 'We are alone, brother. I would not say this if anyone else was present. Lancastrians are everywhere. They've taken over the running of the town, as in London so I hear. Shrewsbury is now garrisoned by young Monmouth on behalf of his father. Henry's place-man has now assumed control in Chester. I know all . . .' He glanced pointedly to where Chandler's robes were neatly folded on a chest.

On top of them lay his leather travel bag and inside it his rescuers must have placed the package containing the booklets.

His latest saviour leaned closer. 'I have seen the bound pages you are carrying. My wife found the package hidden under your shirt when she ministered to you after you were attacked. I

The merchant smiled. 'It's an honour and a privilege.'

Later Willoughby told him he had to go away for a few days. He did not say where but gave the impression he was going on business. He took several armed men with him but most of his men remained behind.

It was shortly before this that Evelyn had come to his bed and been given short-shrift. Since then she had ignored him. Only the ancient leech woman attended to his wounds now. She came every day and was beginning to cluck with satisfaction at his rapid improvement.

'Soon be ready to be on your way, young man. But take care of this'n,' she indicated the sword wound. 'No riding yet for you.'

Chandler was determined to get off as soon as he could. After Willoughby left he went down to have another look at his horse.

A thickset, handsome youth, a horse-master, was always giving him black looks and he picked him out as the current lover whom inadvertently he had been chosen to usurp. Without admitting what had happened he could not put the lad's mind at rest and could only treat him with a sort of deference that seemed to make him even more suspicious.

With Willoughby now away he had reminded the head man that an escort had been promised as soon as he was ready to leave.

The man grinned. 'Fit enough to sit a horse again?' He eyed him. 'You still look a bit rough round the edges.'

'I'll cope.'

'What about the day after tomorrow, first thing? I'll get a couple of men to guide you through the woods to Dieulacres. It's a day's ride and not that easy to find. Hidden away as it is.'

'I shall be in your debt – or . . .' His hand reached for his scrip.

'All in the day's work, brother. The master said to take care of you while he's away. And that we'll do.'

'That's good of him and you.'

'In the same game?' He winked. 'Be ready. I'll have your horse saddled up.'

'By the way,' Chandler turned back, 'when is he due to return?'

'Who knows? How long is the leading-rein on a half-broken horse?'

It was now, as he was going up to his chamber in the attic at Willoughby's, that he saw Evelyn descending the stairs from the upper floor.

Wondering what she had been doing up there he stepped aside so she could pass when they drew level. She had not forgiven him for his rejection. And he had not explained nor yielded.

Now, in order to show her disdain, she brushed by unnecessarily close, her sleeve contemptuously brushing him as she lifted a hand to adjust her coif as if she had not noticed him. She did not speak. He did not give her the satisfaction of speaking either, but something made him take the stairs on to the upper landing two at a time.

As soon as he entered his chamber he knew she had been inside. A scent of rosewater still hung in the air under the pentroof.

A glance showed that his sword in the worn leather scabbard was still lying exactly where he had left it. He went to the bed and searched under his pillow until his fingers found the soft leather wrapping containing the pages of the little books. Something made him pull the package out and at once he noticed that it was slimmer than before. Quickly opening it he counted the booklets inside. Four. When there should have been five.

With an oath he turned to the door and clattered down after her in time to see her hurrying out of the main doors on to the street.

TWO

A few strides took him across the hall, but when he pushed the door he discovered it was locked. Locked! She had locked him in!

Determined now more than ever to pursue her and catch her red-handed, he tried to open one of the windows, but it was sealed shut.

Raging, he swivelled towards the back kitchen, skirting the obstacles and chaos of cooking for a score of men and stormed through to the yard. The kitcheners stared after him in astonishment. Striding rapidly towards the outer gates he shouldered them open.

She had already reached the end of the street and was inserting herself in among the crowds flocking down the main thoroughfare towards the market.

It took only moments to reach the market square.

He glanced about but could see no sign of her. Once in among the stalls and the slowly moving buyers it was impossible to make much headway. Which way had she gone? Left? Right? Was that blue mantle disappearing into the distance the one she had been wearing just now? He took a gamble and, striding between groups of shoppers as best he could, he followed in pursuit.

Where is the witless girl heading, he wondered when he reached the end of a line of stalls and did not see her. She looked as if she knew exactly where she was going with the book. His head ached. She must have an accomplice. Someone who would want what she had stolen. Who here would be bothered about a bundle of writing apart from the usurper's men? Was she hoping to sell it – or was there a more dangerous aspect to her theft?

He thought of the cathedral with its scribes – they would understand what she had obtained – but she was heading in a different direction, north towards the toll gate. Maybe there was a chantry there with a priest who could read and write? Maybe she intended to have it passed on to this new sheriff for a price? He wished he knew the town better.

'Between whom?'

She took a breath and then, as if dealing a winning card, announced, 'The summoner, if you must know!'

If it was meant to impress him it failed. He gave her a pitying smile. 'You do have some interesting connections. Does your husband know?'

'Don't be ridiculous!'

He wondered if she were lying but who else might be interested in paying for it?

He asked cynically, 'So what's in it for you, do you think?'

'Why are you being so hateful to me?'

'I'm being no more than naturally curious. Come on.' He tightened his hold and pushed her against the wall. Nobody took a second glance. Lover's tiff, they would assume. In his dark cloak he could have been any artisan coming to market. 'We can stand here all day,' he murmured. 'You'll find I can be as patient as an ox.'

'I hate you!'

'I know. You've already told me that. I'm not fond of you either, unchivalrous as it may seem. So what's this about the summoner?'

He allowed her to consider his words and after a moment when she saw he was not going to relent she muttered, 'He said he'd run me in for breaking the ecclesiastic law. He told me I could be excommunicated—'

'For fornication?'

'How do you know that! It's not fair! Whether I have or haven't he'll say I have and that will be the end of things. My husband will pitch me out, my life will be ruined—'

'And so will the lives of others if you follow your foolish plan of stealing my property. You don't know what you're doing.'

'You don't care what happens to me . . .'

'Why should I? You betray your husband, you steal from me, you've proved yourself to be untrustworthy and indifferent to the safety of others – yet you expect mercy? He released her. 'I'm not vindictive. I've got my property back.' With the booklet pushed inside his scrip, before he turned away he said, 'You have no idea what deep water you're getting yourself into, Evelyn. This is no game. Men have died hideously because of this new

the yard as the horses were being brought out. His own was frisking with pleasure at the prospect of exercise. Two men and a lad hurriedly threw saddles on to the backs of the other two.

Chandler felt he owed some explanation to the horse-master and took him to one side. 'I found something entrusted to my safe-keeping that had been taken from my belongings just now and guessing who might know something about it, I followed and got it back.' He showed a corner of the package where it was strapped under his robe, then gave the fellow a piercing glance.

Unabashed, he grasped his meaning at once. 'We saw her run out. She's gone too far. He knew she would. She'll be out on her ear when he returns.' Shouting over his shoulder he yelled, 'Pearce? Ready?'

'I am.' It was the good-looking stabler who had given Chandler black looks when Evelyn had appeared with him earlier, still clearly under the misapprehension that he was being replaced as her favourite. If he only knew, nothing could be further from the truth. It made Chandler wonder if there was a reason for appointing him as escort. No time to dwell on such things.

He swung up into the saddle, grimacing at the rearrangement of his aches and pains and hoping he wasn't going to open up the sword wound on his thigh.

'My gratitude, master, and my thanks to Master Willoughby for everything he's done for me. I fear that if I stay longer I may store up trouble for him as well as for myself. He'll know where to find me if necessary.'

With that he urged his horse towards the street followed by his two escorts.

THREE

They headed east from Chester along the drove road, having escaped the city without attracting much attention, and it was easy to keep up a good pace with most of the market traffic passing them by in the opposite direction. Later, they overtook one man and a small cart, emptied of his wares, and he smiled cheerfully as they rode past, clearly pleased with his short but successful day of trading.

When they were about five miles on they reached thick woodland and, after an almost complete silence since getting out on the road, the two escorts reined in when they were deep in among the trees. Chandler raised his eyebrows, wondering if he was fit enough to take them both on should it come to it. He trusted no one at present.

'We'll not stop long,' the one called Ham said. 'I need to have a piss.'

Chandler was quick to notice the two men exchange glances.

Ham dropped down off his horse and led it a little way under the trees, then slipped out of sight into the thicket.

'He's of delicate manners,' observed Chandler, not at all convinced by his excuse. This was the sort of place where a man could have his throat slit and his body secretly buried in a shallow grave, never to be found. His knife fitted snugly into the leather wristband he wore and his sword, should that be needed for any reason, was within reach.

Close at hand a bird called. It emphasized the solitude of the place. It trilled again and to his surprise Evelyn's paramour, if that's what he was, cupped both hands to his mouth and gave a passable imitation of a wood pigeon. In a moment the first fellow reappeared.

'Let's go.' He was back in the saddle at once and without a word led the way at a brisk trot until they were back on the road. Then it became a canter until the road dipped and they were plunging deeper where it led into the thickest part of the woods.

FOUR

The Abbey of Dieulacres

I t was night by the time they turned off the drove road to pick up a meandering track through good sheep country, a track that Chandler would almost certainly have missed if he had tried to find the place himself. Sheep lay across the hillside as motionless as boulders in the gloaming.

Picking their way between them Pearce informed him, 'Only another couple of miles then you'll be in a bed at Dieulacres.'

The track, overgrown but wide enough for their horses to ascend a short hill in single file, brought them out in front of a plain stone archway on what Chandler guessed was the foregate of the abbey. Defensive walls sloped away on both sides into the undergrowth. Over the walls could be seen the silhouette of a couple of slanting roofs and a tower.

When Pearce dismounted and went over to yank at a bell rope, the sound echoed distantly inside the building. After a long moment when it seemed as if no one had heard it, the peephole creaked open and a face peered out. 'What?'

'Guests seeking shelter for the night, brother.'

'At this time?'

'Hard ride from Chester. Our horses are near done in. And so are we, begging your charity.'

'Wait there.' The flap was shut.

Nothing much happened until a sound of movement on the other side brought another face at the flap. A hooded brute peered out. 'How many?'

'Three, begging your leave, from Master Willoughby, a friend of his who needs the help of your infirmarer.'

'Why didn't you say so?'

The first face replaced the second. 'Bring your horses through, then follow me.'

'I need help with a message I must send, ink and vellum is all I need, and a courier some time soon.'

'I'll show you when you wake in the morning. Now sleep.' His genial manner returned as he wished Chandler goodnight.

Now what brought about that change when I asked about the scriptorium, wondered Chandler as he subsided on the bed and shut his eyes.

Tomorrow. All questions would be answered, like who Willoughby is, why that strange look just now, and eventually how Matilda and the master were faring . . . as soon as I can get a message to Pinkhurst or to somebody else I can trust . . . somebody like Brother Daniel say, to let him know where he can send a reply . . . to tell me what's happening in London . . . to let me know where she is now . . . whether she's safe somewhere . . . whether they managed to escape . . .

Someone was shaking him by the shoulder. Sunlight glared straight into his eyes and, dazzled, he dragged himself to sitting.

It was the infirmarer again.

'Here, drink this, brother. Last night you were asking about sending a message? A courier has just come in and will leave for Chester before midday. Are you up to putting on some speed?'

Blearily Chandler swung his legs off the bed, wincing as he did so. 'Your potion last night had a powerful effect.'

'What you needed. You looked done in. Come.'

He walked with a rolling gait ahead of Chandler down steps, along corridors and out into the open, then beckoned to a novice to conduct Brother Chandler to the scriptorium.

Two or three monks were already at work and only glanced up briefly as he was conducted inside. The master of the scribes took his guest to a cubicle to one side out of earshot where the others were working and Chandler explained what he needed and the reason for haste. It was not much later before his coded message to Adam Pinkhurst was written out in the form of an invoice for documents received, sealed and addressed to the stationers in Paternoster Row where Adam would hopefully be picking up mail by some means or other.

'There is another matter, magister,' Chandler told him in a low voice when it was all done. 'It is this. I carry some booklets written by a friend in London. He has entrusted them to my safe-keeping but I fear that, such is the disorder of the times, I may not be able to keep them safe from harm as he wishes and deserves. Rain, wind, the usual weather we can expect these days, as well as unexpected larcenies, all can wreak such damage on anything as fragile as the little books I carry.'

The magister gave him a shrewd glance. 'We Cistercians are greatly in favour of preserving texts, sacred or secular. You will entrust them to us?'

'I will.'

'I have to remind you that Lancaster, our great and novel king Henry IV, does not have the same regard for scholarship as we do. It is becoming generally known that he has begun to send his censors to the abbeys to inspect our chronicles for anything seditious or failing to accord with his view and that of his archbishop of recent dynastic events.'

They exchanged glances.

'I understand,' replied Chandler. 'I chose Dieulacres because you are somewhat sequestered and may not be a victim of the censors. I'm aware of the new laws and it's one of my reasons for throwing myself on your mercy.'

'And the other reasons?'

'I respect Cistercians for their support of the legitimate king and happened to be close by when . . .' He broke off, not wishing to get into a long and maybe, even now, dangerous explanation of how he came to be in this part of the realm.

The magister's eyes began to gleam. 'You said you brought these booklets from London?' When Chandler did not enlighten him he added, 'We are out of the way at the head of this little valley, hidden almost, once you leave the drove road and the recently wasted and burned lands of Cheshire. But we do hear news from time to time. We understand that a repressive law is being given a trial run before being put on the statute books. It puts forward a most barbaric proposal, to tie a living man to a stake and burn him alive in a high place and thereby visible to all, in order to instil fear in the populace, for the sole reason that theological conclusions differing from those propounded by the ecclesiastical authority in the realm have been honestly reached. The burning alive of anyone holding such so-called heretical

men-at-arms went from building to building until they found
what they were searching for.

The scriptorium.

'Why couldn't you have asked?' demanded the monk in
charge when they swarmed inside. 'See, here it is. Where's the
problem? Why all this noise and turmoil? Read it!' He knew they
probably couldn't, but when he thrust the official version of the day's
work in front of them one man, wearing his sword with a somewhat
self-conscious air, stepped forward and took the sheaves of text and
carried them over to a corner desk, calling for more light.

Laboriously, after candles were lighted, he began to scrutinize
what was written in the untidy sheaf of pages thrust into his hands.

'Our daily accounts,' murmured the monk who had chided the
interlopers for their manner. 'If you find anything wrong with
them I hope you'll let me know.'

Chandler, not wearing a sword and looking as like a Cistercian
as anyone could in his worn robes and, moreover, glimpsed only
by flickering candlelight, prayed that the secret place where the
true chronicle was hidden along with Master Chaucer's stories of
pilgrims in a more innocent period, was as safe as he had been
told.

The men-at-arms, their job of breaking and entering done,
were quickly bored and roamed the large raftered scriptorium
like beasts of the field, but there was nothing to excite their
interest. They stayed a few hours until the censor was satisfied
that everything was in order, then caused some damage, demanded
ale, stole a horse they claimed was one of their own, and eventually clattered away under the archway and down into the lane,
back into the night from whence they had emerged.

Dawn was breaking by the time everything was returned to
some kind of order.

'Now that's over,' remarked Chandler to the head of the
scriptorium, 'I had better take my books and find a place that
will not put you in added danger.'

'Do you think they'll return? Now they've seen there's nothing
here?'

'You heard what their captain said as they were leaving? "We'll
be back!" I do not want to be responsible for what happens if
they find these little books.'

FIVE

Chester, again

S o it was, Chandler, after a long day's hard riding with the company from Dieulacres, entered through Chester's town gate and approached the house of merchant Willoughby and, again, hoped to beg his aid.

It was a strange arrival. The town itself, with no market that day, was empty of shoppers and traders, and when they neared Willoughby's place they found it similarly silent and shuttered as if in mourning.

From the open gates they could see that the yard was lacking its usual comings and goings. On the side opposite the wool shed the kitchen doors were closed and the shutters were across. Even the dogs were silent, sniffing at the boots of the riders as they dismounted, then returning chastened to the kennels.

In the street outside the gates, a knot of people were staring in at the yard without the typical gossiping that would normally have gone on.

The arrivals from Dieulacres milled about, guiltily conscious of the noise they were making while they waited for the porter to let them in.

Chandler addressed one of the onlookers. 'Has something happened?'

The fellow crossed himself and almost as if he could not bring himself to speak he muttered, 'A most terrible accident, brother.'

'To Master Willoughby?' Chandler asked, thoughts immediately flying to the new regime and the systematic persecution of King Richard's supporters.

He nodded, and shrugged, 'To him, also. He will never be the same.'

Fearing the worst, a public punishment of some sort, Chandler could not get much more from him until a woman standing nearby asked, 'Surely you've heard?'

'We've have only this moment arrived, mistress. What should we have heard?'

'It's Master Willoughby's wife, poor fellow.'

'What's happened?'

She lowered her voice and crossed herself. 'She's dead, brother.'

'What?'

Instead of answering she shook her head and edged away.

Chandler turned to his escorts. 'Did you hear that?' One or two nodded and a few whispers passed round the group. He said, 'I doubt whether I can disturb Willoughby if this is so . . .' At that moment the merchant himself appeared at the yard door.

Attired from head to foot in black he began to walk briskly towards the stables when he noticed Chandler and the rest of them by the gates.

'Brother! Back so soon?' Arms outstretched in greeting he came over and despite the sombre group of onlookers who were taking everything in, he thumped Chandler on the back. 'And some of my old friends from the abbey,' he added, noticing who accompanied him. 'Well met, brothers. But what has happened to bring you back so soon?'

'We have heard something we trust is not true—' began Chandler, ignoring his question.

Willoughby took him by one arm. 'Come into the house. A long ride from Dieulacres. Join us, all of you. A grim business. But how could you have heard already? News travels fast. Why, it was only yesterday . . .' He frowned. 'But you look bewildered. Has no one told you what's gone on here?'

Chandler shook his head. 'Someone said that Evelyn – but is it true? Your wife . . .?'

Willoughby frowned. 'That's not the whole of it. Come inside and I'll tell you what I know. I only returned from Shrewsbury this morning. Come, follow me. I can offer you only funeral fare as it happens but you must partake. I insist.'

'I'm sorry for your loss,' Chandler said when he understood that Evelyn's death was more than rumour.

'Come in, brother. Later,' he muttered to Chandler. 'I'll tell all. Let's feed and fettle these good folk from Dieulacres before they set off back. I imagine their exeunt is but for a day. Come,

'Tell me what you wish to tell me, Willoughby.'

'John, call me John. I wish you to stay here a little while. I fear there is more to unravel in this matter than we know at present. You told me you regarded yourself as in my debt after that scuffle in the woods. Now I'm calling in your debt. Your advantage is in knowing no one involved. They will trust you, a monastic, with nothing to gain. They will talk to you more openly than to anyone else. You will be able to give me an objective view of the situation. I admit, I'm at a loss. You may, if you do me the kindness of staying, allay my fears.' He called for his steward.

Chandler was surprised to find the fellow had been standing outside the door, possibly all the while the monastics and their servants had been at table. With alacrity he entered and sat down at the right-hand of Willoughby facing Chandler.

'Now, Blake, tell Brother Rodric what you told me when I arrived home late last night,' Willoughby demanded.

'It was yesterday in the morning but not early, not long before the midday bell sounded from St Werbergh's Abbey church when there was an almighty scream and there she was, lying in the yard with her neck broke. We all rushed out from wherever we were but there was nothing we could do.' He crossed himself. 'Poor lass. I'm still shocked. We all are. It was as sudden as a bolt from the heavens.'

'That's exactly what you said to me when I rode in last night.'

'That's because it's exactly what happened.'

'What happened next after you found her there?' Chandler had to ask.

'Panicked a bit. As you can imagine it wasn't something that any of us had ever experienced. We thought it best not to move her. Somebody ran and fetched the apothecary and the bone-setter, for what use they could be, somebody else fetched a constable, somebody else kept the crowd back because as you can imagine it caused a right furore of everybody advising what to do for the best. It was a jostle and a mob. Women crying. The crowd growing by the minute.'

'So you were first on the scene?' Chandler asked.

'Not I, no. I was inside in the counting house but I heard the scream and was getting out of my chair to see what the to-do was when one of the house servants came rushing in to fetch me.'

'I did see a little beneath the surface of what appears to be a well-founded marriage.'

The steward scoffed at that. 'Not wishing to speak ill of the dead . . .' He spread his arms. 'You know how it is then.'

He was about to leave when Chandler put out a hand to detain him. 'Was she alone?'

'To my knowledge, brother, I would have to say yes. But then I was indoors. I did not notice her go out. And I did not notice who else might have entered the yard that morning.'

'And the porter?'

'To our dismay he tells us he left his place to have a piss and then stayed yapping with his mates in the wool shed long enough for anybody to have walked in.'

'And this roof?' Chandler asked. 'Where is that? Can we see it from here?'

'As Master told you, it's between this and the new wing of the house. You get out on to it through a door on the first floor at the landing on the stairs before the climb up the next flight to your attic. You'll find there's a flat section put in and being turned into a little roof garden, or so was Mistress Willoughby's intention. The wing,' he added, 'was only finished a few weeks ago, shortly before you were carried back here half-dead in fact.'

'Was this little garden much used then?'

'Beginning to be. Mistress Willoughby liked to go up there. It's secluded and away from the wool sheds she disliked so much. It gives a view over the rooftops of the town. A pleasant prospect for those idle enough to enjoy such leisure.'

'I'll want to talk to you again but don't let me detain you now. I can see you're busy. I can probably find my way up to this roof by myself.'

Blake nodded and went back to his accounts.

SIX

Mistress Willoughby's roof garden, Chester

The wool shed lay adjacent to the flat roof of Evelyn's planned garden.

It was used for storing the fells before they were sent on to London in Willoughby's fleet of wagons and then, presumably after treatment, being conveyed across the Narrow Sea to Bruges and the money markets, and then on, maybe, to the northern Italian weaving towns. There were plenty of buyers for good Welsh wool in Northern Europe.

In the short time it was stored here it was kept in an enormous structure built against a high wall that separated Willoughby's property from the one next door.

It was out of sight from anyone on the roof unless you stood up and leaned out round an obscuring buttress.

After leaving the steward to his work Chandler had found the little rooftop eyrie with no problem.

The door on to it was what he had taken to be a cupboard during his convalescence. It gave an alarming creak when he pushed it open, giving ample warning, he thought with some cynicism, to anyone contemplating an uninterrupted tryst out of sight of prying eyes in the yard below.

The sound and the stiffness in getting the door to open would also give plenty of warning to anyone up here to conceal themselves behind the chimney stack next to the sloping thatched roof of the new wing, should they wish to.

He crossed the roof with its wooden bench wide enough for two and peered behind the stack.

A trellis had already been fixed to the wall and the beginnings of a creeper was being trained up as if to create an arbour. At present it was no more than a potential shelter from the weather. Wind and rain would be kept off when the vines matured. Mistress Willoughby would have been quite private in such a haven.

This echoing space was empty now. The fells, he assumed, had been taken in the last consignment of wagons. All that was left here and there were a few wisps of greyish wool fibre, a scent of oil, and an aroma of summer meadows.

As soon as he appeared a couple of fellows emerged from the yard behind him as if to find out what he was doing. He explained what Willoughby wanted, then asked them what they had seen. Even though it was an event that happened only yesterday they were vague. At least they agreed with each other.

They had been sweeping the barn out in the morning when the accident happened, they told him. They knew nothing until they heard the scream and a most dreadful thud that would stay with them all their lives.

It was followed by shouts for help from the stabler and one of his lads who must have been out in the yard. Realizing, as who would not, that something was amiss, they had both hurried outside.

'It was a terrible sight,' one of the men said brushing a hand over his eyes as if to wipe it away.

'What did you see?' Chandler insisted.

The fellow gave him a startled glance. 'What do you imagine I saw? I saw the poor young woman lying on the ground in a pool of blood. And she not stirring from where she lay, crumpled up, like a toy.'

'And the stabler?'

'Hurrying up to see what he could do. His lad shouting and running along behind him.'

'And then the crowd gathered,' added his companion. 'Everybody came out from where they were.'

'All employed by Master Willoughby?'

'For sure, brother. Until the passers-by noticed the calamity and their cries brought others to the scene.'

'Can you name any of them?'

'Our neighbours? Yes, all.'

'And they remained outside in the street?'

He nodded.

'Will you let me make a list of them when we go indoors?'

'For what good it will do.'

'It may come some way to explain how it is she fell from the

It was already evening, the shadows lengthening, the yard in shadow, a sense of funereal gloom thickening over the place. No one it seemed was inclined to work. Nobody had told them what needed doing. The wool clip had gone. This would usually be a time when they cleared and cleaned and enjoyed a little respite after the pressure of getting everything off on the road to London, a time when Master Willoughby returned from meetings with his City bankers bearing news of the good prices he had got for their hard work and with rewards for their diligence.

Now Willoughby was hidden away in his private quarters, only Blake, his steward, allowed entry, emerging with a shaking of his head, and returning to the counting house without a word.

Chandler hesitated to ask him if he might see the body. When he entered one of the small chambers in the new wing a trestle had been erected with a sheet covering the body. He felt he had no right to enter without permission but there was only a priest there and a nun with a companion crossing the yard and following Chandler inside. They were soon kneeling and murmuring through a prayer for the dead.

The priest got up and after few words to Chandler went over to the trestle and lifted the sheet to one side. Her body was horribly bruised. Chandler indicated that the sheet should be replaced. It told him nothing. After another prayer, he left.

The housekeeper was watching from the kitchen window as he crossed the yard and the flurried movement as he approached suggested that she was not alone. In fact most of the house servants seemed to have congregated round the big, square, scrubbed table where the kitcheners ate their meals. As one they rose to their feet when he entered.

Again he had to explain about the task Willoughby had given him.

The housekeeper, a wide-hipped, red-haired woman of about fifty, wrapped in a large white apron took charge of him. 'Sit, brother. We are honoured to have the opportunity to help you in this sad and terrible business . . .' And so on in the same tone he had already heard before.

It seemed to be the case that nobody knew anything, no one had seen anything, and they were all shocked and would never forget the terrible sight of the poor young mistress lying in the yard in a pool of blood.

'The devil curses us,' one of the maids said. 'It is a judgement,' and she began to sob.

'Be quiet, Maud, you have done nothing to warrant judgement,' the housekeeper reproved. 'You're always drawing attention to yourself. It's my view, brother,' she turned to Chandler, 'that the poor thing tripped and fell, maybe going too near the edge of the roof in order to watch people passing by in the street. Why else would she go so near the edge?'

'I understand your master had not yet instructed his men to finish their work there? Were they not about to fix up a railing of some sort?'

'I do believe so.'

'We were told not to venture out there until it was safe,' the tearful maid interrupted. 'But Mistress Willoughby liked her own way and said she needed somewhere more peaceful than the noise of a wool merchant's house with carts clattering into the yard all day.'

'And you are . . .?'

'I make the beds and keep things tidy,' she explained to Chandler. 'I was the one who kept your chamber just so when you were unconscious.'

'Really?' He felt ashamed that he had not thought of such a thing. 'I should thank you for your efficiency,' he remarked. 'I remember very little of what happened until later – I am remiss in showing my gratitude.'

'Don't worry about Maud,' the housekeeper interrupted. 'She's as well rewarded as everybody else.'

She gave the girl a dismissive glance and Maud hung her head. She wasn't much more than a child, thought Chandler, with none of the hard edges that would have protected her from a public scolding.

With the same story that nobody had seen anything and they had no explanation to suggest other than an unfortunate accident, Chandler left them.

It was when he reached the door of the main hall he heard a sound and, turning, realized that Maud had followed him.

She put a finger to her lips. 'I have something I could tell you. I'm on duty now but may we meet later, brother?'

'I'm so-so sad . . .' He tried to bite back a sob but his tears trickled down his cheeks.

'Come on, then, brave lad, we must try to remember the good and all the things she enjoyed about being alive.'

He nodded, grasping eagerly at any sort of comfort, meagre and unhelpful though Chandler felt it to be. 'She liked horses,' the boy said when he had dashed his tears away.

'Did she have a special one?'

The boy looked startled. 'Haven't you seen her? Come with me,' he said when Chandler shook his head. Taking him by the hand he pulled him down the length of the stable block where a line of well-tended horses of different colours lifted their heads to peer at them as they passed until they came to the far end. 'There, you see? This is Pasiphae, the one with a queenly expression. She's looking for her.'

The horse, a well-bred mare, might easily have been searching for her mistress because she gave a whicker of inquiry as Chandler and the boy leaned over the rail and fondled her head.

'She is a fine creature,' observed Chandler. He glanced at the boy. 'So we know her name but what's your name, young fellow?'

'Dickon. I'm going to be horse-captain to Master Willoughy when he's knighted,' he said, tears forgotten for a moment.

'And when will that be? . . . Soon?'

'Soon enough, I expect. We have to wait and see. But it's not too urgent because I'm still only ten.'

They petted the mare for a while until Chandler thought it might be reasonable to ask who else was in the yard when the accident happened and Dickon, eyes wide, shook his head. 'Nobody, brother. Just the horse-master running out ahead of me from the stables with a great bellow. The kitchen staff soon appeared at the windows and when they saw something had happened they came pouring out to see what it was. Then gradually everybody else appeared.'

'And did you happen to look up to see where she had fallen from?'

He screwed up his little face and gave the question some thought. 'I think I did. But I'm not sure. I sometimes think I saw a face peering down, but other times I'm not sure. Does that happen to you?'

'I have one or two lines I want to follow, too ephemeral to be called clues.' He considered Willoughby's expression. 'I'm inclined to think it was a simple accident. Something in the street maybe caught her attention and she stepped too close to the edge? I'm told they were going to put up a safety rail?'

'I should have had that fixed. It should not have been left like that. I had no idea she was going up there. Pure folly.'

'I'm wondering how long you wish me to continue here? I have the urgent matter of a book to take to safety. I thought I might go on into Wales with it, out of Henry's reach.'

Willoughby gave a snigger of contempt. 'If his last excursion into the principality is anything to go by it'll be safe enough there. He won't be returning soon. The Welsh gave him a trouncing at Bryn Glas. Even the hand of God is rumoured to have come down and smote Henry's very own tent with a mailed fist. Did you hear about that?' He looked sidelong at Chandler. 'I hope you realize how dangerous it is there for us English by the way? They don't ask our allegiance first. Questions come last. I don't blame them. They've had nothing but trouble from us ever since Edward I's day. Up north they call him the Hammer of the Scots. And so he was. So what do the Welsh call him? They're too discreet to let us know. But they suffered. And it won't be complimentary.'

Chandler agreed. 'It'll be something apt in their own fiendish language.'

Willoughby turned to him. 'You speak Welsh?'

'Not much.'

'Instead of courting danger and discomfort in Wales carrying this book – unless you have other business there – why not let me take you along to meet a friend of mine? I understand the abbot mentioned him?'

Chandler nodded.

He realized he had come to the point when he explained. 'He's a scholarly fellow, this friend of mine, if you know what I mean, Rodric. He has a collection of carefully chosen writings that nobody knows much about except one or two such as myself and our friends at Dieulacres. He can be trusted to hell and back.'

'And you mean I could leave it with him?' Chandler's spirits rose at the thought. It would mean he could get back to London the sooner and find out what was happening there.

Willoughby gave him a keen glance. 'He lives in the town but I'd rather not be seen visiting while the watch is out and the gossips making something of it. We'll go on business and buy a pair of riding gloves tomorrow morning. I notice you don't have any.'

She frowned. 'I don't know. I didn't see him leave.'

'You didn't see him leave. But he might have left after only a few moments?'

She nodded. 'That's true.'

'Had you seen him before yesterday morning?'

She shook her head. 'Never. When I saw a complete stranger walking up I guessed he must be one of Mistress Evelyn's . . .' She hesitated as if searching for a word. Her eyes were guileless when she looked up at Chandler. 'It's what they say, "when the cat's away" and I feel bad speaking ill of the dead but it's the truth. Nobody else will tell you out of regard for the master. It would wound him terribly to know that she . . .' She bit her lip. 'And to know that the whole town knew . . . Well, you can guess it all, I suppose.'

'Where did your mistress meet these fellows?' He cautiously used the plural and as expected elicited no denial.

She rolled her eyes. 'At church.'

Kneeling in the grass, she crumpled the hem of her smock between her fingers. 'And you're wondering how do I know something like that? And I'll tell you. Because I was the one to accompany her to church and saw everything – and I knew the fellows mostly, they were about town, but I had not seen this one before. I saw the others. They came to the house when the master was away. They knew him, merchants' men and such, and often they sat with him and drank ale and he knew they were present mostly on account of his wife and he thought it a good joke and preened himself that he had such a desirable young wife in his keeping. You've seen how very old he is,' she added, with the judgement only the young can make.

'About forty I would say?'

She nodded.

Chandler smiled faintly.

Despite this, he could imagine the scene she described. Evelyn studiedly well-dressed. The grinning merchants, wondering who would be favoured and whether they would get away with it if they tried anything. Although he liked Willoughby he guessed his vanity was something that often came up during confession. It often made men overconfident.

solar. Anyone entering the yard would have been visible through the windows, but what if they entered from the street door? The one Evelyn had locked against him when she ran off with the master's pages? Did the sight-line include these ground-floor windows? If so, that would mean Willoughby himself could see what was going on up there. But he was away. He had said he did not know that his wife had started to use the place as her own private haven. Yet his servants knew it very well.

Her visitors knew of it as well. Or at least, one of them did.

Thoroughly dissatisfied with the situation he went up the stairs to his attic chamber and wondered why Willoughby couldn't sort this out with official help from the sheriff. It was the man's job to look into suspicious deaths. This was surely suspicious enough to have Willoughby call him in?

In fact, he was surprised that there had been no sign of official interest by now. Surely in the crowd of people who had congregated in the yard shortly after the incident there had been some official figures? Hadn't a bailiff been mentioned, and what was the sheriff doing? Where was the coroner? He reminded himself that it had only happened yesterday.

Evelyn had claimed that she was frightened of being accused by the summoner. He knew these fellows. They often had no compunction in dragging someone before the ecclesiastical court if their exactions were not met. Young women, especially attractive ones, could find themselves in deep trouble if they had no one to defend them. As would be the case if the accusations levelled at them held a grain of truth. Summoners gave the church a bad name. They were an evil that the Lollards wanted swept away. But nobody today had mentioned him.

It was obvious he would have to widen his interrogations if that wasn't too grand a term for what he had been asked to do. He wondered how much Willoughby knew about his work at the Tower. Did he know that he was the friar who had caused a sensation by escaping the heretic fire at Westminster when the new statute was being discussed? He didn't know what Willoughby knew.

He wanted to be done with it and have Galfrido's little books hidden out of reach of Henry's greasy paws and then get off back to London.

His longing to see Matilda was growing and although he knew it would be foolhardy to appear anywhere near Westminster to see if she was still there, he was willing to throw common sense to the winds if he could only hold her in his arms again. He lay on his narrow bed and shut his eyes.

Why, he wondered, had Maud said she was frightened?

A chance came sooner than expected to quiz Willoughby further. When he went down next morning, the merchant reminded him that they were to go to inspect some gloves as Chandler had requested. The peculiarity of his words – he had made no such request – caused him to glance out of the corners of his eyes towards the housekeeper who was bustling in on some unnecessary errand. It offered her an excuse to hover in the doorway.

Chandler took his cue from Willoughby and began to describe the riding gloves he was looking for but it misfired slightly when the housekeeper butted in without ceremony and suggested that he send one of the house men to bring back a few samples for him to inspect.

'I rather feel like getting to know the town a little better as it happens,' replied Chandler swiftly before Willoughby could help him out. 'If, John, you would not mind being my guide?'

The housekeeper might have judged this to be an odd arrangement but she said nothing.

Willoughby smiled at Chandler and added, 'I need to stretch my legs a bit. Too long sitting astride a horse over these last few days. A walk with a purpose would suit me very well, brother.'

Once they were outside in the street he turned to Chandler. 'Well, Rodric, you got out of that smoothly. What do you think to her?'

'Rather above herself for a house servant, is she not?'

'So I think too. Someone has been filling her head with nonsense. I'm beginning to mistrust her just as much as she seems to mistrust me these days.'

'The disloyal seem to be in season.'

'Take heed. Nothing is the same since Henry took the Crown.'

'May I ask you about the sheriff and why he has not been called in?'

'I'm letting him take his time. He was put in recently by

what am I doing?' He came to Willoughby and flung his arms round him in a great hug then patted him on the shoulders. 'You poor old devil, you must be heartsore indeed. Have they found out what happened yet?'

Willoughby shook his head. 'This is Brother Chandler. He's doing what he can to give us a clearer picture.'

The glove maker eyed Chandler from head to foot, appeared to find something agreeable in what he saw and gave him a nod. 'Come and sit down here in this arbour of mine while I fetch the jug from inside.'

Willoughby looked round when Nathaniel disappeared. 'What fracas? Do you know what he means, Rodric?'

Chandler shook his head. 'Something must have happened in the town. Your place is situated a little out of the way of things on Church Street. I don't hear anything once I'm in my attic.'

Willoughby lifted his head when Nathaniel brought out a jug of ale and more beakers. 'What's this about a fracas then, Nat?'

The glove maker poured ale all round then said, 'Those sot-witted apprentices again. Thought it might be clever to swipe a few things from the counters as they rampaged down the street just before closing.'

'Didn't you call the constables?'

'They won't do anything. The ringleader was young Smithson.'

Willoughby nodded as if he knew what this meant. Chandler waited to see if anybody would enlighten him but it seemed to be no more than town gossip and he let it go. The question of gloves came up and eventually, after a rather oblique description of what was needed, Nathaniel went out to return with a half-finished sample and offered it to Chandler. 'Try this for size,' he suggested.

When Chandler put his hand inside he had a surprise. Removing his hand he looked at the fine stitching of the lining, with its cleverly concealed secret pocket, and Willoughby gave a chuckle. 'Clever, eh?'

Chandler put his hand back inside and moved his fingers about. 'Neat,' he agreed. 'Do you have a special job for me? I thought it was going to be the other way about?' He glanced at Willoughby, then from one to the other, unsure whether to be annoyed at being brought into something without being given the details, or merely wary, but instead Willoughby tapped him on the wrist.

He turned to Chandler and his face gleamed with defiance in the flickering light. 'The truth will prevail,' he murmured. 'And now, I believe, you have something for me?'

Chandler fished around inside his robe and found the strap binding the master's booklets to his chest. He loosened it and brought out the small package brought all the way from London by way of Dieulacres. With Nathaniel's eyes on him he unfolded the cloth they were wrapped in and spread it out on one of the shelves without speaking.

The glove maker gave a sigh of pleasure as he fingered the pages of vellum in their small bundles. He picked one up. 'A first copying?'

'But hurriedly made.'

'I understand the need for haste only too well.' He opened the pages of Adam's writings and read a few lines here and there. 'A priceless addition. I'll take them, of course I will. How many? Five.' He counted, handling the pages delicately as if too much in awe to lay hold of them roughly. 'And when will they be likely to find a permanent home?'

'That's where you come in, old fellow,' replied Willoughby, with a glance at Chandler. 'He may want to return for them when this wolf tumbles into the pit.'

'Safe here until then,' the glove maker murmured, still handling the booklets with delicate awe, 'and if need be I shall send them on to a safer place in Wales as none of us can scry into the future, to our rue.'

He smiled suddenly. 'Wolf of the East Henry may be but he is not the only wolf. Prince Owain Glyn Dwr as Wolf of the West has more right to the name with his royal Welsh lineage stretching back to the beginning of time. We shall soon see which wolf will prevail!'

He turned to Chandler with shining eyes. 'This is a great honour, my friend. Your trust will not be misplaced. Master Chaucer's work will be preserved. I would take an arrow for it . . . For King Richard—'

'And the true commons,' replied Chandler at once.

TEN

About town, Chester

After they left Chandler felt as if a great weight had been taken from his shoulders. It had not occurred to him that the burden of preserving the master's last work had fallen to him. At first it had seemed merely a response to his rescuer in the chaos at Westminster, at his unexpected deliverance from the flames, the shouts of the crowd, the snorting horses, the bowmen, Matilda seen as he had last seen her standing behind the billows of smoke simply staring after him as the bag of books was thrust into his hands and he made his escape out of the precinct and across the river to freedom.

Only when he had time to rest in relative safety in the greenwood towards Oxford way after their escape did he understand what Adam had entrusted to him. Now the glove maker had brought it home.

The master's last work?

Was it so?

More than ever his determination to return to London one way or another hardened.

He had to know if Chaucer and his small household were safe from the man Willoughby had referred to as the Wolf of the East.

As soon as they were outside in the street again he turned to Willoughby. 'Wolf is an apt name. Henry has no care whom or what he destroys in his lust for the crown. I trust your friend treads carefully. He has in his possession a store of truth beyond calculation by any mortal means.'

'Come, let's behold one of the yapping wolf pups in his lair then, and after that, job done, I'll take you to meet my dear daughter and her husband, then to lie low for a little while as well we may, given my recent misfortune.' He shot Chandler an assessing glance. 'Your own physical wounds healing well?'

Chandler, refusing even to himself that he was still in pain,

and made him sit in the best chair and accorded all the kindness expected towards his new friend, the recently appointed confessor, Brother Chandler.

It was only when Willoughby mentioned that they had been along to see Master Nathaniel for some riding gloves that Ann had shown any concern.

All she said was, 'Father . . .' with enough anxiety in her tone of voice to tell Chandler she knew all about his unofficial activities.

Her husband came in then, a smiling ginger-haired young fellow, introduced as a journeyman to an important goldsmith in the town. They all had something to eat sitting round a big scrubbed table and Chandler thought of Matilda again when he noticed that Ann was also with child.

They discussed family matters, the couple asking a few vague questions out of politeness towards their visitor and avoiding any talk that could be construed as either seditious or heretical.

A quiet, kindly, normal family, judged Chandler, silently applauding their performance. It was only when a name for the baby was mentioned that some discord arose. If it was a boy Ann preferred Dickon despite her father's raised eyebrows.

He reminded his daughter that he had a stable lad called Dickon. Might it not be confusing?

Chester, it seemed to Chandler after this excursion, was secretly smouldering with thwarted loyalty to the deposed and almost certainly murdered King Richard – or King Dickon as his loyal band of Cheshire archers were wont to call him.

On the way back towards the wool merchant's house he couldn't help noticing how often Willoughby was stopped again and again by passers-by wanting to offer their condolences over the death of his wife. He was known everywhere about the city and it was apparent that he was well-liked.

When it came to the funeral a day or so later the abbey church was packed. The Benedictines conducted matters with gravity and grace.

Chandler could get no real idea what was generally thought about this marriage of spring and winter from the solemn faces around him and Evelyn herself was only mentioned in terms of

Now, in the grey stone church, he briefly caught sight of himself in the brass paten as it was displayed after the Eucharist bread was taken. As a beard on day two, it would require patience for him to begin to regard it as anything like an effective disguise.

ELEVEN

Time to leave

The congregation filed out in solemn mourning and stood around in the churchyard for a time, commiserating with Willoughby, renewing alliances and catching up on town gossip.

Chandler, unobtrusively watching everyone who came out, noticed that a handsome fair-haired fellow was not among them. If he had ever existed he had vanished and left no trace.

It made him more convinced than ever that the maid, little Maud, had invented him after talking to the stable lad or vice versa. Someone else must have seen him if he had entered the house that day. But, it seemed, no one had.

He decided to have a final word with Maud before he left.

There she was now, hair scraped inside her coif, clean neckerchief setting off her rosy cheeks, eyes demurely downcast at some solemn remark from another of the kitchen servants. Maybe he would pose an idle question or two, just in passing. He might remark, for instance, 'As I'm leaving shortly, a word or two, Maud, if you will.'

Anyone feeling a twinge of guilt might give a sigh of relief at an end to his questions and relax enough to unguard their tongue.

Just then his glance, floating over the crowd of strangers, alighted on a plump church man daring to raise subdued laughter from a group of young folk, friends of Evelyn, no doubt, then, quickly stifling his own merriment as he took his leave, the fellow glancing round for someone – maybe, judged Chandler, someone of greater civic importance – to ambush by his wit.

The wild-bearded sheriff was the obvious target. With a couple of bodyguards and a deputy they were just now preparing to leave, but the portly fellow instead turned his back and trailed over to have a word with one of the guildmasters, smug in his chain of office.

When he returned to the path he saw Maud coming down as the
Compline bell began to toll and the moment she noticed him she
hurried forward. 'I can't stay long.'

'You don't need to. I just want to know one thing.'

'What?'

'Who was Evelyn afraid of?'

'Oh, not back to her! Haven't we had enough of her? It was
the same when she was alive. Always the centre of everything.
She led the master a merry dance and we were all supposed to
look up to her and call her Mistress Evelyn. She was no more
than I am, a servant, but she thought herself above everybody else.
Now she's dead and gone are we still to put her on a pedestal?'

Chandler, amused by her vehemence, grinned at her. 'I assure
you, Maud, I am not putting her on any pedestal. I am merely
curious as to why a young woman with everything arranged as
she would wish and with a powerful man as her husband should
be afraid of anyone. She could have no worries over money. I'm
confident that Master Willoughby could buy anyone in this town
ten times over.'

Maud scowled.

'Well? . . . Can't you help me?'

'It's no good trying to wheedle anything out of me. Don't you
know we're all afraid? The entire household is afraid. I know I am.'

'What frightens you?'

When she did not explain he asked again, more gently. 'Why?'

'You know why . . .'

He saw her furrow her brow until she hit on an explanation
that might satisfy him.

'It's if we so much as offer up a small curse these days we're
likely to be run in for breaking some new law they've discovered.
Nobody dare speak. Even somebody like you with the abbey to
back you could be hung from the nearest tree for breaking some
church law or other. Something you didn't even know about.
Look what happened to the king! If they can do that to an
anointed—' She broke off and glanced hastily round. 'They could
even do it to Master Willoughby . . .' She dropped her voice to
a whisper. 'Don't you see, none of us are safe?'

'So what is it you yourself are afraid of – you haven't done
anything to break the law, have you?'

'Now you tell me something, brother, before you go. What's that little figure you wear on a chain round your neck?'

'It's a figure of my saint.'

'What's he called?'

'St Serapion.'

'And who's he when he's at home?'

He smiled. 'You shouldn't talk about him with such disrespect. He's a better man than I'll ever be or, indeed, anyone you're ever likely to meet. He was so close to the Holy Cross and its teachings he came to a momentous decision – he decided the best he could do would be to offer himself as ransom for the Christian merchants kidnapped by the Moslems in Spain.'

'And did they take him instead?'

'They did.'

'And I expect they tortured him, being men. Is that how he died?'

'It is. To his glory and everlasting joy.'

She stared at him for a while. Then she said, 'Let's hope you're not holy enough to take Master Willoughby's place should it ever come to the test.'

Before she walked away he asked, 'Seen Evelyn's mysterious visitor again?'

She gave him a look that could have killed, retorting, 'I made him up, didn't you know?' Then she turned away before he could demand the truth.

He walked up the slope towards the house. It was a question of whether the fines, which he believed in easily enough, were for breaking the church code, or for not providing information when requested. He had no reason to think such a thing but it was a question that existed and it was axiomatic that all questions could be answered.

It caused him to wonder, further, how much danger Willoughby was really in. What could his erstwhile wife have passed on to the lackeys of the new regime? What was there to pass on other than general disloyalty to the self-styled king?

Of course, that was often enough, these days, but was there something else? Could Maud's remark about taking his place mean anything?

*   *   *

'Off to Dieulacres this morning?' Willoughby himself came blustering down the stairs into the hall with his indoors gown of figured velvet billowing behind him. Dapper as ever, it was still obvious he had just crawled from his bed.

'I hope to set off in time to arrive before dark,' Chandler replied, up at six and impatient to be on the road. 'No hurry, John,' he added out of politeness, 'I gather you wanted to see me before I left? But if it's too early—'

'No, no, come into my solar, dear boy. You will not be delayed. No, not at all.'

Gown billowing more than ever he swept ahead into the solar and shut the door behind them.

'And how do Master Nathaniel's gloves suit you? I see you have them.'

'They seem incomplete,' Chandler answered.

Chuckling, Willoughby went to a strongbox and unlocked it by means of a key he wore on a chain round his neck.

After tucking it back under his nightshirt he opened the box and removed from it a few pages of parchment. They were octavo size, just right for slipping inside the lining of the new gloves as Willoughby himself remarked with a sense of satisfaction.

'You will not mind doing this small errand for me, I trust? Brother Senlac is ever to be trusted and is waiting eagerly for them so he can have them copied.'

'Brother Senlac? That's who I'm to hand them to?'

'If you will?'

Surprisingly it was a question and Chandler was ready to agree. 'It seems little enough after the kindness you've shown me,' he replied.

'And you have repaid me in full.' He gave Chandler a long, hard look. 'You cannot know the treachery of a small town like this. A place with our boards of dignitaries we may be, but our perspective is as limited as that of any village council – and our punishments are far worse.'

When the pages were fitted into place Chandler put his hand inside the glove and was ready to leave, but Willoughby insisted on having a carafe of Guienne brought in. Then his escort to take him through the woods had to be summoned and the two men who accompanied him to Dieulacres the first time turned

Pearce nodded. 'Both of us,' he said indicating his silent colleague, Ham. 'Pool our ideas? Why not.'

By the time Chandler was being ushered into the abbot's chamber he had taken off his gloves and was carrying them in one hand. When he entered he found Brother Senlac from the scriptorium already waiting and the abbot himself, attended only by one servant, was settled in an armchair carved with fleur de lys facing a plain bench for visitors.

'You may leave us, Oswald,' he murmured, dismissing his serving man as soon as Chandler was seated. As a prelate of the church the abbot was habitually sceptical of the lower monastic orders including friars of any persuasion, regarding them much as a gamekeeper might regard an army of poachers, but his glance took in Chandler's threadbare appearance with mild approval. Most likely the friars of his acquaintance grew fat and prosperous on the alms they squeezed from church tithes likewise eked from peasants poorer than themselves.

'I'm a follower of St Serapion,' Chandler explained straightaway, reading his look and deciding to get the facts out of the way at once. 'I am not a mendicant.'

'No, so I hear. You're a good fellow, I believe. I have recently heard friendly reports of your activities in a more distant part of the realm. I had no idea it was you when you first turned up here. Forgive me.' He smiled. 'I trust your business in Chester received a satisfactory outcome?'

'Somewhat.' Chandler bowed his head.

'And you have something for Brother Senlac and his scribes?'

Chandler extracted the pages from the glove and handed them over. Both men reached forward at once but Senlac allowed his abbot precedence. The abbot glanced at the pages then placed them on his reading stand within reach.

'I believe you wish to remain as our guest until you can return to London, is that so?'

Uncomfortable at how well the abbot was informed he could only agree. 'I beg leave to throw myself on your mercy again, my lord abbot, at least until the situation ameliorates.'

'We heard an alarming story from our fellow Cistercians about recent events in Westminster Yard . . . however, be confident, our

'What can he do?'

'Hm.' Chandler had one or two ideas that had probably already been floated in certain quarters but thought they were best kept to himself.

Pearce leaned forward and spoke in an undertone. 'He knew they'd got a hold over her and was careful about what he allowed her to know. But she liked playing with fire. He knew the nuns had taught her to read, and when she began poking about among his papers that's when his friends at the abbey stepped in . . . You don't need to remind us we can't say a word out of place with this new bunch running the city. Henry's tightening the screws every day. What is it now? We can't mention Calais. Nobody dare say the name John Wycliffe.'

'It'll be worse in London, no doubt.'

'Likely as not.'

'They'll bribe the City into agreement and hang the rest. There'll be no more risings like Epiphany.'

'What they did to those poor, brave fellows after that shows they mean to exterminate all opposition.'

'You paint a black picture.'

'It is black. The only sign of dawn is westwards, contrarily.'

'You mean—?'

'I mean the Wolf from the West. Him. We're close enough to the Marches and can always get into Wales if we're quick enough, but the rest of them are going to have to stay and put up with it – until the day of freedom dawns.'

The two escorts drank more than Chandler thought possible and eventually subsided into a morose silence, not that Pearce's companion had done more than nod his head in agreement. If he failed to shape his ideas into words at least he looked like a good man to have beside you in a fight.

When they eventually lurched to their feet to go to their beds Pearce grasped Chandler by the arm and pushed his face close to his.

'I never thought we'd be accomplices. You're a good fellow despite this.' He plucked at Chandler's robe. 'I will find out about any losel who might have thought it a good idea to pitch her off the roof, whether out of jealousy or for any other reason. I vow to track him down. Trust me.'

THIRTEEN

The abbey of Dieulacres

I t was not unpleasant, the monastic life, Chandler thought, not for the first time. Regular hours. Good food. Wine of some quality. A daily ritual that focused the mind on eternity and kept you from dwelling too much on the barbaric side of everyday life as it now was. But it could not last. He could not allow it to go on forever.

News from outside was grim. Henry had taken his army north to give the Scots a pounding. Except that it was the other way about and he retreated to York to lick his wounds.

Trouble from Wales, in the shape of the Wolf from the West, Glyn Dwr, was seen as an ever-growing threat. The prince was amassing an army of loyal Welshmen who were angry at having their natural rights taken away by the Plantagenet Henry.

News from London was bleak as usual. Everyone it seemed was under lock and key, either out of choice or against their will. Public hangings at Tyburn were a regular occurrence. Curfew was rigorously imposed. Archbishop Arundel flaunted his power as never before.

The free-thinking Lollards continued their activities but in a minor key. The invitation to recant in public at St Paul's Cross was offered and many took it up. As for those who didn't, there was talk of the disappeared. London, ever unsafe for the poor or rootless, was more unsafe than ever. People fled when they could.

A show trial of a man called William Sawtre who had recanted and then changed his mind was announced.

In his corner of the scriptorium Chandler silently pined for news of Matilda and her child without finding any respite. Nor was there news of Adam Pinkhurst, the cook, and Master Chaucer himself. It was a darkness where they were concerned. It was as if they had never existed. His letter to Pinkhurst went unanswered.

The attitude of 'who says?' is to be condemned. Thoroughly. *He* says what is, and what he says goes. End of argument. Until this priest, this nobody, refuses to accept it!

The punishment is burning, declaims the archbishop. And it will take place in what he calls 'a high place'. His idea of the high place is that everyone must see for themselves what happens to the disobedient – if seeing is believing – which of course he does not accept – but so, logic is not his forte nor that of his king.

In fact, his only true belief is 'might is right'. What will happen as sure as Easter follows Christmas is that those who disagree with him will have their ideas burned out of their minds forever. Or so the Archbishop of Canterbury, Lord Arundel, hopes. And probably prays.

It is the second day in March 1401. The fire is lit. The crowd stands in awed silence at first until the shouting begins as soon as the prisoner appears.

Now comes the test – is seeing believing? Many are praying they are wrong.

A house in the Vintry, London, March, 1401

Chaucer's one-time maid, Matilda Nijmegen, is raging against Brother Chandler – the father of her child – and asks Cook and Adam, 'How can I bring a baby into this world? Tell me that!'

They have just returned from Smithfield where they witnessed William Sawtre bravely going through his prayers in the midst of a furnace of flame.

Cook watches her go outside into the garden and gives Adam a meaningful glance. He takes the hint and follows her.

When he approaches she turns to him in tears. 'Why did they let it happen? How could they?'

When he cannot answer she asks, 'Why did they not help brave Sawtre get through his agony? They did not break his neck as you would expect, to lessen his suffering. Why not? How could they be so heartless?'

Adam tells her that Sawtre told them that no matter how weak the flesh nor how he cried out, he wanted to be aware of the moment when the lord God would open his arms to him and raise him forth to welcome him into the celestial realms.

He pauses. 'He did not cry out, Mattie. You did not hear him cry out. His hymns rose to heaven before him. He did not cry out. He was in ecstasy. He defied Henry and Arundel by the power of his purity and courage. The onlookers gave him strength. You saw that. They prayed with him and shouted his name and he died in glory. He showed how we might survive even though they break and burn our bodies. He is a light that will shine forever. His courage, tenacity and purity will last for all time. If he was of the authorized church he would be chief among saints. St William Sawtre. But because he believed everyone was equal and free he will only be remembered as a man among others with courage above the ordinary. But a guiding light, he will always be that.'

Cook has come out into the garden while he is speaking and when Adam pauses he says, 'Sawtre is a warning. Henry is sending us a warning. It's based on a great lie. It is the lie that we welcome the usurper and hate King Richard. But lies cannot live forever. Heroes never die. Truth transcends everything.'

Mattie thinks, This is well but what sort of world will my child inherit? What can I do? How can I protect a baby from all this? What shall I do? Where shall I go? Adam will welcome the fire if it comes to it. He will step into the flames. He will regard a child – and one not his own – as just another soul. The child has only me in this entire world and what can I do?

She thinks of Chandler, again, allowing him to creep back into her thoughts. She remembers – for how could she ever forget – the time they made love in the little chantry near Aldgate, a sin, flouting God's law in a most holy place, but how could she have resisted him? How to resist? He took her back to the chantry, to his secret chamber and she could not resist. She had never met anyone like him. His face, his eyes, his voice, the way his body matched hers and how she felt such bliss and it could not be wrong, such bliss could not be wrong. And now she carried their child and although she knew it was wrong, she could not believe it. It was like being flayed as she imagined it, to have him torn from her side.

Better than being dead, she thought. At least she could think that. Even though it was death to know she would never see him again. She recalled the way he had outfaced Arundel's henchmen, how he had mocked their captain with the forbidden book in his

He was smiling as he went down u

'Mattie!' Adam is holding her b
Sawtre and Chandler and the maste
all and he tries to comfort her.

He tells her, 'He would feel nc
courage would protect him. His ecs

She puts her hands over her ston

Adam asks, 'Are you thinking of

'Of Rodric. How you all saved hii

'Damn and curse him.' Adam is s
against his rival. 'Do you expect hi

She shakes her head. 'He cannot
lives, they will torture him in the
he dare show his face in London again. He will step back into
the flames like brave Sawtre . . . Would you come back?'

'I'd come back for you and our child.'

She feels sceptical, half smiles at his earnestness, knowing it
can never be tested. 'I hope he doesn't try it. They'll arrest him
and they'll not fail a second time.'

Adam had become close in the agonizing months after Master
Chaucer had failed to meet them at the port where they had
intended to take a ship to Gelderland. They did not know what
had happened to prevent him escaping to safety. It slowly dawned
on them that he had been secretly picked up by Arundel's men
and dragged off to Saltwood for interrogation. All they could do
was find a safe house and wait for news. Adam was no more
than a brother to her but he was one she knew she could trust.

The abbey of Dieulacres. March, 1401

A courier did at last reach Dieulacres with news from London.
It was intended for everyone but it hammered straight between
Chandler's ribs and left him breathless with rage.

for H
and f
Ha
It
woul
confe
All
to hin
of dis
He
Ev
Thi
A
regarded?

The monks were silent. They gathered round the courier as if in the hope he could make things better, but his presence has the inevitable aura of death. He knows it.

He goes at once to the church and throws himself at the foot of the cross. His face had been streaked with tears all the long miles of his ride. Now the monks take him into their embrace. He is not the one at fault. After confession he lies for days on end in the hospitium like a dead man. Unmoving. Days and nights pass with the only sign of life the salt tears falling from his eyes. They will not stop.

The monks know how such an act of inhumanity against a fellow human being is to be regarded. They pray constantly. They try to find it in themselves to forgive the instigators. They confess their inability to do so. Some things can never be forgiven, no matter what the church fathers tell them.

They themselves cannot yet know that worse is to follow when Henry destroys their ancient abbey of Strata Florida where all the royal books recording the lineage of the high princes of Wales are kept, where the ancient myths of Cymru are written down. Monks are put to the sword for resisting. But that is yet to come.

Now, one voice manages to raise itself in prayer, ringing to the vault to invite all souls to sit on the right hand of the lord and the evils after the regicide to be remembered for all eternity, world without end. The voice prays that they maintain a faithful record of the measure of the sins of the age and strive without cease to keep the record true.

That night Chandler has a dream of bodies falling from the sky like rain, the sound of their screams wakes him, the way the sound abruptly stops, leaving something that might be called silence. Yet it fills his ears with its aching clamour.

When he fully awakes he hears one of the monks screaming in his sleep.

The darkness continues.

The life of the abbey continues.

The monks write up their chronicle, notably from the Epiphany rising soon after Henry's illegal crown is placed on his miserable head, to the second day of March a year later when, as it was believed, the crown of heaven is bestowed on the head of William Sawtre to his everlasting glory.

This period of roughly the first four hundred and seven days and nights of Henry's reign brings scant joy or honour to the realm.

As it was written in the prophecies of Merlin, the Mouldwarp indeed held sway after the Lamb had been deposed exactly as it was foretold.

Elaborate care is taken to lock their treasonable, seditious and heretical chronicle in an even more secret place that night.

In the privacy of Chapter they discuss a safer, more permanent place, one that will be inviolate for a thousand years. Brother Rodric makes a suggestion.

There are further discussions.

To the abbot and the master of the scriptorium he reminds them of the secret of the riding gloves he wears. A plan takes shape.

ONE

C handler's beard flourished over the rest of that calamitous year of black portents and their even blacker harvest. Autumn came and went. Winter turned to the spring of 1402 and at last he was given his instructions to take his leave of Dieulacres and set out on the long and perilous journey to London.

His beard was intended as a disguise. With his silver talisman to Serapion concealed and with a cloak over his shoulders in plain worsted, he could pass as anyone of little or no importance. His riding gloves looked like everyone else's.

Approaching the city of London at long last he braced himself to queue up at the busiest gate into the City. He couldn't believe his good fortune when the guards did not give him a second glance. Tagging on to a line of fellow travellers he shuffled in after them and then he was through and heading straight for Smithfield to pay his respects.

In all the coming and going the men-at-arms of the new regime, Lancaster's men, seemed to be everywhere.

The ashes of Sawtre's fire had long ago been cleared away and people were encouraged to walk over the burned scarring of the paving stones so it would not become a site of secret pilgrimage, a shrine to courage, truth and compassion.

One stalk of myrtle was lying on the ground but might have been dropped without purpose, carelessly, from the hand of any passerby.

Chandler walked round it, nevertheless.

When he eventually took the ferry up to Westminster later that day he kept his head down when he alighted at the familiar steps but he could not help running a hand over his beard when he noticed some women standing on the quay staring at him.

He did not know them.

He wasn't sure but hoped only that it was because the beard

enhanced his manliness. Judging by the expressions on their faces this might be so. It had been the same in a few other towns he passed through on his journey from Dieulacres. At first he put it down to being a stranger or to his own forgetfulness about what it was like to be seen about in public, until he understood it another way.

Now, when one of the women caught his glance he went up to her and asked as unctuously as any mendicant, 'Maybe you can assist me, dear lady? I wish to find a scrivener to copy some verses in a fine court hand for gifts to my flock. I'm told such a fellow may live somewhere hereabouts?'

'Try the palace, brother. I would.'

'My needs are too humble for the royal clerks to bother with.' He smiled with a deprecating shrug. 'I was told there was a scrivener working here for a pittance . . . but no matter.'

As he began to walk away she put out a hand, 'There was one working for Master Chaucer,' she told him, pointing to the row of houses opposite, 'but that was in the old days. I haven't seen anyone there for a long while now.'

Another woman clipped in, 'Try Paternoster Row in the City, brother. They'll have jobbing scriveners by the dozen there and happen that Adam who used to work for the master has gone back there.'

He thanked them with a flourish.

Taking a closer, but still casual look at the house, he saw that his first impression was confirmed. It was empty although not shuttered. It looked as if it might be about to be leased to a new tenant any day.

So where are they now? All he had to go on was a reply from Brother Daniel. It had reached him at Dieulacres. Couched as a list of cures that any monk would ask for from the old fellow's famous herb gardens, it informed him that the leasehold was now ended and the tenant gone no one knew where if not abroad.

'The harvest,' he had added in a postscript, 'has been brought safely in.'

Such ambiguity was not lost on Chandler. It must mean – he prayed it meant – that Matilda had safely given birth. He yearned to see her. And, of course, their child, no matter how difficult it was to imagine a new, living soul where one had not existed before.

He decided to visit some of his old allies and, taking care to avoid any streets where he might be remembered, he lodged overnight in a Thames-side tenement near the Vintry, and he departed early next morning transformed into a simple yeoman, drably garbed in working clothes picked up for a silver coin from an itinerant ragman.

Satisfied that Arnold Archer, a city coroner, his old school-friend from a different era, would not recognize him, he presented himself at the door of the mortuary like a mourner, which, indeed, in some ways, he was.

Archer frowned at the untidy bearded fellow asking for alms and was about to put his hand in his pouch when Chandler grinned up at him from under his hood. 'Good day, old friend. Still sorting bones?'

Archer gaped, glanced furtively from side to side then stepped back. 'God's teeth! You nearly gave me a fit!' He pulled Chandler inside, slammed the door and bolted it. 'What in hell's name are you doing here? Don't you know they'll have you back on the fire as soon as look at you?'

'Hopefully they won't get a chance to look at me. Where are they all?'

'Come through into my inner chamber. We're dancing on hot coals ourselves these days. Sit down. Drink.' He poured a goblet of wine from a carafe standing by and sat down opposite Chandler, his hands laced under his chin. 'Well?'

'I've been away . . .'

'I'm aware of that.'

'I dare not send a message in case it was intercepted.'

'I guessed as much. I saw you ride for your life from Westminster precinct . . . I also saw you receive a gift from Galfrido's scrivener?'

'Safe. They will not get their hands on it now.'

'Have you heard what has happened since?'

'That's why I'm here. I couldn't keep away any longer . . . and I had a more recent message about – about a personal matter . . .'

'I know all about that. I met her. I attended her, in fact. You need have no worries. She's fine and so is the boy.'

'The boy?' Chandler felt the air fill his lungs. He stifled a shout. For some moments he could not speak. Archer regarded him with amusement.

Eventually Chandler asked, 'So where is she – it?'

'He. They have gone into hiding.'

'I suppose you won't tell me where?'

'If I knew, I might. But they're keeping on the move for safety's sake.'

'Pinkhurst with her?'

'No. He's plying his trade at Paternoster Row as if all's well with the world.'

'So who is protecting her?'

'Cook.'

'And Galfrido with them?'

Archer shook his head.

'What do you mean? Where is he?'

'He told no one he was going into hiding. He was simply not there one day. We know nothing.'

Chandler stared at him in horror. 'Saltwood?'

'We did fear that.'

'Did? And now?'

Archer frowned. 'We know nothing, Rodric. Nothing at all.'

'He will not survive a place like that. Not at his age. Pinkhurst was all but done in when he was eventually released and he's a fit young fellow. But Galfrido?'

'He drew an instalment of his pension shortly after you left. That was in the summer, last June, some time like that, early on.'

'But that's over a year ago.'

'And the rest.'

'But surely –'

'You know what he was like. We believe he sent a coded message in one of his last little poems. It's called *"The Complaint to his Purse"*.'

'So what did it say, this poem?'

'He pointed out that he hadn't received his pension but that if he did he would be able to leave London. I think it was a piece of blackmail. If he stayed and anything happened to him all his high-ranking friends would kick up a fuss on his behalf. Don't forget he's also related through his wife to Henry, the conqueror of Albion as he calls him in the poem.' He gave a sarcastic laugh. 'The poem seems to be saying that if he's paid off he'll cause no trouble. That's how I see it. Remember how he used to moan on that he couldn't write the eulogy Henry wanted?'

'I remember you telling me how Henry managed to frighten some doggerel out of Gower.'

'That arse-licker! He even destroyed his dedication of *Confessio Amantis* to dear Richard as if he had never existed and made it out to Henry instead. I can't stand the smug devil – anyway, that's by the by. Some arrears were in fact waiting for Galfrido at the Exchequer not long after the poem came out, and then silence. He knew it was safest for everyone if none of us knew where he was going. I can see you're looking sceptical – but don't forget that trip he made to Calais back in January before the earls were . . .' His expression hardened. 'Before that catastrophe.' He pulled himself together. 'No point in dwelling on the past. Galfrido was no fool, no sitting duck. He would get out while he could. It's my belief he went over to Calais to fix things up if, or when, it became necessary to flee.'

'So you think this poem was his way of letting everyone who counted know what he was about to do?' Chandler was sceptical.

Archer seemed to change the direction of his thoughts. He asked, 'Do you remember where Matilda comes from?'

'What's that got to do with it?'

'When she arrived in England as a little girl she was a damsel in the retinue of Sir Paon de Roet, a knight from Guelderland, father of Catherine and Philippa, Galfrido's wife.'

Ironically Chandler asked, 'The retinue then of Mistress Catherine Swynford?'

'As was. *La belle Catherine.* My lady of Lancaster. As is. The point I'm making is that Matilda comes from a place called Nijmegen in Guelderland so she still has family there.' He said no more.

Chandler was startled. 'You really think that's where he's in hiding?'

Archer nodded.

'It's close enough to Hainault,' Chandler observed.

'That connection as well. Yes. Nobody would want to mix it with the Hainaulters if they had the aim of harming him. For protection he could do no better.'

'Even so you look worried, Arnie, old man.'

'We are all worried, all the time. No one knows when the knock on the door will come. The bell tolls for us all, every one. Yes, I am worried. And you should be the most worried of all.'

He stayed mewed up at Archer's for a few days while he contemplated the problem of how to deliver the contents of his riding glove to the contact at Grey's Inn.

To be honest, he was also hoping news would come in to let them know where Matilda, Cook and the baby were hiding out but, as Archer himself said, no news is good news and he wasn't expecting to hear from them yet. And so the days passed.

When he could not contain his impatience any longer he suggested that he might go over to St Paul's to have a word with Adam Pinkhurst himself in case he could tell them anything new, but Archer refused to let him out of the house.

'Believe me, you're not invisible. They'd recognize you and have you dragged up before that ecclesiastical court before you could say "the devil be damned",' he warned him. 'Your beard may be making you preen but I can tell you, if you'd given me a second longer I would have recognized you as soon as I clapped eyes on you the other morning, especially if the light had been better.'

He was adamant, even going so far as to carry the key of the main doors around with him. 'You can have it when I say so, you cursed imposter. Now keep out of sight. Tonight I'm having a body brought in.'

'Anyone we know?' Chandler asked, more to calm Archer's sarcasm than in the expectation of an answer and Archer went off, chuntering to himself about mendicants, to prepare the mortuary for an autopsy.

Unchastened about risking going out in public, Chandler wondered if it would be feasible to get some news from inside Saltwood

Castle. He was sceptical of Arnold's opinion that Galfrido had had the foresight to arrange his own escape. Of course, he would have known about the earls' rebellion in its planning stage at the now famous meeting in the Abbot of Westminster's lodging and, fearing their defeat, would have tried to ensure safe passage to thwart the retribution that would inevitably follow.

Even so, something might have stopped him making use of it himself. Look how Despenser, escaping to south Wales after the failed rebellion, had taken ship only to be deposited back in Bristol by the turncoat shipman to face a brutal death at the hands of the Lancastrian guard already there. Just so had the Earl of Huntingdon, heading for a safe ship lying off the coast of Essex, been turned over to the mob at Pleshey by his own mother-in-law.

At Saltwood there would be carters and servants and many other folk going in and out of the place. Somebody would know if there was an illustrious poet like Chaucer, famed throughout Europe, residing within. A word, a glance, something would reveal the truth, he was sure of it.

He waited until later that evening when Archer had scrubbed his hands clean and settled down with a carafe of Guienne and instructions to his cook to bring in a goodly portion of cheese and dried apple, before broaching the question.

Archer, as expected, looked at him as if he were mad. He held out both wrists. 'Where are my manacles?'

'Someone will know who's in there.'

'If he is there. But he's not.'

'Are you just saying that because if—'

'Take my word for it.'

'He's been gone for over a year.'

'So?'

'It's a long time. With no word?'

'Indeed . . . And it's also long enough for a little soul to have come into the world without a father and start to walk and talk—'

'What's she calling him?'

'You can guess.'

Chandler felt shame creep over him. 'I've failed her. What day was he born?'

'You'll have to ask her.'

'But it's not only Galfrido, we don't know where she is either. If I had any idea I would go to her—'

'She doesn't think that. She feels you've abandoned her. She saw you riding away from Westminster and never heard a word afterwards.'

'There were problems.'

'I'm sure there were. But anyway, this is all hypothetical. I've no idea where she is now. With Cook to defend her I'm sure she's safe. It's best not to know these things, Rodric. It leads to needless worry and eventually to ill-considered and hasty action. And, under pressure, can even you be sure you wouldn't give in to the torturers? You surely understand that?'

There was no point in disagreeing. Archer also had his own position to consider. It could not have been easy for a regular orator at the Fleece to convince the men loyal to the usurper's new regime that he was to be trusted as one fully on their side.

Archer said as much. 'I'm giving up being coroner and making way for, you'll never guess, so I'll tell you, Tom, Chaucer's son. What do you think to that? And,' he continued, 'he's also in line to be appointed by Henry as his Chief Boteler.'

'Henry's playing a crooked game.'

'He's no chess player. Arundel will be behind the appointment. If he has silenced Galfrido this is a simple but shrewd move to allay suspicion.'

'Thomas Chaucer. Who would believe it. Doesn't he have any doubts about his father's welfare?'

Archer grimaced. 'Ever loyal, is Tom. Who knows how he'll play it? He's making himself popular in the Commons. But not too popular, we trust.'

He refilled their goblets and chewed on some dried apple and cheese, pushing the platter across the table towards Chandler who asked, 'Do you know what I was thinking when the flames began to lick at my shins?'

'Your immortal soul, I hope. Forgiveness for your many heresies?'

Chandler gave a wan smile. 'I saw a vision of heaven.' Before Archer could ask him what it was like he said, 'I saw myself sitting in the Fleece with you and a bunch of our old ale-mates listening to some far-fetched yarn as we used to do and joining in the verbal scrap afterwards to tear it to shreds. That's what went through my mind.'

'You are surely damned.' Archer scratched his head. 'I'm honoured to learn that I figured in your thoughts at an auspicious moment of your ill-begotten life, Rodric, my dear, dear fellow. Most honoured,' he added. And this time he was not being sarcastic.

So with a visit to the print shops on Paternoster Row vetoed by his host and his plan to stake out Saltwood Castle shown for the desperate ploy it was, Chandler tried another idea.

'You won't advise against going to visit Brother Daniel in his gardens, will you?'

He did not admit that he was desperate to find out whether his sacristan, Martin, had escaped the wrath of Arundel, but Archer gave him a black look and replied, 'I've been thinking about what we might do with you. I understand why you risked coming back but there's little you can do here except put yourself on the roasting spit. If there had been solid news I would have got it to you through Daniel in that code you used when you wrote to him ordering herbs for the abbey infirmarer.'

'He showed you it?'

'Of course he did. It was a clever ruse. I congratulate you for thinking of it. I use herbs all the time. It's my job – even the dead need to be embalmed in a decent manner.'

'I would still like to go out there.'

'What on earth for?'

'To check up on . . . I suppose you didn't see Brother Martin while you were there, did you?'

'Who's that?'

'The one-time sacristan at my chantry. I suppose that's still standing or have they razed it to the ground?' He hadn't thought about it for an age.

'Still there. I pass it often. All locked and barred. Sometimes a few people standing about outside as if they're waiting for you to fling open the doors.'

'One day,' Chandler promised. 'One day.'

'And no, I haven't given a thought to Martin. He was a good fellow but he struck me as only a temporary addition to your work. I didn't know he was down at Hackney.'

'He could have stayed with me forever if things had been different. He'd been thrown out of Oxford for supporting Wycliffe. I was his last resort.'

'Maybe he's gone north and become a hermit like John of Bridlington or fled with other Lollards to some secret place where they can measure the stars with their astrolabes in peace?'

'He could have. Maybe he has. I thought I'd rather like to know.'

'Let's go then. I'll come with you. You can be my mortuary assistant. Your beard fits you for the role.'

TWO

Daniel's herb garden in Hackney

S o, Archer's old mule fetched from the stables at the back of the mortuary for the use of his mortuary man, and Archer himself mounted on a solemn-looking ambler, they set off. Chandler had missed the hustle and bustle of the City. The old streets were hauntingly familiar.

It was here, he thought, as they rode down Aldgate, that Swynford's men-at-arms had tried to drag him off at sword point to do his bidding one morning and he had resisted, earning a sword or two as trophies, and Swynford's grudging respect when he found out what had happened. When they eventually met he requisitioned a good horse for him and the entourage had set off for Pontefract Castle and the imprisoned, doomed King Richard.

There also was the lane leading to the house where Chaucer had dwelt before moving for safety into the enclave of Westminster Abbey that last Christmas he was seen around. It was the house where Chandler himself had made a promise to return to Matilda after they had . . . with a jolt he realized that must have been the very night when the child was conceived – the thought shook him but he anticipated the downward spiral of his yearning and instead remembered the chambers he had rented above the Aldgate gatehouse, just now coming into view.

In a voice unexpectedly thickened by emotion he urged the mule alongside Archer's bigger mount and asked, 'I suppose that old fellow who used to tend the severed heads on the barbican is never short of work? He must be thriving.'

Archer shook his head. 'Gone. Took a knife in the guts late one night. Whoever did it got away. Some grudge or other.' He looked sidelong at Chandler. 'It is not as safe as it was in your day, my man.' His eyes flickered towards the gatekeeper and the guards checking people in and out.

Chandler took the hint and, lowering his head in an as

obsequious manner as he could manage, he held his tongue until they were safely through the checkpoint and riding out into more or less open country.

'And another thing,' he said to Archer when they were out of earshot of any passing strangers, 'seeing the master's old house made me think about your astrologers.'

'Keeping a low profile. What do you expect? . . . Poor Despenser. He was there that night when you were invited, wasn't he?'

'And his wife, Lady Constance. She must be distraught, imagining what they did to him at Bristol. They spared nothing in their descriptions of how he begged to be treated as a prisoner and not be executed without trial.'

'These beheadings by the mob are barbaric, encouraged outright by Henry so he can point to them and say, "Look how much the people are angered by the disrespect shown to me, your one true king." It would never have been countenanced in Richard's day. He would have reached out with both hands and begged them to calm their rage and live as good and reasonable people while they tried to sort out their differences.'

Thoughts busy with Despenser's monstrous treatment at the hands of the Bristol mob, aware of the stories of how their vengeance had been encouraged by Lancaster's men-at-arms with threats and bribes, they rode on in silence until Archer said, 'And anyway, they were astronomers, not astrologers. We're not all trying to turn base metal into something with which to enrich ourselves. Some of us see more value in adding to the store of human knowledge for its own sake rather than destroying what little we do know.'

Brother Daniel, once a successful merchant and importer of herbs, and now a gardener famed for his supply of cures from all over the known world, was tending some small shoots in a row of pots in one of the far lean-tos at the bottom of the garden where the high walls abutted on to nearby buildings.

When he saw a bearded beggar strolling down the path towards him he did not hesitate. With a brief, friendly greeting to Archer, he approached with outstretched arms and took him into an embrace. 'Rodric! What on earth does this mean?' He ruffled his beard.

'How did you know it was me?'

'By your build, your walk, your aura, so many clues, luckily mostly unobservable to those who don't know what to look for. In reality such things can never be disguised. And you? Courting danger as usual? You know you're still on their list? . . . But here, so very welcome, my boy.'

Chandler gave him a close look. 'You're no older than when I left.'

Daniel gave him a sly smile and raised his eyebrows. 'Do I not have my elixirs?'

They all three sat in the shade under a rampant south-facing vine and one of the gardeners brought a cordial and some ripe peaches for them.

'He's looking for news about Brother Martin,' Archer announced when various incidental matters had been resolved and his own herbal requirements had been outlined. 'I warned him it wasn't safe to be on the streets, but you know how obstinate he is. He's avid for news.'

'I am listening to this, Arnold, and I shall remember the disparagement in your tone until I obtain redress.' Chandler turned to Daniel, more seriously asking, 'I hope you have news?'

'I do. As of this morning when I last heard, Brother Martin was pruning fruit trees over there.' He pointed across the garden.

Chandler rose to his feet in astonishment. When he managed to make out a black-robed figure in the distance he strode over without another word.

Martin jerked his head round when he heard someone hail him as brother then did a double-take. His reaction was much like Archer's when Chandler had appeared at his door. 'Hell's teeth,' he muttered. 'How did you get here?'

Greetings done with, smiling from ear to ear, he accompanied Chandler back to the arbour under the vines and all four caught up on the events of the last year. It seemed to Chandler that so much had happened, so much that was worse, even, than the dire news that had reached them at Dieulacres, that he wondered how any of them had the strength to continue.

'I expect Arnold told you that Galfrido's son Thomas has been taken into the Commons and elected speaker?' Daniel mentioned when Chandler voiced his horror at what had been taking place in his absence. 'The Commons are a voice of comparative reason in the madness of the times. The true commons, after all. I see a confrontation between them and Lord Arundel if his insanity continues. They will not countenance more burnings. The entire City is still in shock and it's almost a year since William Sawtre of beloved memory met his Maker.'

'St Chad's Day,' Martin murmured, referring to the seventh-century saint, almost a contemporary of the Venerable Bede, and a great and devout healer up in the north country at Lastingham before the Conquest. 'They chose St Chad's Day, to mock him, maybe? "Come down and pluck your holy martyr from the flames?" The second day of March must always be remembered.'

Martin glanced round at the others in the greatest puzzlement and added, 'It could have been Arundel's choice – to bring spiritual solace and physical healing to the world – instead he chooses violence and the most barbarous punishments ever to be inflicted on fellow human beings. Is this how he wants to be remembered? To be sure, no one will forget his strutting ambition and the barbarous means by which he tries to attain it. But I cannot stop asking myself the same question over and again. Why? Why is it worth the opprobrium? I shall never understand.'

'Nor do we,' Archer folded his arms.

'We shall endure,' replied Daniel. 'Barbarity cannot last forever. It will eventually destroy its own self. Life is stronger than death.'

Unconvinced by Brother Daniel, so dark were his thoughts, Chandler was at least satisfied that Martin was safe and his identity undetected within the sanctuary of the herb garden. Nothing more could be told about Chaucer's whereabouts nor of Matilda, her – their – baby, or Cook.

Before he and Archer took their leave he murmured to Daniel that he had something to ask in private.

When they made an excuse to inspect some new plants recently arrived from overseas and were alone in one of the plant sheds, Chandler took Daniel by one arm. 'You will have noticed this glove wrapped in a bundle . . .'

'To escape observation, yes?'

'It contains pages of the true events leading to the usurpation and these months afterwards. It's written by the scribes at the abbey of Dieulacres. Their scriptorium was invaded by Henry's censors and his armed guards in the first wave of his purge. Fortunately for the preservation of the written record the monks had already thought to hide the true chronicle in a secret place. I have the pages here. They wish them to be kept somewhere where they might be read in safety for the next thousand years.'

Daniel gave a faint smile. 'Should anyone a thousand years hence be interested in the events of these transient days of ours . . . Do they have anywhere in particular in mind?'

'They have connections with Grey's Inn and thought I might try there . . .'

'But you lack the means to gain entry without attracting unwanted notice? . . . Leave it with me, dear boy. One of my lawyer friends from the old days is master there.'

The manuscript was handed over and vanished somehow into one of Daniel's vast but unnoticed pockets in his gardening gear.

As they returned to the others he said, 'There was a most interesting fellow at the Inns a few years ago, a student and later a friend of the master as am I. Name of Owain Glyn Dwr.'

'Ah,' said Chandler. He left it at that. Things began to fall into place.

'You might notice what will happen,' Brother Daniel continued, 'now that this true Prince of Wales has shown what he and his people think of Henry's invasion of their country.'

'I hear Glyn Dwr won his first major victory against Henry's army at a place called Mynydd Hyddgen.'

'A fitting retribution for Henry's bad faith when it came to settling matters after the Tudor brothers took Conwy Castle with a force of only a dozen men!' He chuckled. 'The prince is an orator. His men are fiercely loyal. He has right on his side. Always the strongest defence.'

When he and Archer took their leave they returned the way they had arrived through the Aldgate and were back in Archer's mortuary shortly before curfew.

'I can see you were revolving matters in your mind on the

ride back but as you have not shared your conclusions,' remarked Archer as they separated that night, 'I hope you're not going to do anything foolhardy? Not just for your own sake but for the sake of all of us.'

'What can I do? . . . I will do nothing to put any of you at risk.'

Archer gave him a look from under his brows. 'Fair enough.' He was clearly unconvinced.

THREE

Farewell to London

He couldn't sleep. His question would not be resolved. What could he do? A hundred times, it seemed, he got out of his makeshift bed in one of Archer's attic chambers to stare out of the window at the nighttime City.

Looking at it, sleeping, only a flare here and there lighting up the corner of a wall or a street door far off, the place seemed uninhabited. Maybe that's what the archbishop craved? A dead city. One completely under his control. One that could not raise a question about his own morality?

London, City of the Dead. His image of paradise?

Next morning he was in a lighter mood. Not light. But lighter. Definitely not as dark as his night thoughts.

'Archer. I thank you for your hospitality. Should you ever need sanctuary then come out to Dieulacres and the monks will take care of you.'

'Are you leaving?'

'I think it best. My presence here could easily be detected. It would bring a whole heap of trouble on you and I would never want that. I'm moving on. And of course, discretion is our watchword.'

'So no clue to where you're going?'

Chandler shook his head. He had not concealed his riding glove and its contents but nor had he drawn attention to it either. He would have liked Archer's help but dare not put him at risk. It was safest for him not to know what his own secret purpose was for being here. Brother Daniel would take care of the written pages of the uncensored chronicle as he had promised.

He said now to Archer, 'What you don't know they cannot force from you. You've shown me how I might come to understand that.'

Archer helped load his saddlebags with food for the journey and filled two water bottles for him. Not that they contained only water. He also insisted that his journey might be less fraught if he attired himself in something more respectable, and thrust at him a nondescript houppelande in faded red.

'You won't look wealthy enough to tempt robbers, but nor will you look as if you're a felon, asking to be thrashed for escaping your manor.' He added, 'You can take the mule. It's eating me out of house and home. I shall be glad to be rid.'

'Are you sure?'

'No, no, you accursed sotwit, of course I'm not sure. I don't mean a word of it . . . Just remember you won't get much speed out of it. Go on, get out now before the market makes the streets impassable.' He held the mule's bridle for a moment. 'Listen, if you go to see Pinkhurst, don't mention me.'

'I'm not going to see Pinkhurst.'

'On your way then.'

He was still standing at the door when Chandler reached the end of the lane and raised one hand as he turned on to Cheap.

Guards in twos wearing Lancaster's livery were mingling with the city dwellers trudging to market. He noticed how heavily armed they were, appearing everywhere, arrogantly taking whatever they wanted from the market stalls as by right when they strolled past. He remembered the raucous old market-women in Matilda's time and wondered if they were still wisely keeping away from the City to stay safe and sound on their own homesteads in Kent.

Everywhere he looked there were queues. Queues for bread. Queues for fish. Queues for cheese hacked into meagre slices scarcely worth the trouble. Expressions of hopelessness on the faces of everyone he saw brought home to him how the repression was undermining the normal vivacity of the City.

Beggars were rife.

Barefoot children swarmed everywhere hustling for work.

He led the mule and walked along on foot like everyone else. Only the wealthy rode their cavalcades down the middle of the thoroughfares and not many of those were out yet.

And they said it was King Dickon's extravagance that had

brought the realm into poverty, he remembered, forgetting that it was his predecessor, his own grandfather, Edward III, and his incessant French wars that had bankrupted the realm so that he had to pawn the Crown Jewels! Henry, however, repeated the allegation often enough for it to be believed and used it as a way of getting rid of his cousin. But it had never been as bad as this.

He marvelled that Henry Bolingbroke, eldest son and heir of the richest man in England, had run through his immense fortune after the death of his father in less than two years. He must have realized, cruelly late, that it was an expensive business to steal a crown even though King Richard had practically handed it over gratis.

All those armies to be called out when he docked at Ravenser with only a shipload of his personal retinue – he must have forgotten about the need for pikemen, swordsmen, foot soldiers, cavalry, not to mention the longbow men and the Genoese archers and sundry others as well as cooks, servants, spit boys, vittelers and brewsters, the enablers of any army, once you'd gathered enough men who owed you fealty and ordered them to set out on the long road down the spine of England.

The arrays might owe allegiance to the house of Lancaster, those northern garrisons from the castles old Gaunt had owned, Scarborough, Knaresborough and the rest, but they had to be fed and feeding a growing army of marching men cost more than a king's ransom as it now turned out.

After all that squandering of his inherited wealth to tawdry ambition no wonder Henry was determined to hang on to his prize. He could surely not believe it had been worth it?

Chandler meant it when he said he would not visit Adam Pinkhurst near St Paul's. It so happened he had to pass down Paternoster Row, however, and, glancing into one of the news shops, he could not fail to notice Adam at that moment striding out into the street. The two of them almost collided. To Chandler's satisfaction Adam did not recognize him until he spoke his name.

The scrivener, glancing casually over his shoulder then sidelong at Chandler, strolled on without missing a beat. They fetched up near the platform where the public recantations of the Lollards took place. It was empty today. Adam leaned with one hand on a wooden strut and took out his pouch.

In an undertone he said, 'Let it look as if I'm searching for alms. What are you doing here?'

'Is she and the child all right?'

'You heard?'

Remembering Archer's warning he merely nodded.

Adam gave a faint smile. 'Cook is with her. They've gone out of the City somewhere north of the river.'

'East or west?' Chandler raised his eyebrows.

'I don't know exactly.'

Chandler did not believe him. 'Can you contact me at the abbey of Dieulacres over by a town called Leek when you hear anything new like you did before? I'm going back there. You can even send a message by Brother Daniel, if you will.'

Pinkhurst bent his head as if searching in his pouch and muttered, 'Don't do or say anything to harm her. She's almost happy. She believes you dead.'

They parted.

Chandler had gone a pace or two before saying over his shoulder, 'Thank you for everything, Adam. I'm in your debt. The package is safe.'

He stopped and called to Chandler. 'In the same place you've mentioned?'

'No.' Chandler walked back and replied in a low voice, 'It's with a collector in Chester. If it becomes dangerous it will be taken secretly into Wales.'

Adam nodded. 'Look after yourself, fella. Forget what I said. She might like a word. I'll pass it on.' He unobtrusively clenched his fist.

Chandler mused on the mellowness of his feelings after speaking to his rival. Such feelings of kindness and complicity were a benediction and a grace.

His suggestion that Matilda thought him dead and was happy, were two remarks he could not stop himself from bringing together, however. Which was cause and which its effect? Maybe it was best to keep out of her life now. He would not be welcome.

*   *   *

He had gone only as far as the end of the strand where the convent apple orchards were when he heard a lot of shouting ahead. A tabor could be heard, thumping out a beat at a measured walking pace.

It sounded like a procession of some kind coming from the direction of Westminster Palace. He wondered if it was Henry, back from his drubbing in Wales, making a pageant of his return in a pretence of triumph, when he noted the jeers accompanying the tabors. Shrill whistles became louder as the procession approached.

Hoping his disguise, so called, would serve its purpose, he stepped back against a nearby orchard wall and waited to see who would appear. Horses, nose-to-tail and gaudily caparisoned, rode along on both sides of a group on foot, packed in the middle. When they were near enough Chandler's eyes widened in disbelief.

Half-a-dozen friars in grey robes were being hustled along on foot by men with whips while the horses kept them enclosed in a tight group. As they neared, he noticed one or two elderly ones stumble and the whips from the horsemen snake out to lash them into even tighter formation than before.

They were Franciscans, and their wrists were tied in front of them and knotted on a longer leash held by the rider leading the procession. He kept jerking it for no better reason than it amused him to see his prisoners jolted forward, with now and then one or other falling to his knees. The prisoners' faces were streaked with sweat and they were barefoot leaving a trail of bloodied footprints on the cobblestones.

'What have they done?' Chandler muttered to a fellow standing next to him.

'Spoke up on behalf of –' his glance darted about – 'you know who. Said he was still . . .' He mouthed the word 'alive' and then rolled his eyes and gazed straight ahead as if disowning the words issuing from his own mouth.

'And it's come to this? Just for having an opinion?' Chandler must have raised his voice because the fellow hushed him and slightly turned away.

Out of the side of his mouth he muttered, 'Where the hell have you been all this time, master? Don't you know they've been tried twice by jury and found innocent? Now this third time the powers have got the answer they wanted. They're herding them up to Smithfield to be hanged.'

'What, all of them?'

'The old custom, ain't it? One guilty, all guilty.'

'It seems . . .' he glanced at the fellow and bit off the next word when he saw his features harden. The crowd was continuing on its inexorable progress side by side with the captives and Chandler decided to join them in the belief that a last-minute reprieve must be announced. His informant had sloped off already.

They trailed all the way back along the strand where the large mansions of the barons were situated and where John of Gaunt's utterly trashed Savoy Palace still lay in smoke-blackened ruins after the Great Rising twenty years previously.

That must be a thorn in Henry's side, judged Chandler as they drew level and the crowd began to jeer and hoot despite the presence of Lancaster's harassed and ill-tempered guards. It was a nasty reminder to this benighted usurper what ordinary people in the street thought to the Lancasters now.

True, Henry had been the darling of the jousting circuit a few years ago before he put on weight, but admiration for a competitor on the jousting field was different to the approval bestowed on a just and respected ruler. Maybe Henry was deluded enough to believe that they still revered him as in his sporting days? If so, Chandler argued back at himself, why these punitive measures for the most innocent assault on his self-esteem?

Why was it a crime to believe that maybe, just possibly, King Richard had not been murdered at Pontefract Castle on Henry's orders, but was still alive? It should have restored Henry's good name to some extent, deserved or not, with only Henry himself the one to know the depth of his own guilt, but clearly his delusions about remaining as the realm's favourite son persuaded him otherwise.

Chandler remembered that terrible day at Pontefract Castle when the fight had broken out in the tower chamber and while he was still recovering from a fist in his face someone had hurtled down the narrow spiral stair into the garth below. Had it been Richard, or not? Much as he wished to he could not wind time back to take a closer look at the participants in that sudden burst of violence. It had seemed to mean the death of the king but did these poor friars going to their doom know something to the contrary?

The closer to Smithfield they approached the more intensely Chandler wished he had simply continued on his way out of the City. By the manner of the guards he could tell there would be no reprieve. There was nothing he could do. He could not change the situation one iota.

Helplessness made his anger increase. Why take part in such a carnival? What had possessed him? There was nothing he could do and yet, in some strange way he could not analyse, he had to go on, honour-bound to bear witness to what was about to take place.

Someone close by was mumbling curses under their breath.

'Hush,' his neighbour said to the woman leaning on a stick next to him, 'they'll hear you.'

'I don't give a tinker's cuss whether they hear me or not,' the spirited old woman croaked. 'These are holy men, whatever you might say about some of those other fat friars gulling the poor. I've nothing but good to say of Franciscans.'

A murmuring among the crowd turned to agitation as one of the men-at-arms lining the route turned to stare into the faces behind him as if trying to make out who had spoken out of turn, but no one looked in her direction and with a sneer he turned his attention back to the more entertaining spectacle of a procession of friars being herded to the scaffold.

If the guards were not armed so killingly, thought Chandler, we could resist. There are more of us. By sheer force of numbers we could take them and rid the city of their presence. But we lack arms. Therefore we lack power. We are sheep to the slaughter.

The procession came to a halt and, being taller than most, Chandler was able to report back to those standing behind about what was happening. 'We're being allowed into Smithfield in small groups,' he relayed. 'Being checked for arms by the look of it.'

At this one or two glanced shiftily from side to side and a couple of tough-looking fellows sloped off down a side street.

At a slow pace the procession flowed into the wide open field and it began to fill. A wooden gallows had been erected close to where Sawtre's fire had been built. It was high enough to give everyone a clear view of what was about to take place on it.

The surge of pressure from those following, for by now the crowd had increased massively, pushed Chandler into the middle of the crowd and soon he found they were being pressed up near the gallows itself.

Meanwhile the friars, wrists still bound by ropes, were urged on to the platform where they could be seen by everyone.

Somebody in Lancaster's colours, thinking himself the master of ceremonies, strutted on after them and spoke inaudibly over the heads of the crowd for a while and when he eventually ran out of words some of his men banged their pikes on the ground to make a lot of noise. When they stopped the crowd fell silent.

An uneasy rustling began to take over. No one spoke. Some covered their eyes. The condemned had not been reprieved as Chandler expected. This was no sham exhibition to frighten citizens into obedience. Like William Sawtre, the eight friars were going to serve as an example to anyone who thought to criticize the current regime whether by word or deed.

The guards made short work of dropping a noose round each man's neck. Several of the victims were praying and already in that state of ecstatic submission Chandler recognized from his own near-immolation on the heretic fire. Others were silent. Still others, before the noose could restrict their movements, went up to each of their brothers in turn and gave them the kiss of peace. They might have been offered the chance to renege on the accusations made against them, but none took the opportunity.

Somebody in the crowd asked, 'What happened to the other two?' The silence allowed his words to ring out.

Several voices answered.

'Aye, ten were judged but two escaped.'

'They'll be after them unless—'

Shushing followed as the most senior friar stepped forward to say something. He wore the noose like a wreath of flowers.

'I am the Master of Divinity at the House of the Grey Friars in Leicester where these good brothers were wont to carry out their work. During one of our General Chapters the belief was expressed that our beloved king, Richard II, had escaped his prison in the Castle at Pontefract and still lives. That is our crime, our sin. We believe that King Richard lives!'

Before he could say more and during the small moment when the crowd began to draw in its breath to shout their response, a dozen guards descended on him and dragged him brutally towards the gibbet. He made no resistance.

The onlookers groaned in one voice when he was strung up. His companions rapidly joined him, swung aloft by their necks, feet kicking helplessly as the ground fell away beneath them.

A tall fellow standing beside Chandler demanded, 'Is there going to be any relief for them?'

Chandler knew what he meant. 'Not unless there's a miracle.'

'Then let's demonstrate our belief in miracles, master.' He quirked an eyebrow at Chandler who, for a moment forgetting that he had exchanged his monastic robe for the garb of an impecunious merchant, recovered quickly enough to say, 'I'm with you, friend.'

The man nudged him through the crowd and together they scrambled on to the scaffold and strode towards the hanging, struggling men.

When others saw what was happening they jostled to join them, urging others to help and pull down on the legs of the hanged men to break their necks and shorten their agony.

The crowd was in a chaos of screams and cries, a melee of approval and opposition. Some enjoyed the spectacle of a hanged man struggling to draw breath and turning black in the agony of a slow death and resented being thwarted in their pleasure. Fights broke out. Others were praising those who had risked the wrath of the guards and showed mercy to the eight victims.

In a few moments it was over. Eight bodies swayed on the gibbet.

'Innocent in my opinion,' was the verdict of one of the helpers. 'May they reside with the angels and partake in the glory of God forever.'

Chandler was shaken to the core. He allowed the crowd to drift him without aim back out of Smithfield and along the thoroughfare until he eventually came to his senses and began to look round to see where he was.

He had abandoned Archer's mule somewhere towards Westminster.

When he reached the convent orchards again he saw the creature in the distance placidly cropping grass on the verge. It made no sign that it recognized him when he looped its reins over one arm and began to walk on.

His thoughts were black. The way so many of the mob had jeered when the men were strung up and were writhing in their death throes convinced him that there was no hope for Man. Absolution could not be offered to people like that. They were beyond redemption. Beasts of the field, this mule, even, would show more reverence at the death of one of their own kind than some of the bystanders at the hanging of their fellow men.

He felt he wanted nothing to do with any of them. Days filled with prayer were all that would have any meaning for him after this.

The abbey cloister at Dieulacres had never seemed more desirable. There was nothing more he could do here. He would delay no longer.

FOUR

Approaching the County of Cheshire a few days later he was shocked by the devastation the Lancastrian army had caused after Henry's orders to cry havoc. The ruin of the land was visible everywhere in all the field strips, common land and dwellings everywhere about.

Not a vill had escaped the deliberate destruction by his troops. The thatch of every cottage was burned black, walls were knocked down, animals slaughtered and carcases left to rot if unsuitable for Lancaster's field kitchens. Crops were trampled or uprooted and stolen to fill the pots of the destroyers.

The people who had inhabited these poor dwellings had fled. Or if not so fortunate they had been put to the sword. The bones of many of the old, those crippled by years of relentless labour or by accident or punishment still lay among the shards of cooking pots, of children's toys, of broken-down doors, of rudimentary furniture painstakingly knocked together by local carpenters and now knocked apart again by the army. What poor possessions the peasant farmers had were smashed forever.

This is what it means to cry havoc over a region, he saw. It is no simple shout of triumph but a complete and ruthless extermination of the people who lived here.

This vengeance was taken because the Cheshire archers were renowned for their prowess throughout Europe – and were staunchly on the side of Richard II, forming his own elite two-hundred-strong bodyguard.

In order to defeat his cousin, Henry had had to prise this guard from the king's defence, a feat he had accomplished when Richard was separated from the rest of his army after landing on the Welsh coast during a storm on the way back from Ireland. The storm had dispersed men along the coast, forcing them to take shelter in any haven where they could land safely and Henry, waiting up near Flint Castle, had issued a barrage of lies and misinformation that King Richard was home and had no more need of them.

It had not, however, persuaded Henry from later teaching the army a lesson. To cry havoc against the county that had resisted him was the worst punishment he could mete out.

First Sawtre, thought Chandler, then the Cheshire archers and the Lollards, now the eight Franciscans, would nothing stop his mad killing spree? Who would be next? Rumours that he was about to invade Wales were rife.

He left the burned land as quickly as he could, regretting his decision to make a detour to see for himself what had happened when the invasion took place.

Night was already falling when he entered Chester and he only managed to reach the gates when they were about to be closed before curfew.

Still attired in the borrowed houpeland he reached Willoughby's gates and called for the porter. 'Is the master at home?'

The fellow who appeared looked him over. 'Who wants to know?'

'Tell him Brother Chandler is back.'

The gatekeeper, one of several men in Willoughby's retinue known to Chandler, peered at him more closely. 'Where is he?'

'Come on, man . . .'

Another narrow scrutiny brought a smile to his features. 'That beard's come on a lot since you left us! What you feeding it on? Come. Get yourself inside!' He pulled Chandler into the yard and shut and barred the gates.

'So there it is,' Chandler concluded much later after Willoughby and he had supped alone, 'he is on the rampage and justifying every barbarity he and his men commit.'

'We are warned,' replied his host. 'We are well warned . . . Now tell me, Rodric, what are your plans?'

'I shall return to Dieulacres if they'll have me. A life of quiet contemplation is the extent of my hopes at present . . . I wanted to see you before going out there to find out if anything had happened since I left.'

Willoughby called in his housekeeper and told her to make up Chandler's bed in his old chamber and she went out without a word. 'Forgive her. She is even more deeply drawn to the new regime than ever. I fear I ought to let her go. Her eyes are everywhere. Who knows what stories she takes back to the sheriff?'

'He seemed to want to let you be . . . he looked content to accept you at your own evaluation,' remarked Chandler in an even tone.

'He's a snake. Look what they did to Sir Piers Legh to make way for this new man, and Piers was the leader of one of the most powerful families in the county. I'm nobody. A wool exporter. Expendable. And I was warned, wasn't I?'

'Warned?'

'Evelyn?'

'You see her death as a warning?' Chandler looked at him in surprise. It had been a theory he had entertained himself, especially after talking to Pearce, but to hear Willoughby maintain it now made him sit up and reassess.

'There's more to it,' Willoughby continued. 'Nothing much different to when you were here. I can't follow the ins and outs of the web they weave, but I'm told she got into trouble with the summoner. You know how corrupt they are . . .'

'Master Chaucer told us that, if we didn't already know – and he wrote it all down in graphic detail!'

'No wonder they want to burn his writing.' Willoughby nodded. 'But the point is, Rodric, we never believe it's going to involve us. I try to keep out of all those religious battles. The Church is nothing to me. I do what they ask and pay my tolls and that's an end of it as far as I'm concerned. When the Church does draw me in is now . . .' He frowned and Chandler could see how worried he was, strain etching deep lines over his features.

He continued, frown deepening, voice roughened with emotion. 'The silly child would not guess what he wanted from her. She would not imagine the depth of their corruption. Once set on her trail the summoner would not stop until . . . You see, don't you? Order would have to be maintained – according to their rules. If she failed to keep her side of the bargain –' he gestured with both hands – 'he would call out his hounds.' He gazed despairingly out of the window. 'They have no compassion. They want payment in whatever currency they choose and beware any who cannot or will not pay. We walk on eggshells here. Henry's men have inserted themselves into the network with little trouble. I know I am being watched.'

'So who has he set in her place?'

He shook his head. 'I wish I knew. The kitchen is always full of new faces.'

Chandler remembered Maud telling him that the summoner had tried to draw her into his web. 'But surely you can . . .' He floundered somewhat. 'I cannot encourage you to seek out Evelyn's . . . for want of a better word, her murderer . . . but if you're convinced that it was no accident—?'

'I cannot let them get away with it?' There was a long pause until Willoughby added, 'And if I seek revenge what will their retaliation look like?' He shook his head again. 'I have a daughter and soon I shall have a grandchild. I have to tread carefully, Rodric. I believe my men to be loyal. But you know what they say about enemies?'

'Keep them close.'

'And that's why I haven't yet thrown that woman out on to the street.'

He rose to his feet. 'It's good to see you back. Safer, I would think, to get out to Dieulacres as soon as you can.'

Spirits brought low by Willoughby's predicament, Chandler made his way into the yard for a breath of air before turning in. Torches were being lighted as the day drew to an end. Across the yard the great doors of the wool shed were closed. The stables were quiet but for the intermittent shifting about in their straw of the horses. The last of the servants retired once the lamp-lighter finished his job.

It was quieter than in London but underneath the surface the power shifts and secret alliances were just as dangerous.

Chandler leaned against the wall and wondered if there was any way he could help Willoughby. He liked him. Now he felt he might know him at last and was convinced he was on the level. But the situation was difficult and a solution seemed out of reach. What had happened was yet another injustice brought by the change of regime. Another cross to be born. Any reckoning would be down to the merchant himself if he could only accept the murder of his wife as part of the much bigger game that was being played out. He would have to tread with the utmost care to survive.

Chandler could not see him ignoring what had happened, not Willoughby. He was not some all-forgiving passive religious fellow who could easily turn the other cheek. Quite the contrary.

He remembered how powerfully he had come to his rescue in the woods when he was first on his way here and beset by those desperate men. But for him Galfrido's books would have been stolen and no doubt tossed into the River Dee unless some astute fellow had been able to read and realized they were worth something. Of course, Willoughby hadn't known that at the time. But he had acted to prevent the murder of a stranger by a gang of ruthless outlaws without a thought for his own safety.

He felt he would be forever in his debt.

But what could he offer in return now Willoughby's suspicion had hardened into a conviction? He might discover the identity of his wife's killer. But was there anything more rash than to engage in reprisals for her death if it were true?

Chandler thought of Matilda and the child. How far would he go to avenge them if anything happened to them?

He had no idea.

After risking the danger of being recognized in London, Chandler was confident that now he was far away almost in the Marcher country his disguise was hardly necessary and he was free to trim his beard somewhat.

Next morning he shaved it down almost to the skin, cut his own hair, albeit roughly, and put on his spare monastic robe. The housekeeper had taken the houpeland he'd worn all the way from London for a good scrub in the river with the rest of the household's regular wash. It was now drying over a bush in the heat of the sun. Then he went to find Pearce to ask about escorting him back to Dieulacres.

'Willoughby said you might.'

Pearce grunted an assent. Greetings over.

There was a pause while each waited for the other to say something. Finally Pearce said, 'She still means more to me than what you might be thinking.'

'I know it.' Chandler hesitated before asking, 'Has nothing turned up?'

Pearce looked off into the distance. 'Somebody must know something.'

'If it wasn't a simple accident.'

'It was no accident.'

'Did you find out who the fellow on the roof was?'

Pearce gawked at him. 'What?'

'The fellow who was seen on the roof that morning?'

'I don't know nothing about – what did you say?'

'Didn't Maud tell you? She said she saw somebody up there . . .' Chandler gripped him by the arm. 'Did she not say?'

'The little bitch!' Pearce exclaimed. He stared at Chandler for a long moment with his mouth open. 'Why did she not say anything to me?'

'You'll have to ask her. It was when I questioned her—'

'Let's find her! . . . Where is the little devil?' His rage erupted so suddenly Chandler feared for the girl with Pearce already stalking off, bellowing her name and startling everyone out of their work.

'She's down by the river seeing to the washing,' somebody called.

Pearce began to stride down the side of the wool shed towards the meadow. Chandler followed.

A group of women on the riverbank were still pounding garments on the stones while others were rinsing them and wringing out the moisture before draping them on bushes to dry and folding them when ready into baskets to take up to the yard. Maud was nowhere to be seen.

'Where's that Maud?' Pearce demanded loud enough for Chandler to hear halfway up the meadow. Somebody evidently muttered a response because Pearce swerved towards the thicket separating Willoughby's domain from the burgage next door.

Chandler anticipated him and swung off the path and dived into the trees higher up. Almost straightaway he heard somebody chanting. When he came to the edge of a clearing he stopped to watch.

It was Maud. She was chanting and walking round and round in a small circle she was wearing in the grass. He listened.

'Out sickness! Out!' she chanted. 'From marrow to bone – from bone to skin – from skin to hair – from hair to stone!' She repeated this incantation several times and on the final word picked up a stone from the middle of the circle and hurled it into the bushes where it disappeared.

Pearce loomed on the other side of the grove. 'You come here, you little witch! What's this about some fellow on the roof?' He lurched forward and gripped her so suddenly by the shoulders she gave a scream and, seeing who it was, kicked at him and tried to wriggle free.

'You vixen!' He tightened his grip as Chandler stepped forward.

'It's all right, Maud. You're not in any trouble.'

'Who says she's not? Why didn't you tell me about this fellow?' He shook her. 'Who was he?'

Maud began to weep with a mixture of fear and rage. 'Because you didn't ask me, did you? How was I to know you'd be interested?'

'You knew how it was between us!'

'I know she was the master's wife! That's what I know,' she snarled.

Chandler saw that she needed no help but he went over anyway. 'Come now, both of you. This can be sorted out quite amicably. Maud. You can see Pearce is worried that if someone harmed Mistress Evelyn he would want to know who it was.'

'I told you I didn't know. I'd never seen him before.' She gave a reproachful tear-stained glance at Chandler. Her expression softened. 'I didn't know you were back.'

'I arrived last night, for what it's worth. Now tell Pearce what you told me.'

'Tell him to take his hands off me, then!'

Chandler nodded to Pearce who immediately removed his hands.

'Go on. Tell me what you told him.'

'It was that morning when she fell – I was shaking up the bedding in the attic and about to come downstairs when this stranger appeared and went straight through that little door on to the roof. There now –' she turned to Chandler – 'isn't that exactly what I told you?'

'Almost exactly,' he replied with a faint smile. 'You said a little more about what he looked like.'

'Go on,' muttered Pearce.

'Young, smiling, bounding up the stairs from the hall. There!' She glared at Chandler.

'And you told me you had never seen him before,' he reminded.

'It's true! I hadn't! Nor have I seen him since. How would I? I never leave the house!'

'Mean anything to you?' He addressed Pearce.

He shook his head. 'But he soon will. Somebody will know him.' He glared at Maud again. 'Who was with him in the hall?'

'How would I know.'

'Didn't you hear voices?'

She shook her head. 'If I had I would have told you.'

'I doubt that. You didn't tell me anything until the brother here forced it out of you.'

Maud flounced off a few paces. 'Can I go now? I've work to do.'

Chandler took a step forward. 'Maud, is there anything else because if so it's important you tell us now.'

She frowned down at the grass.

'Come on,' he coaxed. 'Anything at all, no matter how unimportant it seems.'

'I only heard what he called when he stepped through the door.'

'What was that?'

'He said, "Lyn?".'

'Is that what the mistress was usually called, Lyn?'

She shook her head.

'I've never heard anybody calling her Lyn.' Pearce scowled.

'Just that one word?' Chandler insisted and when Maud nodded he said, 'And in what sort of tone? Was he friendly? Joking? Surprised to find her there?'

She shot a glance at Pearce. 'He sounded loving.'

Pearce looked into the distance. Chandler could see that Maud was pleased she had wounded him.

'His tone, of course, is nothing more than a matter of opinion after all this time. Do you have any reason to suppose they were intimate?'

Maud smirked. 'Not really, brother. But I wouldn't be surprised.'

Pearce turned away muttering something about hunting down the vermin who had harmed her and began to walk briskly back towards the path up to the yard.

Chandler gave Maud a quizzical glance. 'Is that true, Maud, or is it just you trying to get your own back against Pearce?'

'It's true. I wouldn't lie with you standing there.'

'What have I got to do with it?'

'You being next thing to a monk?'

'What was that little ritual you were doing when I first came up?'

'It wasn't anything bad, honest!'

'I didn't think it was. It was a banishing ritual. I just wonder who taught you it.'

'You won't . . .' She bit her lip. 'If you tell anybody they'll think I'm a witch.'

'I'm not in the habit of telling anybody anything even when they ask until I know them and trust them. Any secret you tell me is as safe as an oath made before God. I thought you knew that?'

She began to walk backwards, watching him, as wary as a wild animal. 'If you must know it was my grandame. She knew all kinds of healing spells. I wanted to get rid of the darkness. It lies all around like a sickness. It's choking us. The master is beset by shadows. They are drawing nearer and none of us are safe. Even you, brother. She had the sight and I think some of it rubbed off on me. It doesn't do any harm. It makes things better. I don't like it but what else can I do?'

For once she looked transparent with honesty. He thought he had got her measure, until now. This binding of spells was a surprise but it made her no different to many young girls who lacked education and believed in the existence of Nature's powers as strongly as if they really existed. In fact, it was not much different to Archer's astronomers, intent on piercing the veil of mystery by which we are all surrounded.

Maud looked as if possessed. Her transparent blue eyes held his as she continued to back from the grove.

The last he saw of her was as she was edging through the

trees towards the riverbank where the women were still pounding the washing with stones in the bright and exalting sunlight.

When he reached the yard he saw Pearce in conversation with Willoughby. The latter was listening intently with a frown on his face while Pearce waved his arms and kept looking towards the gates. Willoughby caught sight of Chandler and beckoned.

'You've heard this, have you?'

He agreed he had if it was about the visitor. Something about the story had made him fail to pass the information on to Willoughby. 'It seemed more fantastical than true,' he explained, while he wondered if it was so. 'Nobody else had seen hide nor hair of the fellow. I assumed that if he existed he would be something to do with you.'

'These maids,' agreed Willoughby with a bland expression. 'Who can guess what goes on in their heads with their fantasies and dreams and their ability to make something out of nothing. I'll get them all together and see if anybody else saw him. Someone must have let him in.'

'It's the first time I've heard of him,' Pearce said.

'And I won't ask you what you have to do with it,' Willoughby replied. He turned on his heel with a curt nod that implied much and went back inside the house.

Pearce gave Chandler an angry scowl. 'You might have to get yourself another escort through them woods,' he muttered. 'This'll be me out on me ear.'

'I'm sure he's merely grieving for the fact that he knew so little about what was going on. He will not blame you.'

Chandler was not so sure about Willoughby's intentions. Pearce could be expendable.

On the one hand the merchant appeared to have been indulgent towards his young wife, ignoring her small betrayals, as satisfied as someone can be with a bauble others covet.

On the other, maybe he was secretly smitten by a young and beautiful woman he knew did not care for him, his heart broken by her perfidiousness. It was usually folly for an older man to imagine he was the beloved of a much younger woman.

Chandler considered the matter of beauty and decided that

Evelyn had been beautiful enough if you did not look too closely into her nature. He did not doubt that she would have enjoyed making the older man jealous.

Whatever the case, it was for Willoughby to deal with and he would take his advice and get off to the abbey as soon as he could for the contemplative life that drew him now any alternative was lost.

FIVE

Willoughby's house

I t was not to be. Events next day prevented it.

The horses were being brought out. Pearce and his silent companion had been instructed to escort Chandler back to the abbey. Chandler, bag over his shoulder, ready to leave, met Pearce in the stables. He was in a strange, wild mood, slapping the horses rumps, kicking a bucket across the stalls, banging about and showing every sign of repressed rage.

'Look, Pearce.' Chandler went up to him. 'Is it about this visitor Maud mentioned? Just forget it. She probably imagined him. You heard what Willoughby said yesterday.'

'We're getting nowhere! One of those vermin will know something.'

'Do you include Willoughby in your list?'

'What? The master? Why would he not say if he knew who it was?'

Chandler didn't answer the question but instead said, 'Let's pool our knowledge.'

'What knowledge?'

'Tell me this. Who was it Evelyn went to meet at the chantry by North Gate?'

'When was that?'

'When she stole something of mine from my bag. She took it there in the hope of getting a price for it, I assume.'

'That's not something I'd be knowing, is it?'

'Why not?'

He gave him a long-suffering stare. 'For the reason that I'm employed here to work. She played while I worked. Who do you think she met?'

'I don't know. Don't you have any idea?'

'I don't.' He bunched his fists at some name that might have entered his head.

'Was it the town summoner?'

'She wouldn't go looking for him. He'd find her.'

Chandler stifled a shudder. 'I'll take a look down there myself.' He turned to leave.

'You think there was somebody . . .' Pearce gave him a wary glance.

'It's worth a look.'

'What about these 'orses?'

'Let's go later. We'll set out when I come back.'

'If we don't leave now we won't be there till nightfall.'

'I don't mind.'

'I do. Just me and 'im –' he gestured towards his silent companion – 'against who the hell knows who, roaming wild in their own outlaw territory?'

Chandler, aware of his own useful sword, considered the three of them – against unknown odds – and said, 'Tomorrow then, if it suits you better? Why not delay and get this matter sorted?'

'Work's a bit slack now the clip's been sent on.' Pearce jerked his chin in a sign Chandler took to be agreement.

He left.

Pearce was either naturally surly or suffering in the inner recesses of his heart for the death of his lover. For Evelyn's sake he hoped it was the latter. She deserved some fond remembrance. Everyone did.

Something made him ponder the feelings Willoughby, the husband, might own. Pride in possession did not have the same sting as love, he decided.

The chantry was a well-built little place erected side-on against the city wall near the gate to the open country and when Chandler strolled up the doors were wide open.

He hesitated, trying to look as if he was wondering whether to go inside, but a quick glance up and down the street showed nobody of any particular interest other than shoppers plying back and forth to market and, taking his time, his presence unremarked, he went to stand under the porch.

From here he could see the whole length of the short nave, with its plain flagstones and the small altar at the far end. Four stone pillars held up a roof decorated with surprisingly delicate fan-vaulting. He wondered who had paid for it.

There were two people inside, a tearful old woman kneeling amid her shopping baskets, and a young priest doing nothing very much apart from lighting a few candles at the far end. Of the fellow he had seen sweeping the porch when Evelyn had been here that time there was no sign. The go-between, she had called him. Between whom?

He went in and sat down on the stone ledge against the wall at the back.

Almost on cue two men entered. One took a seat on the opposite side of the nave to Chandler and stared fixedly at him while the other sauntered down the nave towards the priest. When he drew level they exchanged greetings.

The priest glanced towards Chandler and the other fellow. To Chandler he looked nervous when he went behind the altar and lifted the cloth draped over it. He took something from underneath at the back. He returned to his visitor and glanced about once more.

Chandler, with his head down, clearly saw cash change hands. The visitor stuffed it in his pouch then turned to leave.

When he drew level with Chandler, instead of walking straight on, he came to sit next to him.

Chandler kicked himself mentally for not recognizing him at once. Portly, somewhat sweaty, but today wearing a dull fustian houepeland with a wooden cross in the open neck, he was less dapper than when he had attended Evelyn's funeral.

He smirked at Chandler. 'I know you.'

'You do?'

'Yes, I do. You're a friend of Master Willoughby, I believe.'

'And what is that to you?' Chandler felt no obligation to be pleasant.

'To me it's a point of interest. Shall I tell you why?' Before Chandler could say yay or nay, the fellow went on. 'It's because I'm the summoner of this town. It happens to be my business to know everyone within its walls and everything they do that might contravene church law.'

Chandler said nothing. For some reason he wanted to punch the fat, smug face confronting him, but with difficulty held himself in check.

The summoner gave another smirk. 'So what, my friend, is your business here in this town of mine?'

'I have no business here, as you put it. I am merely passing through.'

'No special reason to visit Master Willoughby?'

'If I had it would be between myself and Willoughby.'

The summoner regarded him with an odd smile. 'I do believe you're being insolent in a way that reflects badly on my office.'

'I do believe you're trying to harass me which reflects badly on my authority as a free man.'

The summoner's pale blue eyes widened slightly.

In Chandler's opinion he must have too easy a ride in the town. Were people so afraid of him and the threat he carried to answer him in kind?

Chandler smiled. 'Now, perhaps, Sir Summoner, you might answer a question from a stranger in this fair town of yours.' He smiled again. 'Tell me, is law and order so slack that a young woman can die in suspicious circumstances and nothing is done about it? I understand that my friend, Master Willoughby, is grieving for the death of his wife with no visible assistance during his period of affliction.'

The summoner puffed out his cheeks as if affronted. 'It is hardly my responsibility to concern myself with the bodily welfare of the citizens. I am concerned only for their souls.'

'And their behaviour which includes their material selves?' Chandler corrected.

'That, of course. So what, may I ask, is your interest in the woman?'

'In Mistress Willoughby?' Chandler corrected.

The summoner frowned. 'As you say. Whatever. She was unknown to me. One of many young wives. I cannot lay claim to know every one who dwells here.'

'But I understand you knew Mistress Willoughby rather well?'

'Did I? What gives you that impression?'

'The way she spoke of you,' Chandler replied.

'Why, what did she say?' The summoner stood up as if in a hurry to go on to his next visit.

'Nothing much. Enough to make me believe you had an arrangement of some sort.'

He bent down to bring his face close to Chandler's and snarled, 'Listen, friend, keep to your own pitch, wherever that might be. Get it? Keep out of my business. It's off limits. And so are you. On your way, brother!'

A shadow fell across Chandler's vision as the summoner's henchman glowered into view. He said nothing at all but merely stood deliberately too close with his thumbs in his belt.

Chandler stared him out. When the man dropped his gaze he rose to his feet and found that he was taller than both men. He gazed at them in as gentle a manner as he could muster. '*Pace tanti nominis.*' He bowed his head and left.

So the summoner was taking his cut from the chantry alms, was he? If he ran true to form he would no doubt take a cut from every small undefended church and place of worship where he could exert his influence. The sooner they were all swept away, the better. The Lollards surely had right on their side to desire an end to the church and the commercial extortions made in its name.

He had just slipped down a narrow alley off the high street to get back to Willoughby's without having to weave through the market crowds when he felt someone push him from behind as if in a hurry to overtake him.

Turning to remonstrate he saw something out of the corner of his eye flashing towards him. Instinctively he ducked but it caught him full on the side of his head. It was a fist, mailed and, but for his timely reaction, it might have caused a lot of damage. As it was he could only see a constellation of stars in the blackness before he shook his head and cleared it somewhat. By then his assailant had vanished.

Guessing he could only have dodged back into the busy thoroughfare he strode back to the entrance, glancing left and right when he reached the street. A few men in Lancaster's colours were lounging about on the other side of the road but as soon as they saw him emerge they began to walk away, laughing and nudging each other. Five of them, thought Chandler. He was no fool. He turned back into the alley and continued on his way.

When he entered Willoughby's yard a few jeers and remarks about friars not being the peaceful fellows they made out to be greeted him until he growled something back. He went over to the water trough and sluiced cold water over his face and blinked a few times. With water droplets flying everywhere he glanced up to see Maud standing with her mouth open.

'Who did that?'

'One of your fellow townsmen.'

'Does it hurt?'

'No, it just looks as if it does. Why aren't you working?'

'I'm offering you sympathy instead. Would you like some arnica cream to put on it?'

'Got some?'

'Come to the kitchen.'

She marched off and Chandler followed.

It was cool and clean inside. With the sun blazing from a cloudless sky the shade was welcome. Maud proffered a sliver of mirror glass and he peered at the damage. A bruise was already showing. He cursed under his breath and handed back the glass. 'Is Pearce around?'

'With the horses.'

After dabbing on the cream she offered, he went in search.

Explanations were soon over. It seemed Pearce didn't need to be told what had happened. He had, he claimed, expected it. 'If you go poking around wherever that summoner is this is what you can expect.'

'Doesn't anybody stop him?'

'Like who?'

'The sheriff?'

Pearce lips twisted. 'Likely.' He held his hands out. 'Here's the hand –' he lifted the right hand – 'and here's the glove.' He put the right inside the left.

'Is this why Willoughby appears to want to let things take their course?'

'They'll do that, don't worry.'

'And I suppose you know the summoner is taking his cut from the chantry?'

'No, but I suspected as much. Is that why you got that?'

Chandler nodded. 'Evelyn was involved in something, wasn't she?'

Pearce nodded. 'I see that now. I thought it was – I don't know what I thought. It's this story of the fellow who visited her on the roof that made me doubt her.'

Chandler left him to work that out. It wasn't for him to reassure a man if his carnal desires led him to tangle with the wrong woman.

He didn't doubt that the proscribed pages of Chaucer's *Tales* breaking the new censorship laws were not the first piece of marketable material that had come Evelyn's way. Willoughby admitted that he had not been careful in concealing the books that passed through the house at first. If he had held them long enough Evelyn would have discovered them.

Inevitably Willoughby himself got to hear about what had happened. 'I cannot protect you, Rodric. You should have left for Dieulacres as I advised. Leave first thing in the morning. You see now how things are here?'

'I never had any doubts. It was only the details I knew nothing about. What are you going to do? Are you letting them get away with it?'

The merchant spread his arms but made no reply.

Maud brought him some more arnica later on and as she took the lid off the little carton and dipped her fingers into the cream to smear it over the bruise, he said, 'I'm glad you had the sense not to get mixed up in all this like Evelyn. She was a silly young thing if she imagined she could get the better of such men.'

He glanced at her out of his good eye when she stopped dabbing at him. 'Maud?'

She bent her head as if concentrating on putting the lid back on.

He took the carton containing the salve from between her fingers. 'Maud, what is it?'

She lifted her head. 'What's what?'

'You.'

'What about me?'

'You haven't done anything witless, have you?'

'I don't know what you mean.'

'I hope for your sake you're being sensible.'

'Anyway, that eye should heal up quickish now. Do you want to take some of this with you?'

'I'm sure the herberer at Dieulacres can supply some – it's very kind of you to ask.' He took hold of her hand as she took the salve from him. 'You will tell me if anything worries you?'

'How can I? You'll be gone tomorrow morning.'

'I mean sooner than that . . . Like now.'

She looked down and a blush turned her cheeks pink. 'I'm not worried about anything.'

'If you think of something before I leave, let me know and I'll sort it out for you.'

She put the little carton into her apron pocket and stepped back. 'The skin's not broken, much.'

'Does that mean it is?' Chandler grinned. 'Ouch!' he said, making a lot of it. 'Ouch, ouch, ouch! No more smiling ever again, it hurts too much! Ouch!'

Before she turned to go he said, 'I mean it. You'd tell me, wouldn't you?'

'Oh, stop making such a fuss. I'm not a child!' She stormed childishly into the kitchen.

SIX

To Dieulacres

As he set out with his two escorts shortly after dawn next morning the dew was still on the leaves. Their horses snorted with pleasure at the softness of the day. It was a moment of beauty before the midday sun turned everything to a crisp.

'Perfect travelling weather.'

Chandler turned to Pearce and to the silent Ham although he did not expect an answer from him. 'That fellow Maud saw must have left town long ago. Or somebody would have reported seeing him.'

'I reckon.' Pearce was riding on one side and the other fellow was on the other.

'She's convinced she saw someone,' he persisted. 'Her description of him was detailed enough.'

'Aye. Mayhap he'll show his face one of these days . . . if he's unlucky enough to have the stars against him.'

As the track slipped down towards the woods Chandler said, 'These fellows who give us safe passage – who are they?'

'Friends,' replied Pearce. 'Outlawed through no fault of their own.'

'I'm surprised the sheriff doesn't clear them out.'

Neither of the two replied.

It was before they reached the trees that there was a shout behind them. Glancing round, Chandler had already put his hand on the sword concealed under his riding cloak when he recognized the rider galloping to catch up with them. He was shouting something, but only when he was close enough could they make out what he was saying. 'Master sends for you to come back!'

When at last he was able to ride alongside them, he demanded, 'Is that Maud with you?' Seeing that she wasn't he added quickly, 'She's gone!'

'What do you mean "gone"?' Chandler frowned.

'Vanished off the face of the earth,' he replied.

Pearce said, 'Why do we have to come back?'

'It's only what I was told to say.'

'Who by?' Chandler frowned.

'Master Willoughby's instructions, brother. Nothing to do with me.' He paused and added, 'It's all hell back there. You'd better come quick!'

Chandler turned his horse. 'Dieulacres will have to wait once more. Let's go!'

He was filled with a dark premonition and all he could remember was the way Maud's hand had stilled yesterday when she was seeing to his black eye and he made that casual remark about Evelyn's lack of common sense. His thoughts flew to the summoner and his illicit dealings. Surely he would not take out his vindictiveness on an innocent maid? And anyway, why should he target Maud? She had said she had rejected his suggestions and she wasn't the only maid at Willoughby's.

Yet something had happened. He had guessed it yesterday and now cursed himself for not insisting on her confession.

He forced the pace on the way back despite Pearce's protests and the fact that the messenger had not been able to keep up the same speed on the return journey and urged them to ride on ahead without him.

They arrived in the yard to a hubbub of servants with Willoughby standing in the middle of them looking grey with concern. 'I am their victim,' he kept muttering as Chandler asked him what had happened. 'They are aiming to ruin me and destroy my business. No one will work for me if there's a curse on me. It has to stop.'

Chandler took hold of his arm. 'Steady, tell me in simple words what has happened.'

'She has gone. The house and barns were thoroughly searched when she failed to appear to break her fast.'

'Was her bed slept in?'

'Certainly.'

After demanding to know if his men had searched the riverbank, which of course they had, as they vehemently declared, adding that they were not dolts, he was as much in the dark as any of them.

Willoughby had already instructed men to search downriver in case her body had been washed up in the reed beds, but they had returned shaking their heads and looking grim.

Undeterred, Chandler asked, 'Has anybody been over to the other bank to see if she's there?'

'No, we haven't for the very good reason that our boat is missing. And she in it with her captor, as we assume.'

'Then find another boat, can't you?' Chandler was impatient with their manner and reminded them that she must be found.

She had been missing since the household had gathered first thing that morning. He himself with his escort had left shortly before it all started.

Willoughby gave Chandler a sidelong glance. 'There was some tittle-tattle about witchcraft. That makes it the summoner's business.'

'Has anyone been to see him?'

Willoughby nodded. 'My steward went to report the matter but he claimed to know nothing about it and that these girls inevitably turn up after committing their nighttime sins. He would hear her confession, he said, if she presented herself to him as soon as she appeared with her fine ready to pay and was able to express true contrition.'

Chandler felt a similar rage as when the summoner had pushed his face into his and tried to threaten him.

'Come to my solar, Rodric, if you will.' Willoughby barrelled ahead of him into the house, called for a jug of wine and when the servant left, kicked the door shut behind him, then threw himself into his chair, indicating that Chandler should pour them both a cup.

'So, Rodric, my deep apologies for recalling you. I needed Pearce and Will back here. They're my best swordsmen. Did you see anyone on the road?'

Chandler shook his head. 'No one remarkable. One or two travellers riding towards town. A carter or two.'

Willoughby could not remain still. He got up and walked about the solar, sat down again, then almost immediately rose to his feet and walked back and forth between the window and the door. 'They know I'm successful. They covet my trade. Now the new regime is encouraging them to try to bribe my contacts. They want to take them over, take my business away from under my nose. They'll run me into the ground. There's no one to put a stop to them.'

'Why would they do that?'

'To bring me to heel under their blasphemous rule. And this . . .' He rubbed the fingers of his right hand over the palm.

'You seem to be certain it's a plot against you.'

'She would not leave without a word. It's too much of a coincidence to be credible.'

'Meaning?'

He gave Chandler a haunted glance. 'Evelyn.'

'If you think it's an attempt to drive you out of business is there an active guild down here to support you?'

He gave a disgusted curse. 'We're on our own. I've sent a courier to my nearest contact. Who knows whether or not he's bribable? He's always been trustworthy but with the king dead – or merely dispossessed and living safe up in Scotland as rumour has it – these new men are jostling for supremacy under Henry's protection. They'll stop at nothing to grab as much power as they can. You've no idea what it was like when Henry called havoc on the county. Richard's archers were still in Wales. Henry's men rampaged through every vill, burned every cot and grange, trampled the crops, set fire where and when they could.'

'I saw it for myself when I rode back from London.'

'You didn't see the people who were made homeless. They were forced to flee and live in hiding, starving in the woods, old men, women and children. The very woods that King Richard's father gave to the county under his protection for their faithful service in France are now their only refuge.' He thumped one fist into another. 'If Prince Edward were alive today he would cry to heaven to see how this Bolingbroke pretender treats the loyal troops who always gave England such heroic service. Who wouldn't aid them?'

'And now?' Chandler asked. 'Do you really believe King Richard is alive? Can he be put back on the throne?' A brief image of the eight friars hanging by their necks at Smithfield for even broaching such an idea floated into his mind.

Unaware of it, Willoughby stood in front of him, nursing his wine cup. 'This is Henry's constant fear – that someone will bring Richard back to dispose of him as cruelly as Henry himself disposed of the men of Cheshire.'

He continued to prowl the chamber. 'Did you hear about the metal contraption somebody placed in Henry's bed? A game-keeper's man-trap sort of thing. Either he was imagining it or it was a story to make everyone believe that God and all the angels were protecting him by letting him find it before it could do for him.' He sat down again and put his head in his hands. 'Nobody knows what to believe. We are drowning in lies.'

'We shall find a way through it.' Chandler had no more idea than anyone else how the current barbarism might be survived other than by showing even more endurance than ordinary life usually demanded.

These were dangerous times. He could only tell himself that darkness cannot drive out darkness. Belief in the power of the light might be hard but he could only believe this period of destruction would give way to a new dawn when the forces of darkness were exhausted.

'Let me know what I can do, John, if anything.'

Willoughby reached out and gripped him by the arm with desperate strength. 'I know I can trust you.'

Chandler had a question. 'May I ask what your boatman was doing when his boat was taken?'

Willoughby shrugged. 'Ask him yourself. He'll be down there now, weeping and wailing.' He nodded towards the door. 'He says he saw and heard nothing.'

It was true. The old fellow, sparse strands of grey hair flying wild about his head, tottered to his feet with a cry when Chandler approached the jetty. 'Has he told you about my boat?' he demanded at once. 'Gone missing. And that poor lass with it.'

'Where were you when they took it?'

'Up in that hut of mine, asleep . . . at my age,' he excused.

'Was anybody else in the habit of taking the boat out?'

He shook his head. 'It's my job, is that. What do they know about tides?'

'I've seen somebody take it.'

The boatman goggled. 'Who would that be?'

'That's what I'd like to know.'

His puzzlement cleared. 'I thought before, it's been tampered with. It was a puzzle. The way it was tied. Not my way.'

'So it was always brought back?'

'Aye, none the worse, I have to admit.'

'And you've no idea who could have taken it?'

The old fellow shook his head. 'I'd have given him what-for if I'd caught him. What did he look like this one you mention?'

'I didn't catch sight of his face. He had his hood up and his back towards me. Nothing special to notice, really.' Chandler shrugged. 'I thought he was a guest at Evelyn's funeral. It was back then. I thought he'd maybe decided to leave early.'

He strolled down to the water's edge and looked about.

The tide was running and the shoreline was scuffed with the many footprints of those who had started the search for Maud. A few reeds grew about on the edge of the slip leading to the jetty, some of them snapped off and trailing in the water. Signs of a struggle, maybe, or merely the numbers in the search party treading without care? It was impossible to tell. There must be something, he told himself.

He walked across the planking to the end of the short wooden structure and gazed up and down.

On the far side of the river a few people were standing on the bank like himself. One man had a fishing line in the water.

He was about to turn away to suggest that they send someone over there as soon as possible when he told himself that it was at this moment he would find something helpful. His glance roamed the long grass higher up the bank, sharpening but to his disgust alighting on nothing out of the ordinary.

He walked back to where the boatman was standing with his arms folded. 'I'll never see that boat again,' he told Chandler. 'Not now. That's me out of a job.'

'How long have you worked for Master Willoughby?'

'All my life. My father before me worked for his father. We go back, we do.'

'I'm sure he'll replace the boat and keep you on.'

The boatman grunted. 'Mayhap.'

As he was beginning to hobble up the path towards the meadow he stopped suddenly and glanced back at Chandler. 'Well, what do you make of that there?'

Chandler's gaze followed to where he was pointing. He couldn't see anything out of the ordinary. 'What?'

'That, look, that wasn't there when I put my boat to bed last night.'

He indicated something shining in the undergrowth where the sun had moved round enough to pick out a different colour in all the greenery. It blazed forth. Something red. Chandler climbed a few paces up the bank towards it. He did not touch it but bent to peer more closely to see what it was.

It was a fragment of cloth. It had caught on a branch and was hanging underneath one of the bushes. The sun blazed down on it, picking it out with sudden intensity.

The boatman hobbled up and bent to take a closer look. He straightened. 'Well, what do you make of it?'

It was red wool. It had been torn from a much larger piece of woven fabric.

With nothing else to observe he carefully disentangled it from the bushes where it was caught and held it up. The threads floated where they had been ripped away.

'Are you sure it wasn't here yesterday?' Chandler asked.

'Sure as I'm standing here. I'd have noticed. 'Sides, it rained a patch or two on and off last night. See here? This is dry.' He took hold of it between thumb and forefinger and rubbed it, just to make sure.

'And let me ask you this, have you ever seen anybody round here wearing anything of this colour?'

The boatman screwed up his face with concentration then slowly shook his head. 'Not down here. Too showy for us.'

Chandler urged him to recall anything at all about anyone he might have seen loitering on the riverbank, but again the boatman shook his head. 'I know everybody from the household.' He gave him a sly glance. 'Thinking it was the fancy fellow you said took my boat out, do you?'

'It could be.'

Chandler felt a cloud of grief settle over him. The little stable lad, unsure if he had actually seen anyone on the roof when questioned, might really have seen someone after all. It was Maud who had mentioned the capuchon. He placed the scrap of fabric in his pouch. If so, the stranger could have been there when she fell – or even been the cause of her fall. Back to that. And now he was going to – or had already – drowned another young woman, actually no more than a child. He kept his thoughts to himself but the boatman gave him a quizzical glance.

'I heard about the mistress and some stranger.'

Chandler gave him a long look. 'And who told you about him?'

'The little lass who's gone missing. That's who. She was down here asking.'

Observing Chandler's expression, he crossed himself and began to mutter a prayer.

Chandler made his way back towards the yard.

SEVEN

Willoughby's

The household was already in mourning twice over, once for Mistress Evelyn and once more for the state of the realm. And now this third reason. Little Maud had been popular with everyone.

Even worse for the general public was to witness the violation of the king's sovereignty and then have to live through the violation of his memory. It was almost too much to bear for those loyal to him. They had to endure the situation from day to day because nothing could halt the battle for power that threatened the realm. Many fell into a grief-stricken and helpless silence.

Meanwhile the sycophants who adorned Henry's court, his bought and paid-for vassals, were exultant at the success of their own lies, seeing them turned to 'truth' by constant repetition, until the volume of people who hurried to declare their allegiance to the usurper grew too large to ignore and swept truth into oblivion.

The more blatant the lies told about Richard – the unfounded accusations of vindictiveness, for instance – were turned into self-evident truths merely by the frequency with which they were repeated.

No one could tell you anything factual against him other than what any ruler would have done in similar circumstances.

All they endlessly repeated was the old whine about Richard Arundel, Archbishop Thomas's elder brother – conveniently forgetting that the earl had plotted Richard's assassination, been arrested, charged before a court of law, was found guilty, and paid the traitor's penalty. Vindictive was not a quality that came into it. It was the law.

But this is no help to Willoughby, thought Chandler now. He is on the wrong side of the power struggle that has driven everyone mad with their paltry and ephemeral ambitions.

If they had nothing else in their lives, could they not simply keep the ten commandments? No covetousness, no killing, and above all, abandon hate and instead, love thy neighbour?

It was simple enough. Surely it was simple? A child could manage it.

It was as he was standing in the doorway of the stables, glancing round to see if he could catch sight of Pearce, that he heard a sound from the hay loft and looked up. It came again and he took a step towards it. He called. The sound stopped.

With no sign of Pearce or any of the stable-hands back from the search of barns and meadows he mounted the ladder into the loft. It would be a rat, he told himself when no one appeared. But something made him want to make sure. When he reached the top he stood for a moment in the sweet-smelling, sun-speckled hay. It was as quiet as the grave.

About to turn away a small sound came again.

'Maud?'

In two strides he was across the floor and dashing handfuls of hay to one side. He stared. A frightened little face peered out at him.

He recalled the lad's name. 'Dickon? What are you doing here? Are you hiding?'

The child was so frightened he could not reply. His cheeks were grubby with tears.

Chandler held out his hand. 'Come now, there's nothing to frighten you here.'

It took time to coax him out of his hiding place and even though he still looked ready to make a bolt for it he whispered, 'He held her down in the water when she wouldn't go.' He seemed to frighten himself with the little croak issuing from between his lips.

Chandler crouched down to his level. 'Let's get you out of all this prickly hay and find you something to eat and then you can tell me all about it. How long have you been hiding in here, Dickon?'

The boy was reluctant to answer but with some coaxing he admitted, 'Since this morning. When I saw him.'

He made a guess. 'This is the bad fellow who has harmed Maud, is it?'

Dickon nodded. 'They were saying she was a witch but she's a good girl.'

'They?'

'The men when they came in here to look for her.'

'You mean the master's men, don't you?'

He nodded.

'And they didn't find you?'

'I made myself very small and didn't breath.'

'You mustn't believe what folk say, Dickon, old fellow. They often get it wrong. Now they've gone why not come out and tell me all about it? I'll protect you from them if they come back. You don't think they would harm you, do you?'

He shook his head.

Chandler threw some of the hay aside but Dickon was still reluctant to come right out.

'Look,' Chandler coaxed, 'let's sit here on this bale for a moment until you feel stronger and you can tell me what you saw, all right?'

Scrubbing both fists into his eyes to wipe away the shame of tears he eventually allowed himself to be prised from his hiding place and, clinging on to Chandler, was hoisted on to one of the bales of hay and began to tell him in a rush of words what had sent him into such a fit of fear that he had sought safety in the loft.

'She was poking round near the jetty as she sometimes does in the early morning and this fellow calls to her and asks her to go out in the boat with him. But she refuses, so he grabs her and they scuffle. She put up a real fight, Maud, she wasn't going to go, but he was bigger and stronger and after pulling her by the hair he pushed her down into the water then got her into the boat and began to row into the middle of the river. And I was watching and she kicked him and before he could grab her she dropped over the side and he kept poking the oar into the water to find her.'

'And did he find her?'

'She drowned.'

'And what did the man do?'

'He rowed away.'

'And what made you yourself so frightened? It wasn't your fault that you saw all this.'

'It is my fault. I was too frightened to help her.'

'You could not have helped her. It's not your fault. He was a big, vicious man, too much for even a strong lad like you.'

'And it's what he was shouting at her as well. "You won't live another minute to tell folk about me!" He was yelling at the top of his voice. "Nor will anybody else live who sees me." That's why I'm frightened.' He gave Chandler a careful look. 'I've seen him.' His eyes were like saucers. 'Is it like a magic curse? One look and you're cursed to stone forever?'

Chandler couldn't help smiling. 'Such things like that don't happen outside stories,' he told him. 'And anyway, Maud saw him and she didn't turn to stone, did she?'

Despite his reassurances, he was filled with rage at what the boy had told him. Eventually he said, 'You need have no fear of magic, Dickon . . .' He paused. 'There is a stronger magic. It's this, look.' He showed him the little cross of St Serapion he always wore. 'Be strong and believe in the lord of light and his servant Serapion will protect you.'

'Will you stay with me until – just a bit longer? To make sure he's not coming back?'

'Of course I will. And maybe you'll be able to remember if you've ever seen this bad fellow before?' He cocked his head on one side.

'Course I have,' Dickon said at once. 'It was the same one who was on the roof when Mistress Evelyn fell. I thought I hadn't imagined him . . . but then . . .' He shrugged as if faced by a great mystery. 'Then I thought I had.'

Chandler took this in without surprise. 'Come on, let's go to the yard and get you sorted out with that dirty face of yours. Then I expect the kitchen will be a good place to find something to eat. Have you lasted since last night without eating?'

'It wasn't too bad. I sucked on some straws.'

Again the wearer of a red capuchon had turned up. Someone, somewhere, must have seen him and knew who he was.

Someone, concluded Chandler, was shielding him. He considered the possibilities.

* * *

After he had the kitcheners sort out some food for the new, shiny-faced Dickon and had made them swear to keep him safe beside them for the rest of the day, he went in to find Willoughby.

When he entered the solar one look showed him that now was not the time to give him the details of Maud's fate. An empty flagon of wine stood on the table next to him.

He would let the foreman know what had happened instead so that they could redirect their efforts in their search for what was now almost certainly her body.

For now he said, 'I regret my offer to help you, Willoughby. I've failed. I know as little as anybody who was making accusations of witchcraft against an innocent young maid.'

Willoughby waved this aside.

Chandler continued. 'The big question is whether the one who took the boat is known to anyone here?'

He waited to see what he would reply but his manner was distraught, his usual control gone.

Almost before Chandler finished speaking a servant entered with another jug of wine. Chandler sat down opposite and waved it away when he tried to pour some into his own goblet.

After the door closed he leaned forward. 'Listen, have you had your housekeeper brought in to answer a few questions? You say you believe she spies for the new regime.'

Willoughby gave him a bleary glance. 'She?' He tried to rouse himself. 'What can she have to do with it? You think she knows anything?'

'Work it out.'

Willoughby slumped back in his chair. Chandler took out the piece of torn fabric from his scrip and placed it next to him on the table.

Willoughby picked it up and stared at it as if it would tell him the answer to its owner's identity.

'The boatman found it earlier by the river and was sure it had not been there the day before. Young Dickon says he thought he saw a man on the roof the morning Evelyn fell and Maud saw someone wearing a red capuchon visiting Evelyn also that morning. I didn't think much to this as evidence. Dickon admitted he might have imagined the whole thing – and of course, we don't have proof that this visitor had anything to do with Evelyn's fall – but it's likely he can at least tell us something about how it happened.'

'Fetch that woman in, she might admit to seeing somebody like that,' Willoughby suggested. He half rose from his chair to do it himself but the effort was too much and he slumped back again.

'Ask her a few questions in a roundabout way when you're feeling more yourself,' Chandler advised. 'Meanwhile, I'll see if anybody else can shed light on his identity.'

As he got up to go he said, 'Come on, John, old fellow, stop drinking yourself under the table. It's now we need all our wits about us.'

He went out.

The kitchens were busy preparing the midday meal. Vats steamed. Aromas of fish and meat mingled with the sweet and sour of different sauces. Willoughby did not stint on his responsibilities towards his household. No plain pottage for them. Was it enough to keep them loyal in the present situation when there were advantages in paying allegiance to the other side?

The housekeeper looked up from her basting. 'Brother, what may I do for you?'

'I'm rather anxious about the master,' he replied. 'Will someone attend him – and maybe take away the replacement jug that was just brought in?'

'I'm sure there's nothing wrong with it . . .' she began to flare.

When he merely smiled as if he understood the duress she was under and still expected compliance she changed her tune. 'Very well, as you like, brother. He won't be flattered to think you believe him a drunkard.'

'I believe him a man suffering extreme grief for his wife and servant,' he replied smoothly. 'I'm sure you understand, mistress. Your kindness towards him will be much appreciated when he's himself again.'

Unexpectedly she glanced down as if chastened. 'I'll go in and see him,' she replied shortly.

After she swept out Chandler turned to glance across the hall towards the solar to watch her go inside. To his astonishment

she bent over Willoughby and with great familiarity stroked his
hair. She had forgotten to shut the door and Willoughby himself
was in no state to do so. Chandler saw her bend to kiss him on
the brow and to his further astonishment Willoughby placed one
arm round her hips to pull her against the side of his chair in a
gesture of open familiarity.

Chandler moved out of sight. So that's how it was. Or was it
more a matter of keeping his enemies close?

He took the stairs up to his attic for some solitude. As he reached
the landing with the door on to Evelyn's roof garden he hesitated.
Hoping it might bring some inspiration to have another look, he
pushed the door and stepped outside.

From up here he could look out over the entire domain.

It gleamed in sunlight through what was turning out to be a
long, hot summer. From the distant meadows the source of
Willoughby's wealth, his sheep, could be heard with their lulling
plaints, and in his fields the arable crops were already being
brought in, such was the master's typical good management. His
men worked with zeal and confidence under his aegis. It was
odd, then, to see that moment of apparent weakness through the
open solar door.

Was it merely the familiarity of a drunk with an attractive
female within reach or was it something that had been going on
in secret for some time? Did anyone else know about it? Had
Evelyn known? Is that why she took it as a sign she could behave
with the same freedom?

He stood on the roof and noticed that he could look straight
in through the solar windows, as also into the kitchens and the
rest of the offices needed for the daily running of the place.
Nothing was hidden.

The steward was hard at work among his accounts. On the
other side he could see the new building standing empty and
wondered what it was to be used for. In other circumstances he
imagined it would be an ideal nursery for a whole string of little
Willoughbies and their nursemaids. What had that made Evelyn
feel? Was it a threat, or an assurance of her status?

Before he turned away he noticed two figures in familiar white
robes enter the yard through the side door. They spent some time

in the shade talking to the gatekeeper, then made at once towards the house where the steward came out on to the step to greet them.

Chandler recognized both Cistercians. They were monks from Dieulacres. One of them, Senlac, worked in the scriptorium and knew that Chandler had been entrusted to take the pages of the secret chronicle to London.

He went back inside and had started down the stairs to the hall just as one of the house servants began to climb up.

'There you are, brother! Two visitors for you.'

They met in the steward's chamber but after greetings were exchanged they seemed to have nothing much to say to him until the one who Chandler had down as the bodyguard on behalf of his more bookish companion suggested a walk in the yard. The steward nodded and turned back to his ledgers.

'So what is it?' Chandler asked as soon as they were outside.

Senlac smiled faintly. 'We bring thanks from our lord abbot for the message you sent to inform us the mission was accomplished.'

Chandler acknowledged this.

The monk continued, 'We have, however, another request.' He frowned. 'But before we mention that we gather that things are not as they should be here at the master's house? The steward also mentioned that it was a difficult time?'

The bodyguard added, 'We have not yet set eyes on the master but gather that he is somewhat indisposed?'

'Grieving for the mysterious death of his wife, yes,' agreed Chandler, 'as well as for one of his servants. You can get all the information you need from the others. They're in great turmoil today because a young maid is believed drowned . . .'

'And we understand a rumour of foul play is going round concerning both females. Is that so?'

'It is.' He marvelled at their speed in getting to grips with the situation. 'Before you ask, I have no idea who the perpetrator can be beyond the fact that he may wear a red capuchon.'

The two monks pondered this for a moment. 'Sadly our abbey is too far away to give us the privilege of understanding local animosities. Praise be to the lord! Apart from that one brief invasion by the censor when you were with us we have so far remained blessedly unvisited and unharmed.'

'We're well-placed on the road to nowhere,' agreed the body-guard. He turned to Chandler and gave him a searching glance. 'We're told you were returning to Dieulacres when you were recalled by Willoughby?'

'He really wanted the strong arms of my two escorts,' he told them. 'I would have come on to save you a journey if I'd known. The household here was engaged on a fruitless search along the riverbank for the missing maid. There's little I can do that they cannot. I might have come on alone and risked the outlaw element. I'm sure by now they realize I have some protection in Chester.'

'Despite the situation here we deem it an honour to escort you back to Dieulacres ourselves.' The scrivener indicated his companion. 'Brother Wilfrid is used to these ruffians and knows how to speak to them.'

Whether he spoke to them verbally or by physical means, Chandler did not ask. Before he could decide whether to accept their offer Brother Senlac came to the point of their visit.

He glanced from left to right to make sure no one could overhear. 'We have a new matter for the glove.'

Equally quietly Chandler asked, 'And the destination?'

'Not London this time. In the other direction.' He lowered his voice still further. 'We need it taking into Wales. To be put into the hands of Glyn Dwr himself.'

Chandler felt overwhelmed for a moment.

He recalled his promise to the three longbowmen and their protege, young Aethelstan. So far he had not been able to find any way of fulfilling such a promise. Now he asked, 'So what's afoot?'

The two monks lowered their heads. 'He is elected Prince of Wales now, you must know that?'

Chandler nodded.

'He is amassing forces to repel an invasion. Lord help us all and we pray that it will never come to pass but if it does we will, of course, support any opposition against the usurper.' He gave a lugubrious chuckle. 'Even he can't hang us all!'

'Does it mean I must return with you today?'

'It's late now. We left just after matins and could use some sleep. We can leave tomorrow if that suits us all better?'

They left as unobtrusively as they had arrived with the information that they could be found at the Benedictine guesthouse at St Werbergh's.

'Good cover, is it not?' murmured Senlac.

'Take care. The town isn't as placid as it seems. I've been threatened by a punch in the face by the summoner.' He thought it worth warning them but they burst into wry chuckles.

'I'd say that eye has received more than a threat!'

'If you hadn't been warned off we'd have assumed you were too lowly to warrant his attention.'

Senlac was still chuckling as they took their leave and headed for St Werbergh's for the night.

EIGHT

Farewell to Maser Willoughby

Later on, Willoughby had sobered up a little when Chandler went in to see him.

'Forgive me, Rodric. I'm at my wit's end. Any news?'

'About your maid?'

He nodded.

'Nothing, as far as I know.'

'Do what you can. I resent having the curse of death hanging over the place.'

'But what if I say I would like to leave with the monks from Dieulacres tomorrow?'

'Go, let me not hinder you. If this fellow is more than mere coincidence he will emerge from the darkness, we can be sure of that. I shall attend to our defences in every way I can devise.' He brushed a hand over his face. 'It's just the death of that poor girl . . .' His face sank into misery and for a moment Chandler thought of his wife. 'My serving maid,' he added. 'A direct stab.'

Before he stepped back into the hall Chandler took it to be as good an opportunity as any to mention what Dickon had told him.

'But did he mention the red headgear this boat-stealing fellow was wearing?' Willoughby demanded.

Chandler frowned. 'I don't believe he did.'

When their eyes met they were equally blank.

It had been a long and emotional day. Chandler took the opportunity to lie on his bed and think things through. If her body was swept back by the tide he wondered if it might turn up close to Willoughby's jetty where it had started from. He could not bear to think of the child being swept back and forth like nothing more than a piece of unregarded flotsam until someone found her and dragged her body ashore to give it a proper burial.

He had a wish to remain in Chester until she was found, but matters in Wales sounded urgent.

He realized he had been staring at the ceiling as if to discover whether the troubled and confused state of mind he was suffering could be called sleep, and when he realized it could not and he was as wide awake as ever, he rolled off the bed.

It was still light enough to check the tide with the old boatman and return to the riverbank when it was due to flow back in. It would be near midnight by then he guessed, but if they took flares with them they would be able to see anything washed up among the reeds.

He felt he owed it to her.

Before that he would go to the parish church to send up prayers for her. It was no good going to the chantry again only to witness the summoner picking up his tolls and probably getting his other eye blackened at the same time.

St Werbergh's was busy when he entered into the cool shadow of the nave before Compline and no one took any notice of him. He knelt in the lady chapel and spoke heretically into what he suspected was nothing more than a void filled with the yearnings of desperate folk like himself who were certain of only one thing, their own mortality.

Then he began to wonder if the prayers of a heretic mattered anyway. Would they rise up with the same potency as those of a believer?

He decided he could only offer them in trust and humility and leave the rest to fate. While he was indulging in such hope he would add the names of several other people he believed might benefit from divine help – those uppermost in his mind after what the monks had told him being the longbow men.

He wondered if they had managed to get through safely to Glyn Dwr as they had intended and were now numbered among the bowmen in his army ready to defend Wales from Henry's expected invasion.

And he would add Matilda of course. And Cook and Adam and Master Galfrido. And Matilda. Always Matilda. He added her. And the baby. Of course, the baby, poor little soul.

His mind veered away from the latter. He could not imagine

he had a child somewhere, a living creature struggling for survival in this horror-filled place. How could the little being ever be safe in such a hazardous world?

'You're intending to do what?' Senlac looked at Chandler as if he had taken leave of his senses.

'It's going to be a difficult task in the dark.' Brother Wilfrid added his opinion. 'Why not wait until morning?'

Chandler looked from one to the other. How could he say because he couldn't stand the thought of Maud's body lying in the river all night?

He was sorry he had called at the monastery now. It had not been his original intention. He had no idea what had led him to approach the porter's lodge and ask after the two Cistercians. And there they were, standing in the garth. He could not avoid them.

They caught sight of him at once and came over, all smiles and with their usual warm greetings. When he told them what he must do before he could travel back to Dieulacres with them they were sceptical.

They pointed out the obvious difficulties to echo Chandler's own misgivings.

With no duties other than to please themselves now they were outside their own abbey's jurisdiction, the two monks strolled back to Willoughby's with him and he showed them the path beside the wool shed that led down to the riverbank.

The old boatman, perhaps making up for his negligence in being asleep when Maud went missing, came out of his hut to greet them.

Chandler quizzed him about the tide and he told them exactly when high-water mark would be reached.

'Trust me, that's your best time to find anything swept up from lower down.' He gave Chandler a pitying look. 'It might be worth a try. They still haven't found hide nor hair of her. Likely the body got caught on some underwater obstruction.' He paused and wrinkled his brow. 'Though if yon lad is sure about when he saw her go under she would have been in the fast stream in the middle or thereabouts, when it was on the ebb. Mayhap,' he added, 'she was swept on down to the estuary. Which in that case means you won't find her for days, if ever.'

The monks made no comment until they were out of earshot. 'A cheerful soul,' remarked Wilfrid eventually.

Senlac merely pointed to the river. 'The tide's on the turn already. Where do we see about these flares we'll need for later?'

Chandler led them back up to the yard and the headman came out, calling for Pearce when he noticed Chandler, and willing to do what he could to help.

Chandler explained their purpose, citing the boatman as his guide for the best time to make a search of the bank again.

'My fellows have found nothing but old boots and an empty flagon floating in the water,' he told them. 'It's probably as the boatman says but these staunch fellows won't give up just yet. Witch she might have been, if you believe in such riddle-me-ree, but she was a neat little lass and everybody's favourite.'

He went into one of the store sheds and roused somebody to prepare enough flares to make a thorough search when the tide came up around midnight.

The monks returned to the bank and watched for anything that might give them hope, even though the water was only drifting gently back upriver at this time and could have brought in nothing with the weight of a human body in its gentle current. The boatman came out to join them.

Darkness was already falling as he passed round some hunks of crusty bread while they waited for the tide to gather strength.

They patrolled the riverbank in both directions from Willoughby's land, but the short summer night yielded nothing.

There was no moon, but the sky at this time of year was never quite dark and it shed a glow over the rippling surface of the water.

Small sounds became magnified as a fish or unseen river monster rose to the surface and splashed back again.

They could see torches moving on their side of the river as men quested methodically back and forth along the shoreline. Brief excitement was caused when a dark shape resembling a body was seen swirling towards them. Flares lining the bank could be seen clustering together as someone called for more light and waded into the shallows to drag something ashore. Expectations were thwarted when they discovered the body was nothing more than a log that had got loose from someone's yard further down.

'Stout oak, is that,' one man observed, but it was sent back on its way to be floated down again when the tide turned.

Disappointed that their vigil brought them no nearer to finding Maud they waited until the tide was well on its way out again just to be sure. By then dawn was breaking. The monks walked back up the meadow in the gloaming with Chandler leaving the men to make a final patrol before returning to the kitchens to break their fast.

'Time to start on our way back to the abbey if you're ready, brother?' Senlac turned to Chandler.

'I'll get my bag and join you. Are your horses stabled with the Benedictines?'

'We thought it would be more convenient to keep them at the town stables. We'll pick them up on the way.'

So the decision to return was made. Chandler tried to put thoughts of poor little Maud aside.

It was as they reached the yard that he noticed Dickon hanging on to the apron of the housekeeper. She was gossiping to someone, giving instructions for feeding the men when they returned from their night's search.

The lad seemed delighted to see him and showed how the housekeeper had tied him by his belt to her strings – because you said to keep me safe, he told him – and as she talked she kept pulling at them as if he were a misbehaving dog on a lead. He gave Chandler a long-suffering glance every time she did it.

Something made Chandler ask, 'Want to ride back with us?'

His little face broke into a beaming smile.

'Get everything you need.' He turned to the housekeeper and interrupted her. 'Where's his mother?'

'Dead from the plague. Why?'

'His father?'

'Run off with a fancy piece.'

'So he's next to being an orphan?'

'So are many,' she replied without emotion.

'I'm leaving for Dieulacres now but I'd like to take the lad along to help us with the horses. Will you mention it to the master when you next see him?'

She huffed and protested but was easily cajoled into an agreement and unloosed the boy before Chandler changed his mind. 'I'm not sure I should be doing this,' she muttered. 'But I'm fair sick of him. Questions, questions, all the time without cease.'

'I'll speak on your behalf. I don't want to wake Master Willoughby as early as this.' He didn't add more although he thought it.

'I'll be glad if you'll take him off my hands, to be honest. He's the sort who never stop fidgeting,' she grumbled. 'Needs a bit of house-training in my opinion.'

Freed, Dickon slipped his hand into Chandler's. 'How shall I start, brother? Shall I fetch your bag down?'

The monks looked askance when they heard what was happening. 'How's he going to keep up?' Wilfrid asked.

'He'll ride with me,' said Chandler.

A few moments later while Dickon had disappeared into the house to fetch Chandler's bags he explained, 'Bearing in mind what he told me about this murderous fellow by the river he'll be safer with us. I don't like to think of him being the next victim on that fellow's death list.'

The monks understood and when he reappeared with Chandler's small bag and a grin on his face at the prospect of an adventure, they asked him his name and how old he was and generally made a fuss of him. Then together they set off.

The sun was halfway to the meridian.

Dickon was marvelling when Senlac told him how far the abbey was from Chester. 'I've never travelled this far ever in my entire life,' he said. 'How much further do we have to go? Are we near London?'

'Work it out. We're nowhere near. We'll be nearer to a place called Leek. We've done twenty miles already, more or less.'

'A lot, then.'

'If we've already done twenty miles and Dieulacres is thirty miles away, how much further do we have to go, do you think?'

'How do you work it out?' the lad asked.

Senlac was just beginning to give an explanation and also how he knew it was thirty miles in total when they were hailed by a voice from the trees.

'Stand! We have you in our sights!'

They drew to a halt and glanced about.

'Up there,' murmured Wilfrid, drawing his sword and indicating a tree overhanging the track.

They stared upwards.

An archer appeared in the branches with an arrow already in the nock. At the same moment two men pushed through the undergrowth beside the path and made for their horses. The animals reared. Wilfrid slid to the ground. Chandler drew his own sword and jumped down. Senlac calmed his horse and attempted to ride away, but one of the men grabbed the bridle and dragged his mount to a halt, pulling Senlac out of the saddle at the same time.

None of them could go either forward or back without making a fight of it.

'What do you want?' demanded Chandler as a preliminary.

'Your lives,' sneered the one in the lead. 'Or anything of value.'

At this point, adept at talking to types like this as was claimed, Wilfrid lunged at the nearest fellow and taking him by surprise disarmed him and sent him fleeing at once for cover. Roaring, he followed.

Chandler set about the man nearest to himself and they had a brief, brisk conversation as Wilfrid might have called it, with swords doing the talking, until the third fellow, jumping down from the trees, with his bow slung over his shoulder, and noticing Senlac was unarmed and thus an easy prey, grabbed him round the neck and began to throttle him.

Before Chandler could go to his aid Senlac fumbled in his belt and there was a sudden scream of pain as his attacker fell back, both hands clutched to his face and blood streaming from between his fingers.

Senlac fell to knees and to everyone's astonishment started to beg forgiveness for causing harm.

Chandler dragged him to his feet and pushed him towards his horse. He forced him to mount then leaped astride his own horse and, before their opponents could recover, Wilfrid reappeared, flung himself into the saddle and, shouting to Chandler to follow, swiped Senlac's mount on the rump causing it to leap forward before spurring his own horse away.

Chandler had lost sight of Dickon in the heat of the moment and now saw him scrambling out of the bushes at the sound of the retreating horses. Scooping him into the saddle he spurred his horse after the others without delay.

Soon they were galloping along a narrow track far from their attackers and when they were satisfied there was no one in pursuit they slowed enough to express their astonishment about what had happened.

'Beyond Willoughby's jurisdiction,' muttered Wilfrid, ambiguously.

But Senlac was in a fever of contrition. 'I have never blinded anyone with my penknife before, so help me, God,' he exclaimed in dismay. 'I cannot believe I did that. To use it as a weapon, an instrument only invented to create beauty. What made me so vengeful?'

'He was about to murder you, Senlac. He was throttling the life out of you. It was no more than he deserved. It was self-defence.' Chandler tried to calm him.

He still mumbled and prayed and looked white-faced and would not be consoled.

Wilfrid urged him to be practical.

'It was either you or him. Who is doing most good in this sorry world, you with your beautiful manuscripts spreading truth or that blamed fellow, fighting and stealing with only hatred in his heart? I know the answer to that, even if you don't. Our lord God knows it too. He is saving you for more important tasks.'

Chandler thought to relieve the situation by adding some humour. 'And think of the trouble you've saved us from having to carry your corpse back to the abbey with us!'

Wilfrid laughed out loud then turned to him. 'How's the lad? Good thing he kept out of it.'

'Not very far out, brother,' Dickon piped up as he jogged along on his perch in front of Chandler. 'Those felons will have a long walk home. I used my eating knife to hack through their hobbles and set their horses free.'

After they had congratulated him for his quick thinking, Wilfrid grinned. 'Four against three? They hadn't a chance!'

Was it the boy they were after, wondered Chandler as they rode on. The fellow in the red headgear as Willoughby referred to him had sworn to silence anyone who had seen him. It must be common knowledge by now that Dickon was one such.

Was it likely those three had been following them?

He tried to remember who had known he would be leaving with them for the abbey. It was a futile task as mostly everyone searching along the river last night would have found out the moment they returned to the yard.

The housekeeper, whichever side she was playing, was hardly the type to keep the reason for his absence to herself. Had there been time to inform her spymaster, whoever he was, that Dickon had got away? In fact, he asked himself, was there even a link between the housekeeper and the fellow with the red capuchon or was it merely his own assumption?

NINE

Dieulacres at last

In a mood of subdued jubilation they reached their destination without further mishap. Brother Senlac went at once into the church to pray and seek out his confessor. Brother Wilfrid accompanied Chandler and the boy to the abbot's lodge.

'Well done, men,' he observed when he heard what had happened. 'They encroach too often on our lands. I shall have to send a few bowmen out again.'

He was well-known for his determination to maintain their independence and his forerunner, Abbot William, had earned quite a local reputation for armed defence of monastic property. He was robust too in his defence of any of his men involved in the protection of the abbey, who were hauled before the courts as had already happened several times.

The abbot and Brother Wilfrid discussed the purpose of the attack and decided that it was probably no more than the usual travellers from elsewhere looking for their daily pickings.

Chandler was unconvinced. He was glad Dickon was now safe within the abbey precinct. It was agreed that he should join the oblates at their lessons and see how he liked monastic life.

The glove was discussed. Or rather, its eventual contents.

'Can you be prepared to leave at short notice, brother, whenever that might be?' The abbot turned to Chandler. 'It may not be until the end of summer, however. We are making arrangements to remove a small but valuable collection of writings to a safer place as soon as it can be conveyed in secret. We're waiting for confirmation to be passed back along the line that they are ready to receive such treasure in a place safe from harm. The consignment consists of some of our own books and some belonging to a glover I believe you have already met?'

Chandler assumed it was the same man Willoughby had introduced him to and nodded.

'We're having everything sent into Wales,' the abbot continued. 'Given Henry's lack of success on his so-called campaigns there it should be quite safe from his depredations.' He smiled. 'You, if you will, must take a message to the prince to confirm our side of things and offer certainty of our support.' He steepled his fingers. 'That the day has come when we have to protect our written records from barbarians of our own blood! Who would ever believe it? However, the Lord sends these challenges to try us and we shall not fail him.'

While the conveyance was being built by which the books could be taken into Wales, Chandler was forced to kick his heels. He had no real function here and waiting was something he had never had the patience for. He wondered if it was worth returning to Chester to see if he could find out more about Evelyn's death and whether Maud's body had been found, but he knew that the task the abbot had asked of him meant he had to be ready to leave at once. And anyway, he thought, what possible use would he be in Chester? He had to school himself in patience.

Meanwhile, couriers were arriving almost daily with news from all parts of the realm as the situation outside the walls of the abbey came to the boil. Self-styled King Henry IV was facing problems from all quarters, they heard.

A courier arrived from Westminster bursting with the news. 'It's this new tax,' he told everyone when he was invited into the guest refectory and plied with ale.

Chandler and several others came to listen.

'What new tax?' Chandler asked.

'This one brought in to counter the rising cost of wheat.' The man wiped the back of his hand across his lips after downing a stoup in one gulp. 'He's got to feed his army, hasn't he, and he needs money to do it. But the tax is causing riots. Why? Because nobody feels they should pay a tax merely to fulfil Henry's wicked ambitions. They see it as outrageous when his claim to the throne is based on his promise of better financial management – not on theft of their own. And anyway,' he ran the argument on, 'how can they pay when they cannot sell? Money is simply non-existent. It can't be summoned from the very air, can it?'

Two other couriers had arrived at more or less the same time and trailing the scent of sweat and horseflesh as they came over to join the group as soon as they heard their colleague putting his point of view.

They agreed with him at once. 'Everyone but Henry's most avid Lancastrian supporters can see he's failed utterly,' said the first as he flung himself on to one of the benches.

'So much for his oft-repeated promise to put the country back on a sound financial footing and restore what he calls good government,' added the second. 'He hasn't considered the practicalities.'

Another courier had recently arrived from the north. 'Another thing,' he interrupted as he joined them. 'King Dickon had the sense to listen to the advice of his Chancellor, Michael de la Pole, a fellow who knew all about the money exchanges from his father – after all, he was a wealthy wool merchant in Hull and he knew what was what. Young de la Pole advised Dickon well when he told him how he could solve the problem of the silver shortage.' He jingled the coins in his leather bag which all the couriers carried to protect their sealed documents. 'He knew we had a desperate need for silver in the markets. He told King Dickon he could acquire all he needed by gaining access to the Bohemian silver mines. It was de la Pole who suggested a dynastic marriage to the sister of the Holy Roman Emperor, owner of Kutna Hora, the largest silver mine in Europe!'

'It was the best dowry Good Queen Anne could have brought,' his companion added. 'King Richard's carping enemies were sore at heart by the praise he received when it became known he'd made such a profitable alliance.'

'They didn't like him to have such a resounding success. Remember how they used to whine endlessly about the fact that dear Anne brought no actual dowry with her?'

'Even when the truth of what she really brought to the realm became widely known they still carped and complained for another decade in their small-minded desire to bring him down.'

'It stuck in their baronial craws to discover that de la Pole, a fellow they disdained as a mere merchant without a drop of royal blood in his veins, had been able to make such a lucrative arrangement with the Emperor.'

'No such luck for royal Henry! His once over-filled coffers were emptied almost as soon as he invaded Ravenspur!'

Chandler agreed. 'He spent his inheritance like a profligate – buying the massive army he needed to maintain his grip on his illegal rule,' he observed to general agreement. 'And, judging by the continual uprisings against him and the never-ending hangings and incarcerations so vindictively ordered by him that have followed, the situation can only get worse.'

The first courier said, 'Where this continual expense is going to come from has only one answer, it'll come from massive taxation of ordinary folk, starving and destitute as many of them already are.' He spat into a corner and glared round. 'What is to be done?'

He was met with a gloomy silence.

To add to Henry's self-inflicted wounds the rumours that King Richard still lived would not go away, as another of them pointed out. 'The monastics, Cistercians especially, and the friars, both Franciscans and Augustinians, are openly opposed to a man who can murder his rightful king to put himself on the throne. It's as straightforward as that.'

There was quite a group of them now, having travelled from different courts and towns, fetching up for a few days respite at Dieulacres as it was so centrally placed. One who had been more or less silent glared round at everyone. 'The point is this, Henry's problems are made worse by the abhorrence his actions are causing throughout Europe. I've just come over from France. His allies are non-existent. Nobody wants to be tainted by an accusation of regicide. The French are wild in their condemnation. After all, the new queen poor Richard married when his beloved Anne died, is their own little princess Isabella, no more than an innocent child. Now where is she? A prisoner – or guest, as Henry likes to put it – at Wallingford Castle!'

Somebody asked, 'What are they going to do with her, poor little maid?'

'It's looks as if she'll have to stay there. Henry can't afford to pay back her dowry. He's already spent it. The French are on the brink of retaliation. Such duplicity! That a king, self-styled though he is, has failed to keep his word! They're shocked into astonished rage. It bodes ill for the future.' He told them that the French had already recaptured thirty castles Henry had held in Aquitaine and Perigord but that without ready cash the earl he sent to retake them was unable to do more than wring his hands and cry to heaven for aid.

'Finance,' said Chandler to murmurs of agreement, 'is not Henry's strong point. His only way of not losing face is to increase the violence and arbitrary attacks on individual people who are brave enough to point out his failings.'

The open barbarism of beheadings and mass hangings were becoming the norm. Both monastic and secular critics came in for the same vindictive treatment. Chandler reminded them, as if they needed reminding, that Henry had clearly demonstrated his vengefulness at Smithfield with his vile punishment of the unarmed friars of Leicester.

The only success he managed was in the north at the battle of Homildon Hill. Even this was down to someone else. It was Northumberland's son, young Harry Hotspur, who restored Henry's hold on Northumbria in a battle at which many Scots were slaughtered, but the Earl of Douglas came over to Hotspur's side with the aim of dislodging the usurper and re-establishing a legitimate king.

Henry's biggest problem at this time, however, was in Wales.

One of the couriers newly arrived from Caernarfon mentioned how Glyn Dwr's army had repelled Henry's last failed invasion and now held the castle as a bargaining piece against the exorbitant taxes demanded to foot his misplaced ambition. He gave a sardonic smile. 'But to finance a man who would use your money to pay for an army to destroy you seems like strange logic to those many who understand what he intends.'

When the ironic laughter subsided, somebody added that the only hope of a change for the better lay in the Prophecy of the Six Kings. Given that it had predicted the destruction of the Lamb – King Richard – by the Mouldwarp – Henry – it went on to say that the Lamb would eventually triumph and the realm would be divided into three and live in peace.

To Chandler all this rumour and counter-rumour, all these failed campaigns of Henry's, causing such death and despair to so many, could only lead to one thing. None of Merlin's prophecies were necessary to predict where it would lead before Henry was finished.

It could only lead to war.

TEN

The abbey of Dieulacres basked in a summer of good weather with enough rain to keep the crops from drying out and sun enough to ripen the fields of wheat that had struggled back to life after the cry 'havoc!' had lain waste the earlier harvest.

Despite this the clouds of war lay heavily on the horizon and could not be ignored.

As far as Chandler knew there was no change in the situation at Chester. Pearce's vow to find the killer had come to nothing.

It was also difficult to work out what was being planned at Dieulacres, for such was the abbot's discretion Chandler was not included in the discussions in Chapter, and he gathered only that Glyn Dwr's movements depended on where and when Henry would attack. It was merely hinted that the monks were waiting for more information about the final destination for their secret cargo of precious books. He understood that it was to be sent somewhere over the border, to Caernarfon, perhaps, or even to Anglesey.

The problem with the latter destination was that Anglesey was an island, cut off by the unpredictable straits from the mainland.

The safe place there was a friary near the town of Llanfaes, a once great and noble stronghold on the island's south-east coast. A port thriving on trade in ale, wine, wool and hides and, with a lucrative fishing industry, it was a major market town until Edward I destroyed it to rebuild his copycat fortified town and the castle he called Beaumaris. Designed to take over the rich-pickings of the Llanfaes trade it was mightily successful.

The priory built there had been revered because it was the final resting place of Llewelyn the Great's wife Joan, daughter of King John. It was Llewelyn who had the priory built and Edward II who had it rebuilt after his father's destruction of it.

It was there, it was hoped, the books would be safe.

If Chandler expected to be asked to accompany the treasure

trove on its eventual journey the word did not come. Instead came only murmurs about having to wait and see.

Henry's forced marches at this time were restless enough to confuse everyone. Nobody quite knew where he was going to appear next. It was impossible to work out his battle plan if any.

When he did make his random assaults the upshot was the same: destruction, a victimization of any public figure who made a murmur of protest, and the brutal hanging and quartering of any who dared suggest that his phantom enemy, King Richard, was still living and breathing in the material world.

Chandler fretted to be out on Glyn Dwr's trail with the message, or whatever it was that would be entrusted to him.

A few months earlier he had longed for the placid existence of the cloister, but it was not enough now his wish was granted and there was nothing to stop him from sinking into a routine with only prayers demanded from him. He wondered again whether he would be better employed at Chester should news or more likely no news come in. But it was not practical when departure was imminent, even though he was itching to get out and on the move again. To add to it, rumours of Henry's planned invasion of Wales were growing.

The secret conveyance for the books turned out to be a special cart being built down in the abbey wood yard during this long and uncertain period of waiting. Only a few monks were allowed in to see it and offer their advice. Chandler was eventually included and along with several others was given a demonstration of how it worked.

What was special was that it had a double floor which slid back to reveal a deep cavity into which it was hoped the books from the Chester glover would fit.

One of the carpenters slid it back and forth to show how easily it worked.

Tightly bound bales of hay with loose hay piled on top were to conceal this floor even though everyone doubted that the secret partition would ever be noticed in the turmoil of resistance. Because, of course, whoever was driving, if attacked, would resist.

Brother Wilfrid was hoping to be chosen and was positive on that point, citing the holy wars to justify the shedding of blood, but there was no shortage of contenders for this dangerous honour.

Chandler fervently wished he was going with them but soon began to realize that he would be travelling alone and in a different direction to the main cargo. It rankled so much that he was being kept in the dark that he tried to find fault with the plans made so far.

'When you get to Caernarfon,' he asked in a tone dripping with scorn, 'how do you propose to cross the Menai Straits? Can you walk on water?'

Wilfrid patted him on the shoulder.

'We cross by ship, of course. Do you imagine there are no loyal shipmen in Wales?'

At last a message came through that the cart was to be driven to a meeting place halfway between Dieulacres and Chester. It was unnamed. The negotiators clearly had a place in mind known to both parties without having to name it.

Brother Wilfrid, to his delight, was appointed as head driver and as if to show there were no ill feelings between himself and Chandler asked if he would like to come along as well.

At least, that's how it was put to him.

Mollified, Chandler agreed with enthusiasm. He wore his riding gloves in case it was a ploy by the abbot and he would have need of them even though he still had no idea where they intended to send him other than to find Glyn Dwr.

The head carpenter insisted on jumping on to the cart and giving the secret panel one last check before being completely satisfied it would do, then the cart was loaded with the books wrapped in kidskin for protection and hay from the granges was piled on top of the secret cavity to conceal it. Finally, with a hymn or two from the gathering monks who assembled to see it off, it creaked out under the archway and on to the foregate.

Several lay brothers astride some of the abbey's most mettlesome horses followed at a distance down the lane as if unconcerned and in no way aware of the importance of the cart and its contents.

Escorted in this way they reached the woods.

Chandler noticed a visible straying of hands to half-concealed weapons. The lay brothers tightened their formation around the cart. Horsemen all, and well-muscled from their days in the fields, they were a reassuring sight as the cavalcade approached the first dip in the track. It was particularly well-screened by thick undergrowth hereabouts and had become a familiar place in the past for the laying of ambushes, but they trundled down one side of the slope and eventually, unscathed, ascended the other to drive deeper into the dark depths of the wild wood.

Wilfrid, attired in rough secular clothing, was whistling between his teeth like an old carter himself by now. Chandler could see how much he was enjoying the mission and silently chided himself for his envy.

His doubts arose not only from the desolate woods they had to traverse but, when he saw how slowly the horses laboured along, his doubts stemmed from the casual seeming planning that had so ordered things too. The abbey horses, although the best the abbey could afford, were unlike the deep-chested mounts of Henry's cavalry that might be encountered on the long road into Wales.

He wondered if the unworldly monks really understood how devastating an attack by professional cavalrymen could be, or how many miles they would have to labour along like this until they reached the safety of west Wales.

Eventually they drew to a halt. Water bottles were passed round. Riders slid from their saddles to allow their mounts to munch the grass in the shade.

It was a day of blazing sunshine. Once the wooden wheels of the cart were stilled the only sound to break the silence was birdsong. Some were calmed by it and exchanged glances, others were unsettled as if expecting the unnatural silence to be the warning of a trap.

After a while a figure emerged from the bushes and hailed them in a cheerful voice. It was a lad of about twenty wearing fustian and carrying a bow over his shoulder. Chandler guessed he was offering a password because Wilfrid replied at once with the strange observation that, 'My leaves are green!'

The lad beckoned to some unseen watchers behind the screening trees and came on until he was standing next to the cart and looking up at Wilfrid disguised in his borrowed garments.

'Be there a Brother Chandler accompanying you, master carter?'

Wilfrid gave Chandler a quick glance. 'Who asks?'

'Master Willoughby's man, Pearce.'

Chandler announced himself and jumped down from the cart. 'What's this about?'

'He asks you to return to Chester with me, brother.'

'And why should I do that?'

'I know not, brother. I only know that I was asked to put this request to you, then escort you back to Chester.'

Brother Wilfrid nodded. 'Go, the lord go with you.'

'But how did Pearce know I would be here—?'

Just then several men followed the lad from out of the woods and soon there was quite a group clustering round the cart with their cudgels and knives. Something seemed to be happening among the trees and with a little subdued shouting and the sound of broken branches a few men appeared carrying what looked like several small coffins. On seeing them the lay brothers from Dieulacres began to move aside the bales of hay and with their guards peering into the trees on all sides the newcomers ran to heave the coffins where indicated as the secret panel slid back. It seemed to take only moments.

The Chester men disappeared as quickly into the trees as they had appeared and the bales of hay were replaced, Wilfrid whistled to the team of horses, raised his whip in a valedictory salute to Chandler, and the whole cavalcade turned in a great arc to take to the road again.

Chandler rested his hand on the hilt of his sword under his robes and watched them leave until he and the lad were the only two remaining.

To anyone riding by now it would look as if there had been no meeting and no transfer of anything at all, least of all several boxes of banned books. Only the fading creak of the loaded cart betrayed its existence but even that soon faded into the distance.

The lad turned to Chandler. 'I have a horse hidden by for you, brother. Come.'

*   *   *

He could get nothing from his escort as they rode side by side on the road to Chester. At every question, he merely shook his head.

His secrecy made Chandler the more keen to find out what had happened.

Pearce?

Why him?

Was it a trap after all? Had the glover's secret haul of dissident books been discovered and were the little wooden coffin-like boxes being taken with their illicit contents as evidence against him and the abbey men? More confusing, how had Pearce known that the books were being handed over and that Chandler would be present? The lad had even been instructed to bring a horse for him. Who was behind all this? The abbot? Willoughby? Someone else, unknown to him?

Chandler examined every possibility until he was tired of it. Instead he allowed his thoughts to dwell on Matilda and how beautiful she was, and how trusting, and how badly he had treated her, and then he thought of their baby, a son, no less, and how he could fulfil his duties as a good father, and what the little fellow was like, probably bawling its head off at this very moment as his father rode along in the sylvan shadows of the path towards his destiny.

When they reached the edge of the woods the invisible lookouts made a token call which the lad answered, murmuring afterwards, 'God's speed, to you, fellows.'

He grinned at Chandler out of the corners of his eyes, then spurred his horse with joyful yells all the way to the city gates with Chandler, resolved to face whatever should transpire, following closely behind.

When they reached the houses along the north street within the walls he told him he had to go to his mother's, and Chandler thanked him and began to head towards Willoughby's house.

Before he could enter the street where the wool merchant's property lay, a man with a hood pulled over his face stepped into the path of his horse, dragging at the bridle to bring it to a halt.

Before Chandler could raise his whip the fellow said, 'It's me. Pearce. Hold off!'

Seeing no one else around to cause alarm, Chandler dismounted. 'What gives?'

'Something has turned up. Or I should say "someone", but I'm not saying who. Will you come with me?'

'Is that all you're going to tell me?'

'I think it's important. They might know who murdered Evelyn.'

So it was now definitely murder, was it? 'Aren't you going to tell me who it is then?'

He eyed Pearce suspiciously in the descending gloom just as the flares outside a few important houses along the street were starting to be fired up for the night making the shadows between deeper still.

Pearce peered into his face and muttered, 'I can't. They have not spoken to me. I suspect they will only tell you.'

'They?' Chandler queried.

But Pearce would say no more. 'Follow me. It's important no one recognizes you. We'll go the long way round.'

Chandler pulled up his hood. He knew he should be treading carefully but there was nothing to suggest that Pearce was playing him false.

He began to follow him along the street towards an open stretch planted with cabbages and peas. A path ran alongside it and the River Dee was visible like a light-stippled silver fish between the roofs of a few single-storey dwellings lower down fronting on to the water.

He suggested that Chandler leave his horse in the burgage of one of the cottages with the gruff words, 'I know who lives here. He doesn't mind.'

Then, becoming nothing much more than a blur in the failing light, he began to head for the riverbank and to a path that ran along behind the houses before eventually petering out.

It was completely dark now and Chandler was calling himself all kinds of fool for trusting Pearce. Confident that he could take care of himself if it came to it, he was not so sanguine at the thought of a reception committee of more than two or three armed ruffians.

He followed in an alert silence.

Pearce turned off the narrow way along the bank and struck

out into the shadowy mass of the undergrowth and a vague familiarity made Chandler hesitate. It was too dark to see properly but something about the lie of the land was not new. It was surely Willoughby's domain?

Pearce turned his head. 'Stay here. I'll be back in a trice.'

With whose army, thought Chandler, now prepared for anything.

He made sure he had a tree at his back then settled to wait.

ELEVEN

The riverbank

Night sounds crowded round him. His hearing became acute, every small sound identifiable. A bird. A fish rising in the river. The scuttling of a weasel. The lazy thump of a rabbit not far off. A dog barking in the distance.

Then something human seemed to join the wild, a movement that no animal could make. He imagined it as Pearce returning but then he heard him threshing back and forth in among the trees further off as if he had lost something.

Chandler's night vision was slowly improving and he could make out the row of hawthorns sheltering Willoughby's domain from his neighbour's land, and a great tree that stood as a sentinel on the riverbank, and further along he knew he would find the wooden jetty. From there, walking up the slope towards the meadow he would eventually find the wool shed, the yard, the house.

He wondered why Pearce had brought him here when they could have walked openly across the yard and down the path.

With a sudden shock a figure loomed in front of him, materializing like a wraith out of the shadows. 'Come on up. I can't find it.'

'What are we looking for, Pearce?'

'It's a shelter. It wasn't here when you left. I came across it the night before last. It was good fortune I knew about the exchange and I guessed you'd be with it. I want you to see something.'

Without asking any more of the questions that were clamouring to be answered, Chandler followed Pearce through a tangled barrier of brambles and hawthorn stubs until they emerged into a clearing. He recognized it at once.

It was where little Maud had been discovered pacing out her banishing ritual before issuing that strange trance-like prediction about dark forces closing in.

Pearce was crawling about on hands and knees but stood up almost straight away. 'I can't find it. Like an animal hide.'

'Is this to do with Maud?' Chandler asked.

Before Pearce could answer he remembered where she had thrown the stone at the end of the little ritual and it had landed with scarcely a sound after flying over a screen of bushes. 'Well, is it?'

'I found her coif.' Pearce drew something from inside his pouch. 'It might not be hers . . . but I think it is. I think she's back.'

'That cannot be.'

Moving quietly Chandler pushed his way deeper into the undergrowth and had to force an opening to allow himself through, but there it was, a clearing surrounded by thick undergrowth and on the edge of it, screened by broken branches, a shelter someone had built for themselves.

Pearce was right behind him. 'Lucky,' he observed, but Chandler did not correct him.

Crouching down he pushed aside the curtain of leaves and whispered, 'Who's here?'

An animal of some sort gave a sharp rustle of alarm, then froze. Into the darkness Chandler spoke again. 'Who's here?'

He put out a hand and touched something warm. No animal fur nor feathers. It was as smooth and warm as human skin. A stifled scream followed and the creature pressed back into the darkness out of reach.

Unable to believe it he whispered, 'Maud? . . . Is it really you?'

A breath came, fast with fear. 'Who is it?'

'It's me, Rodric Chandler . . . Maud? Are you hurt?'

With a jolt something hit him hard in the chest and he fell back, righted himself and, kneeling, took the whimpering child in his arms where she was clinging to him and heaving great gulping sobs.

'No, don't cry, you're safe. Maud, I can't believe you're here. We feared you were dead. We thought you must have drowned. Dear child, don't cry, you're safe, there's nothing wrong.'

He held her while she sniffed and sobbed and clung to him as if she would never let go. He rocked her back and forth. 'Pearce knows it's you hiding out here, doesn't he?'

'I saw him come into the grove and look about and I thought he'd found my hide so I built another one deeper in the thicket when he'd gone. I didn't know what to do.'

'Why don't you go up to the house?'

He felt her shudder and draw back. It made him begin to suspect a possible reason but decided he would let it come to them in its own time.

Pearce crouched down beside them. 'It is her, isn't it? I daren't believe it. And I couldn't catch a glimpse. She's as frightened as a mouse. She knows something, doesn't she? That's why she's in hiding.'

Chandler disentangled the girl's arms from around his neck and tried to push the hair back from her tear-stained face. 'Come and tell us what happened, Maud. You know Pearce, you know us both. Will you tell us how you got here?'

Apparently Pearce held no fears for her now and, though still clinging to Chandler, she allowed him to lead her to a little rise in the ground backed by thick bushes where they could keep a clear lookout for anyone approaching and talk in safety.

Chandler had a question to ask Pearce before anything else. 'Tell me briefly, how did you know I would be with the contingent from the abbey?'

'They sent a message on ahead to tell us so.'

'Ah . . . Nothing else I need to know?'

'Yes. This is of the utmost importance. You must go to the master glover's house before daybreak to have your gloves inspected.' Chandler could make out in the gloaming the ironic twist to Pearce's mouth as he said, 'I won't ask you what it means but I'm sure it makes sense to you . . . After that,' he added, 'you must not come back here but follow the instructions you receive.'

So it was all beginning to start up as expected. The abbot had arranged things rather impressively after all.

Now for Maud's story. He put his coat round her shoulders and gave her a hug. 'We cannot express our joy at seeing you safe and sound, Maud,' he began, 'but I, for one, am at a loss to know how you survived. Living rough. Dickon told me what he saw that morning and how you disappeared over the side of the boat.'

'I was not going to be taken by that horrible man and dumped out to sea. I played dead, and when he was sculling us into the middle of the river I lashed out with both feet and kicked him hard where it would hurt. He gave a howl and while he was clutching his treasures in agony I dropped over the side and swam under his boat. I knew he'd start to poke around looking for me so I came up on the other side, took a breath and went under again. While he was peering about and groaning with pain I kept coming up for air. It was like hide and seek. He started to scull with his back to me so I swam partly underwater in the opposite direction to the current. He was being drifted downstream quite fast by then, but I've always been able to swim, I'm half-sister to a fish my ma always said and I could beat my elder brother at swimming any day.'

She stopped for breath.

'I was carried further downriver than I'd expected but came ashore near the common land and decided to lie low in a copse there to avoid the searchers that came out later. They were really close at one point and one of them looked straight at me where I'd crept into the bushes, but the sotwit didn't see me though I must have been as plain as day to any but a blind man. And it's thanks to my guardian angel and the good lord that I was made invisible, kept safe by an old cottager woman downriver for a while until I managed to get back here.'

'Why didn't you go straight to the house?'

She gave him a frightened look. 'In case Master Willoughby found me.'

Ah, he thought, now we come to it. His old suspicions surged back. 'But wouldn't he have been pleased to know you were safe?'

'Not with what I had to say. You see, I know what happened that morning Evelyn died. Master Willoughby would not want it known.'

'And that was a reason not to go up to the house?'

She nodded.

He looked thoughtful. 'But you came back.'

'I didn't know what else to do.'

'You're a brave and resourceful girl, Maud. Now tell me this, where is your ma and your brother? I think we must let them know you're safe.'

'I wouldn't bother. They're in a hamlet miles away and will not have heard that I'm dead.'

'Are you dead?'

She giggled. 'Can't you see I'm just a wraith from the other side?'

'You're a wicked girl. What are we going to do with you?'

'Don't mention taking me up to the house again. Master Willoughby knows more about Evelyn's death than he lets on.'

'So what makes you think so?'

'I believe he knows this fellow. He called me a spying little bitch, poking my nose in where it didn't concern me—'

'Who did, Willoughby?'

She shook her head. 'No, this fellow I kicked. He said he was going to shut me . . .' Her voice wobbled for a moment and she had to force herself to continue, 'He said he was going to shut me up for good.'

Pearce made a rustling movement, its suddenness showing how still he had held himself as he listened to her account. Now his voice was shaking when he asked, 'Maud, what connection can Willoughby have to Evelyn's fall?'

'I'm not sure. You're going to have to find this fellow with the red capuchon. He must have come ashore somewhere. He knows the truth. He may even have been the very one who pushed her off the roof himself. I told you, brother –' she turned to Chandler – 'about seeing a stranger hurrying up the stairs to the roof. It was the same man as the one in the boat.'

Chandler frowned.

Pearce put his head in his hands. When he eventually looked up he said, 'He's going to wish he'd never been born.'

While Chandler was thinking what they could do to protect Maud she began to tell Pearce a little more about her abductor exactly as she had recounted it to Chandler, but before he could add anything to what she had told him the sound of voices, loud and not making any attempt to conceal their presence, floated down from the meadow path.

'Is that Willoughby?' Chandler murmured.

Pearce grunted an affirmative.

'Don't let him get me!' Maud grasped even more tightly onto Chandler's arm.

'He'll have me to contend with if he tries it. Let's get away before he sees us, just to be on the safe side. It sounds as if he has a small army with him.'

'He's got that old boatman along of 'im as well. He must have lost his boat again.' Pearce was full of contempt.

Further up the meadow the flash of torches appeared intermittently between the boles of the trees.

'Listen,' said Chandler to Pearce, 'will you take her for safety to the guesthouse run by the Benedictines? Don't allow her to go anywhere near Willoughby's until this has been sorted out. Tomorrow morning can you then get a message to Dieulacres and tell them what has happened?'

'I can and I will. What's more, I'll ride there myself and take young Maud with me. Them monks will shelter her, won't they?'

'If you explain the situation I'm sure they will.'

Pearce urged Maud to hurry out of the clearing towards the river path and Chandler followed, feeling he might have to act as a back-stop should Willoughby and his men decide to interfere. He wondered who had alerted them or whether it was some other alarm that had brought them out so late.

Before they parted Pearce whispered, 'Remember where your horse was left, brother? Knock three times on the door and him inside'll give you shelter for the night. He won't ask questions.'

With a further vow to hunt down the nameless wearer of the capuchon Pearce took hold of Maud firmly by the arm and drew her along with him, then the three figures melted into the shadows.

Further back among the trees the group with the torches ranged back and forth. Something had disturbed them but Chandler could not see how it could have been themselves, unless someone had been secretly watching from the riverbank when he and Pearce had first walked up.

TWELVE

Leave-taking

Dawn. Used to the night offices, the same in all abbeys throughout Christian Europe, Chandler found no difficulty in snatching a couple of hours sleep before waking shortly before sunrise. It was Prime, the first Office of the day. It was imprinted into his being.

He collected his small bag, careful not to wake his host.

Leaving a few coins for his hospitality he let himself out into the luminous dawn light and whispering to his horse to quieten him, led him stealthily back alongside the dew-shimmering cabbage field towards the town.

Already bakers were beginning to light their ovens and wood-smoke drifted into the pristine air. Others were moving like sleepwalkers about the streets on their way to their own private business of the day. The shutters over the shopfronts were not pushed back yet. A lone dog sniffed its way along the street.

The glover's was in darkness when he arrived outside but a push at the door opened to reveal a short corridor with a candle burning at the far end. The glover was waiting for him.

When he recognized Chandler he reached out for his riding glove, fitted something neatly inside the lining, and handed it back.

Without saying much else he placed a small parcel into his hands. 'Bread, cheese and our thanks. Now you must make the short ride to Hawarden to a certain house where they'll tell you how to find you-know-who.' He lowered his voice to conclude his instructions, saying, 'Remember, you carry something meant for his eyes only. Go well, friend!'

As soon as the town gates were opened he was waved through as just another mendicant plying his trade and someone the city was glad to be rid of.

He rode on towards the foothills of the Marcher country.

*   *   *

Over into Wales was only another six miles or so. At Hawarden, instead of being sent on to Sycarth, Glyn Dwr's stronghold in the Berwyn mountains as he half expected, he was directed to the market town of Wrecsam. Apparently Glyn Dwr was being called in to defend the town lest it fall into Henry's hands as he moved his army towards it.

At Wrecsam he expected to find Glyn Dwr's own army camped outside the walls, but found no sign of them. He guessed they must have moved on but he slept in the shelter of a belt of trees to wait for the town gates to be unlocked, then, with the vaguest idea where his next contact lived, he made his way there through the unfamiliar streets towards an inn called the Star of Bethlehem, entering a stable yard at the back as unobtrusively as any itinerant.

The horse-master, already at work alongside his men, ordered someone to see to his horse, then without asking questions led him in to meet the innkeeper.

He was a genial fellow. News picked up the previous day, he told him, was that Henry and his army were now quartered at Worcester. Where he would strike next was unclear. Maybe it wouldn't be Wrecsam after all. Glyn Dwr would be making his own plans accordingly.

'Maybe Henry has no idea of his plans himself,' observed Chandler's contact with a chuckle. 'Judging from the way he's to-ing and fro-ing about the border he doesn't know whether he's on the moon or back firmly on earth. Mayhap our noble resistance forces will make sure he's soon down on, if not in, the earth – and preferably the latter?'

Chandler agreed though mourning the folly that led men to fight when there was really no need.

'Glyn Dwr has the upper hand after that first major success at Mynydd Hyddgen,' his contact added. 'You heard, no doubt?'

Chandler admitted that he had had other matters to deal with in England at the time but of course they had heard a rumour of something to add to Henry's discomfort. 'Free comment,' he added, 'was beginning to be discouraged in London at that time and people with little heft at court were cautious about being seen to be spreading information that Henry would construe as critical of him and his grab for power.'

'Well, I'll tell you then. It was quite a victory, there at Mynydd

Hyddgen, three hundred Welshmen mounted on hill ponies against ten times that number of English and Flemish mercenaries mounted on cavalry horses. Two hundred of their men killed and only fifty, God rest their souls, of ours. Such is the justice of our cause.'

From there Chandler was advised to go to Sycarth where the latest news of Glyn Dwr's whereabouts would be known.

And so it went, in similar vein, from one contact to another, the secret letter hidden inside the lining of his riding glove, and his destination changing and uncertain. Only Glyn Dwr himself, the Prince of Wales, acting like a lodestar, drew him ever deeper and more dangerously into the heart of the principality.

After travelling for some time and still some distance from Sycarth, he was directed to the Cistercian monastery of Valle Crucis and when he arrived was told he would be able to reach Glyn Dwr's stronghold in less than a week.

The hot summer days were giving way now to cooler nights and down in the valleys the greenwood was burnished to autumnal shades of light gold and deepest bronze. It was a lonely pleasure to ride under the deep canopy of the trees with only the regular, muffled thump of his horse's hoofs and the occasional high, heartbreaking sweetness of a blackbird's song to accompany him.

Sheer persistence kept him picking his way over the confusing, seemingly endless miles of steep mountain country, that and a wild sense that the fight against injustice must triumph over the evil that had been unleashed in both realms. He thought of Pearce back in Chester and wondered if Maud had been able to shed any light on Evelyn's death, but mostly he dreamed of Matilda with a feeling of resigned longing.

Guided by the local knowledge of his contacts, he kept to the narrow unfrequented tracks alongside deep, serenely flowing rivers wending their way through isolated valleys, and as far as he could he avoided farms and villages and the many Norman castles built to subdue the populace. They were always sited on the high crags with armed men patrolling the battlements. The sinister glint of sun on steel came from lookouts posted on the roofs of the highest towers.

Alone, he had time to dwell on dreams about the future when this current madness was over. Matilda appeared to him, smiling and lovely, and he imagined them both sometime and somehow meeting once more.

They might choose to live in peace and loving bliss in a sequestered valley like the one he was riding through, he imagined, away from the stir and bustle of the towns, and the more he thought about it the more he knew it was a dream and nothing more. His son was real but was himself in Chandler's deepest heart nothing other than a dream, a not-quite-real figment of his imagination.

War was the only reality in these dark days waiting for Henry's invasion. Rumours of his army on the march were constant everywhere he went.

When Chandler took his leave after a day's rest following his last long trek when he mostly slept and eased his aching muscles, he set off with his speculations about Glyn Dwr's whereabouts somewhat more certain.

Sycarth was mentioned without having to be coaxed into the conversation and he felt his days of being tested were drawing to an end.

'Go there,' his latest contact advised him. She was a woman this time, broad and bonny with a brood of dark-eyed children at her knees and an astute-looking sixteen-year-old son trying to look as if he hadn't noticed their visitor was armed and was not eyeing him as if trying to read his thoughts.

'News comes,' she continued, 'that Henry has finally mustered enough men at Worcester to give him confidence about facing our army. The guess is that he plans to invade by marching straight through the middle of our country to reach Aberystwyth and the coast.' Her lip curled. 'He no doubt hopes to cut our ancient realm in twain so that he can more easily destroy us. North against south. We true Britons descended from the heroes of Troy to be set against you invading Saxons and Norman descendants of barbarians!' She gave him a quick smile. 'Not that you can help that, brother. I don't blame you personally!'

'My father was Castilian,' he explained as if it made things better.

'There then,' she murmured, looking at his black hair and deep dark eyes with approval. 'The south is standing firm and the men of Gwynedd will never surrender.'

He thought of a cart laden with forbidden books, creaking its way towards the west. He had no real idea of its destination but thought to ask, 'What of Anglesey? Is that strong for Glyn Dwr?'

'Always and forever,' she replied. 'Those Tudor boys are from there and held the castle *and* got a price for it. Whatever Henry does to them they will never give in.'

He thought about asking for more information about the place whose name had been mentioned at Dieulacres when Brother Senlac had spoken of Llanfaes.

From the little Senlac had said, Chandler still believed that this was the most likely haven to be sought. It was already a famous and holy repository for valuable documents although not as famed as the great Cistercian abbey at Strata Florida deep in the heartlands.

He thought better of saying anything in case by mentioning such a place he would jeopardise both the safety of his contact and of the secret cargo searching through Wales for a home.

Maybe, he thought, I've been sent from pillar to post these last few weeks to be tested for the strength of my allegiance and my ability to keep my mouth shut and not endanger the enterprise by gossip.

Encouraged by his reticence, she said, 'You best go by back roads to the abbey. You'll be halfway to Sycarth and will find exceptional hospitality from those Cistercians there. But here, take this little offering for your journey and go well.'

This friendly Welshwoman whose name he was never given had one more thing to say before he left. It was about Henry's ally, Edmund Mortimer.

As they of course both knew he was a marcher lord and held a vast reach of territory in the Marches around his stronghold at Wigmore Castle. King Richard's legal heir to the English crown was his seven-year-old nephew, also called Edmund, who had been pushed aside by Henry and at present lived as a 'guest' at Windsor Castle with his younger brother, Roger.

'Guest? Captive is a more honest word,' she told him. 'We all know he's a captive, he and his little brother. But maybe someone will have the courage to set them free and try to put the elder on the throne as the rightful king, if Richard, God save his soul, is truly dead?'

'I believe him to be dead, more's the pity,' Chandler mumbled, memory going back to that day in the great tower at Pontefract Castle.

'We live in hope,' she persisted.

Everything she said was seditious. Chandler trusted that there was no way anyone could overhear her. It would be the worse for her if there were traitors around. Not everyone wanted the dream of an independent Wales when they could obtain richer pickings by supporting their English neighbours.

Avoiding any possibility of coming across Henry's outriders Chandler made his way along local back roads as instructed, north in the direction of distant Sycarth where, if Glyn Dwr was not actually present, his men would know where he could be found.

As he rode away her words returned and he mulled them over in an attempt to draw some sense from the confusion that befogged everything. The Mortimer boys' father had been King Richard's lieutenant in Ireland but had been murdered at a skirmish there which some saw as a ploy to get him out of Henry's way in a place distant and little known by most of the hangers-on at the Lancastrian court and for that reason unlikely to have interrogators swarming about looking for his murderer.

The two young boys had been forced into Henry's custody as royal wards, hostages in order to maintain their uncle's loyalty to the usurper.

A power in the Marches, Edmund's genealogy was as old as Henry's and indeed his own father had briefly ruled alongside Queen Isabel when she rid herself of her husband Edward II. How Mortimer now squared his allegiance to Henry Lancaster puzzled Chandler and he longed to have Arnold Archer's common sense analysis of the situation.

But there it was, two ambitious families each riven by alliances, betrayals and bad faith, and their grab for power continued and would do so until one or both sides were destroyed.

* * *

He reached the long, green valley with its overhanging cliffs and the narrow track that wound along the bottom to the foregate of Valle Crucis.

Before he rode down he dismounted and took a long look at this Valley of the Cross. The Cistercians always built their abbeys to a similar plan and from a distance this one looked to be no exception.

He could see the high towers of the church in the middle of several sloping grey roofs. They would belong to the dortoir, the hospitium, the lay-brothers' quarters, the Chapter House and other necessary buildings. He had heard about the scriptorium, famed throughout the Cistercian world.

It was said to be almost as famous as the abbey of Strata Florida which housed the chronicles of the princes of Wales and other royal records. There – it was Senlac again who had told him – was a copy of the famous *Mabinogion*, the collection of ancient tales from the beginning of written records when Wales was recovering after the time of the Romans, England nothing more than a wild realm at the mercy of warring tribal invaders.

Musing over the past which we cannot know even as we cannot know the future, he stood beside his horse for some time lost in thought.

He was reluctant to join the company of other folk. He did not speak the language well enough to take part in general conversation and found it exhausting to try to make sense of its nuances. He feared offending his hosts and being thought disrespectful of their language and customs. At least the monks would speak Latin.

About to urge on his horse to walk it down the hillside, a shout from somewhere over to one side of the glade alerted him.

Before he could move several men emerged from between the trees. They were carrying cudgels, and he noticed a broadsword or two, and the colours of Henry Bolingbroke, before he was surrounded and briskly disarmed almost before he could draw breath.

The ambush was so unexpected he did not even shout out. In moments he was trussed up like a cockerel to market.

They began to force him into a run, jostling him on all sides, yelling something in their own language, and somebody decided he deserved a punch in the face.

Stumbling he tried to shout questions, wondering if he had been mistaken for another traveller, but they ignored him until they reached a wooden redoubt of some kind, a cabin erected on the very edge of the cliff overlooking the abbey. Briefly he had a glimpse of a distant group of lay brothers working the arable strips outside the walls.

The great gates under the stone arch behind them were wide open. If he had had time he might even have caught a glimpse of the quiet courtyard within with a few monks in contemplation in the cloisters. Another blow knocked such thoughts from his head.

The rushing captors slowed to a halt near the cabin and a man appeared and stood in a shaft of sunlight looking out. Squat and, by the colours of his hauberk, a follower of Henry of Lancaster, he offered no greeting except to stroll up to Chandler to stare up at him with an expression of intense dislike.

He said something in his own language then slapped Chandler across the face with the back of his hand. 'Speak English?'

Without waiting for a reply he said, 'Hand it over.'

Chandler was too knocked about to reply at once and the fellow hit him again and held out his hand. 'Give me what you carry . . . you courier? What you take and to whom? To this accursed abbot? Give me.'

'I have nothing. I have no idea what you mean. I seek only hospitality at the abbey this night,' Chandler managed.

The fellow gave him a sour glance. 'Nothing for us?' He turned to his men. 'String him up,' he said in English for Chandler's benefit following it with a stream of Welsh that made no sense to him but from its tone only boded ill for him.

One man produced a noose from somewhere with such speed it must have already been in his hands and with equal alacrity he strung it round Chandler's neck despite his struggles to resist, useless while in the grip of the three others.

He felt a sudden chill. All energy to fight back drained from his body. He could not fight, tied like this. He thought, that it should end here. In some miserable forest clearing.

The futility of it, the absurdity, made him draw in his breath and release it in a great bellow of curses. That some of it was in Welsh made them draw back as if the curse of a dead man might mean something.

But their captain urged them on, cursing them in his turn, and they, fearing his magic more than the stranger's, cautiously tightened the noose round his neck and began to hustle him towards a suitable tree.

A beech, with one thick branch ten feet or so above the good earth reached out towards the light. He could tell it had been used for a similar purpose already because the bark was grooved at the point where a struggling man's boots would have kicked out at it as he fought to free himself.

How many am I going to join? Chandler wondered, unable to halt his curiosity. This is their hanging tree. How many have gone before me?

He remembered St Serapion and silently called on him.

The two men gripped his arms behind his back despite the fact that they had already tightly trussed him up. It couldn't stop him from kicking out at them. He heard the snap of a bone as he found the place at the front of the knee where he knew its weakness.

He was almost able to do it a second time to one of the others until the man ran back to a safe distance. With one fellow howling on the ground and gripping his leg in anguish, the others circled their prisoner, as wary as wild animals choosing a safe distance from an unsubdued prey before they closed in for the kill.

Three beefy fellows on the other end of the noose were given a shout by the captain watching from the doorway of his hut and they began to coil the rope ready to get a grip so they could haul Chandler by his neck off the ground.

He tensed, ready for the jerk and pull, the swing into the air and the gasping grasp as his lungs tried to refill themselves. The noose tightened.

THIRTEEN

Before anything happened a voice roared, 'Stop there!'
So commanding was the order that the men faltered.
The noose slackened.

A big, burly, smiling fellow accompanied by one only slightly shorter but muscled like a bowman swaggered into the clearing.

'We heard you were heading for Valle Crucis, brother. Greetings! Forgive the king's men their famed hospitality.' Turning to Henry's underlings he snarled. 'If you do not make yourselves scarce you will pay for it with your lives. I have this sacred grove surrounded. Now get out!' He repeated it, Chandler assumed, in Welsh.

Glancing up into the trees he next called, 'Jack? Show them!'

At once an arrow flashed across the open space to hammer itself into the wooden wall of the cabin so effectively and so accurately it pinned the leather breeches of the captain to the timber behind him.

He struggled to free himself, like a wasp in honey, in terror of another arrow to come. When he found that the one pinning him was too deeply embedded in the timber to be wrenched out, he yanked forth a dagger to slash himself free, then, crouching, torn breeches flapping and both hands shielding his private parts, he fled from the grove.

Chandler was still trying to make sense of this apparition strolling towards him when the rest of the attackers melted away into the undergrowth, dragging with them the wounded man still groaning over his knee.

'You promised to meet us at Sycarth, but we couldn't wait so we came to fetch you!'

It was Will, the Cheshire bowman who had rescued Chandler from the flames of a terrible death on the stake in Westminster Yard.

'You're making a habit of keeping me away from those pearly gates,' replied Chandler, rubbing his neck. 'I'm beginning to feel you're simply jealous that I'll get there before you!'

The two men fell into each other's arms and thumped each other heartily on the back as if they would never stop.

Will eventually unloosed the rope round Chandler's neck and threw it to one side. 'We can't be doing this all the time. Don't you know there's an invasion about to start?'

He was accompanied by Fulke who was grinning from ear to ear. 'We've been trying to catch up with you all day, brother.'

'I'm glad you eventually managed to get your timing right,' Chandler replied. They did the same exchange of thumps, then stepped back, grinning and confused and astonished.

'And me!' a high voice called. 'It's me, Brother Rod! Don't forget me! I'm the tracker round here. These dolts got themselves lost in the woods.'

A spindly figure came streaking out of the undergrowth and threw himself at Chandler. He had grown in the year or so since they had last met and the boy wore his bow across his shoulders as nonchalantly as any seasoned mercenary.

'It can't be Aethelstan, he's only a little lad no higher than an imp – oh, heavens forgive me, master.' Chandler fell back in mock astonishment then lifted him up and swung him round several times.

'Stan the Man,' he said, setting him down and recalling his teasing name for him when they first met in Westminster Yard – before the business with the boat and the book he had thrown into the Thames and the near burning that followed.

'He's shaped up nicely, brother. We could have left this entire rescue to him.'

'Jack Underwood is still up his tree. Come down, Jack!' Aethelstan shouted.

'I thought you had the grove surrounded?' Chandler asked as Jack slithered down from his perch unaccompanied and began to stride briskly towards them with a wide smile.

'Nah,' replied Will. 'I said that to encourage you and scare them. We don't need nobody else, us. We were on our way to join the prince when we heard about you. At least, we thought it was you from the description. On your way to headquarters at Sycarth by way of Valle Crucis with a message, we were told. We're going down there now ourselves –' he nodded towards the abbey – 'to pay our respects to the abbot and wait until Henry makes up his mind where he's going to attack so that Glyn Dwr can send for us and set up his defences.'

'I will show my gratitude to you fine fellows,' said the abbot when they were seated in great and welcome luxury round the vast table in the refectory where the monks were dining.

A scent of rosemary and mint filled the air. A vielle player sang a Welsh accompaniment naming hero warriors of the past and a silver wine jug of subtle and skilled workmanship to match the silver goblets raised in regular and convivial toasts to these heroes was circulated and filled and refilled without stint.

The abbot continued. 'That rabble horde of armed men mustered by your so-called King Henry are as irritating as a swarm of wasps on a summer's day. You bowmen have done me a great service in clearing them out of our woods. So far they have been unable to ruffle our feathers and we have been able to keep our demesne mostly free of them, but I fear for the appearance of a larger army if the usurper decides to bring his mercenaries this way. We know from our brothers elsewhere how they destroy the crops and kill the cattle in their passing, demonstrating their deliberate and unconscionable malice against us.'

He frowned. 'We are not built for defence. We are not a castle. We are an abbey. Henry seems not to understand the difference.'

'We intend to point it out to him,' replied Will. 'All we need is the opportunity.'

'Pray that it will not be long in coming.' The abbot was a vigorous though elderly monk, a lord of good rule and hospitality as Chandler now witnessed.

He was erudite and the conversation turned to text and scripture and a dispute over the meanings of various words that would have delighted Wycliffe if he had been alive. The Welsh Cistercians had their own translators and the scriptorium at Valle Crucis was no exception. Shortly after arriving, Chandler had been taken up to have a look.

Fingering the vellum pages he felt like an unlettered peasant staring at the neat lines of incomprehensible script.

Exhausted more than he expected by another close encounter with death, his neck somewhat sore, now he allowed the conversation to continue without him. He would learn Welsh, he decided.

He had no trouble with Latin and the Romans had left many of their own words to swell the mellifluous cadences of the bardic tongue.

It was happiness to hear some old fellow get on to his feet and stagger into the space below the abbot's table and when the hall had fallen silent declaim in his own tongue some mythic story from the past. Roars of approval followed. Laughter resounded at what must have been jokes.

Chandler tried hard to imagine such a scene in an English monastic house, maybe among one or two Cistercian abbeys in the north, he decided, but at court, never.

Only for Master Geoffrey Chaucer had similar occasions existed when he read from his popular tales and then his readings were often seen as an excuse for gossip, matchmaking and a show of the latest fashions.

He wondered where the old poet was now. Did he find a safe place in Guelderland as they hoped he might? Why else make that dash across the Narrow Straits and back, shortly before the Epiphany Rising when the earls were about to make their doomed attempt to free King Richard? Surely, as Archer had suggested, it was to ensure a safe passage out of Henry's realm should the earls' plans fall apart?

What other reason could he have to go to Calais just then? Maybe it was something to do with the wine trade? But Chandler doubted that. He had handed over his share of the family business to his son Thomas who had no poetic ambitions.

He hoped he was safe. He longed to have news of him.

And of the others, of course . . . Definitely.

'Brother Rod, wake up!' It was Aethelstan, shaking him by the shoulder and rousing him from his sleep. 'We're leaving before Prime and you're coming with us. We have somebody to meet!'

By the excited look on the lad's face, Chandler guessed it was something to do with Glyn Dwr, maybe even a meeting with the great man himself. At last, he thought. He could only half believe it would ever happen. He checked his glove for the hundredth time. It would be good to hand over the letter as soon as he could.

Several horses were bridled and ready to go when, after nightfall a small group of well-armed men set off into the darkness.

FOURTEEN

The Wolf from the West

Glyn Dwr was as magnificent as Chandler had been led to believe. They called him the Wolf from the West with good reason. As if to emphasize this title he was attired from head to foot in a long wolfskin cloak that swept the floor.

Not a tall man, as such, compared to Chandler, that is, he nevertheless had great presence.

Wherever he was in the hall a light seemed to shine. Men turned to him. Made way for him. Deferred in a manner that was both familiar and full of reverence.

Chandler had no difficulty in seeing how he inspired so many to follow him wherever he chose to lead. They loved him and in a way he could not describe he loved them. It was different to the rule by fear that prevailed in Henry's court.

When he and the bowmen, with Aethelstan tagging along for once silent and awestruck, were taken towards the high table, they walked between crowds of his followers parting before them like the waters of the Red Sea until they stood at the foot of the dais and looked up in expectation.

Glyn Dwr rose at once to greet them. He even stepped down off the dais and as if they were long-lost kinsfolk took each of the bowmen warmly by both hands much as King Richard would have done in similar circumstances. He had a quiet word with each one and thanked them for their work and finally called for the servers to attend them.

When he came to Chandler he looked him up and down with a piercing scrutiny, searching out his fealty, questions already forming.

Chandler took off his glove. 'I have something for you from the abbot of Dieulacres in Shropshire, sire.'

He drew the letter from inside the secret lining and handed it over. He felt amazed that somehow, at last, the letter was safely in Glyn Dwr's hands. As the prince's strong fingers closed over it Chandler felt a wave of satisfaction at a mission achieved.

A lawyer trained at the Inns of Court in London, Glyn Dwr read quickly to the end, then smiled. 'My dear brother,' he murmured, 'this is most welcome. Our resistance to Lancastrian rule grows apace. Are you commissioned to deliver my reply?'

'Most surely.'

'Then tomorrow, when we are all rested, we will have our scribe pen a suitable response.' He placed both hands on Chandler's shoulders in a sort of benediction, then shook them affectionately. 'Good fellow,' he said, 'I hear you've had a time of it, chasing me about the country, first here, then there. I know every step of your way. I'm sorry I caused you so much trouble. Let me make amends.'

He indicated to a passing serving man that Chandler needed drink, then pointed to the bench on the dais. 'Come and sit by me, tell me about Mortimer and what he thinks he's doing, taking his men into battle under Henry's captaincy.'

'A puzzle and a mistake as he will surely come to understand,' Chandler replied when they were seated. 'But the two children, his nephews, are at Windsor. For that reason I would imagine he feels he must tread cautiously for their sake.'

'And how is Henry's expression of contempt for the earls who would have rescued Richard being regarded?'

'As barbaric. As a desperate attempt to strike terror into Richard's allies and stamp out any support for the true king, rest his soul.'

Glyn Dwr looked askance at this. 'He still lives, surely?'

Chandler shook his head. 'No one knows.'

'We heard he was in Scotland, waiting for a sign that he might be restored?'

'Henry knows the terrible truth but cannot admit how he knows. His step-brother Swynford was given his orders and Henry of course knows what those orders were. It drives him mad with fury to hear folk claim that Richard is still alive and about to reappear when he himself knows better. You heard what he did to those friars for suggesting such a thing? They were not even preaching but discussing matters in the privacy of their own

Chapter House.' The horror of Smithfield, the row of hanged men, the stricken crowd, flashed before him.

Glyn Dwr put his hand on Chandler's sleeve. 'We heard.'

'Thomas Swynford was made constable at Pontefract,' Chandler explained. 'Henry trusts him implicitly to have done the job he was sent to do. I was taken from London in Swynford's retinue. That's how I know. I was present at Pontefract, to my rue. I saw the king. Henry's own claim to the crown is illegal as we all know. The son of a third son with the heir still living has no legal right to the English crown. A child would not be convinced if you set out the arguments he uses. He and his advisor, Archbishop Arundel, were arrogant enough to imagine that the citizens of London and elsewhere would be convinced by their sophistry. The sad thing is, unconvinced as they were, only profit persuades them of anything. They'll believe pigs walk on the moon if it means they'll acquire gold from saying so. They are but merchants and the rest of the citizens see only Normans squabbling for power among themselves as usual. They cannot understand how their own freedoms will be curtailed by the measures that are being passed, the burning law, for instance—'

'*Haeretico comburendo*.' Glyn Dwr narrowed his eyes.

'And all the banned texts and who is and is not allowed to read them, so many limitations being quietly imposed they do not even bother to resist. I fear Arundel has Henry under his thumb. He can make him do anything he wishes if it renders his stolen crown more secure. Henry was never known for his intellect. He's even duller now and relies on Arundel to do his thinking for him. Too many assaults on his wooden head in the lists, some say.'

Glyn Dwr nodded. 'And it's always difficult to outwit the witless. A man of logic can never fore-guess which way their minds will wend.'

'They say you have special powers,' Chandler suggested.

'My only power lies with the people of Wales, their love of freedom, and the prophecies of Merlin.' He gestured to a dark, silent, old fellow sitting close to him on his other side. 'Iolo, give our friend your song about Merlin's prophecy, will you? Let him hear what gives us heart. This is my bard,' he explained to Chandler. 'Listen to him. He will translate for you afterwards when you have the spirit of his song inside you.'

It had needed only that one gesture to bring Iolo to his feet and make the hall fall silent.

The men jampacked inside must have heard the song a hundred times but they hung on every word as if for the first time as the bard took to the floor and began to sing.

Something changed as his voice rose and fell, something like a magical incantation filled the hall with its high, swooning notes and humming bass. The words were as lost to Chandler as much as any words heard in Muscovy or Cathay, but the lyric beauty was as beguiling as if it were sung in his native tongue in the language closest to his heart.

As the last word faded it was breathed into the bone and marrow of the listeners as they let the silence grow and Chandler knew he was at one with their cause and would be forever.

The bard reached across Glyn Dwr when he retook his seat and tapping Chandler on the wrist to attract his attention gave him a twinkling smile. 'Get this fellow out of the way and I'll tell you what it said in your own tongue. Go on, Plant, out of it.'

Chuckling, the prince rose to his feet, replying in English, 'I have my captains to instruct, you rogue, and you know it.' Giving Chandler a final nod he left him in the hands of Iolo.

'It's like this,' said the bard, bending his head close to Chandler's. 'The song of Merlin. It tells us that the Tudor brothers will go from Anglesey into England, they will be horsemen and skilled in the magic arts, and when the king dies, that is, the son also called Henry of this usurper strutting around now in his stolen crown, the French widow of the son will fall under the spell of Owain Tudor . . . for so this usurper's son Henry, the fifth of that name, will follow King Richard's example and marry a French princess, but Owain will not become king by virtue of this but his son's son will be called King Henry VII and found a dynasty in England which will bring both sides of these troublesome Plantagenets together, like one rose with many petals. So will it be. The Tudor kings and queens of England will hail from Anglesey. And these Welsh monarchs will rule the conjoined realms of England and Wales for a hundred years until it's the turn of the Scots.' He added, in a matter-of-fact tone. 'We will not live to see it but it will be so.'

His expression had an invincible look that made questions

irrelevant. Chandler accepted it. Sometimes he believed that all things were true at the moment of speaking.

His beautiful silver goblet was refilled and he lifted it to his lips to drink.

Sure enough, next morning, late, as it happened, due to the previous night's carousing, someone came to Chandler with a letter, the ink dry, the wax seal of Glyn Dwr still tacky and, without further instructions, he inserted it carefully inside the lining of the glove and prepared to leave.

Aethelstan came to him. 'Will and the other two are going on to follow Glyn Dwr but I . . .' He bit his lip and looked ashamed. 'I have something to ask, Rod, but it's all right if you say no . . . I . . . what I mean is . . .' He tailed off and raised his eyes to Chandler's. They had a worried lustre.

Guessing at once Chandler asked, 'You wouldn't by any chance want to come back with me to England?'

His mouth dropped open and he nodded eagerly. 'I'm . . .' He still found something difficult to put into words.

Chandler tried to help out. 'What is it, Stan?'

The boy bit his lip.

Chandler bent his head. 'Are you wanting to go back to London? Are you missing your mother? You left her in quite a hurry, for my sake, for which I am most grateful and I feel I owe you a debt of honour which is still unpaid. I wonder that she might be thinking of you and worrying, you know how women are?'

'Are you going on to London?' Aethelstan asked, eyes widening in hope. 'Do you think you might?'

'Eventually. I may have one or two things to sort out in Chester first.'

'Can I come with you? I can be a help on the way. I could travel as your esquire, perhaps?'

Chandler gave him a long look. Then his face broke into a smile. 'I think there's no perhaps about it. Indeed, I command it!'

As if some weight had been shifted if not removed from his boney shoulders, Aethelstan gave a shout of triumph then ran off to tell the others and gather his things, hallooing like a huntsman.

*   *   *

While Chandler was getting ready to leave he asked Will, 'Tell me, mate, what's this about Spindleshanks? He's got something on his mind, hasn't he?'

'He's longing to get back to England. He's desperate to go back. He'll tell you why if you take him with you. You will, won't you?'

'I've already told him so. That's what he was shouting about. But there's more, I feel.'

'There is but you won't regret it. He's handy with a bow and he's an all-round useful little brat. We'll miss him when he leaves us but I can tell his heart isn't in it these days. He's seen too much. He does nothing but talk about London as if it's the centre of the universe.'

'To some it is,' Chandler remarked. 'I'll be happy to take him along with me.' He watched Will carefully. 'And where are you going next?'

'I can't tell even you, brother – you know how it is, Henry has his spies everywhere – not that I'm thinking you might be one, but we even suspect the blades of grass to whisper Glyn Dwr's plans.'

'No blame there. He has to be careful, his forces are so small compared to Henry's—'

'But we make up for that in loyalty – we'll go wherever the prince leads us. I can tell you one thing, there are rumours about another Cistercian monastery out west called Strata Florida. It's where they keep all their royal records, their ancient chronicles, the entire memory of their forefathers and the stories they built their nation on . . .'

Chandler told him what he had been told on his way here by one of his contacts, although he did not say who it was and Will nodded.

'He could do that, Henry, plough through the middle of the principality and set one side against the other – but not with Glyn Dwr as their captain.'

Will accompanied Chandler to where his horse was hobbled and turned to him with a grin. 'You know how much store he sets by learning. Maybe we're going to be taught to write a fair court hand and draw those little figures in the margins of the manuscripts?' He chuckled. 'How much more peaceful my life would have been if I'd paid more attention to the dame instead of spending all my time at the butts!'

'You'll do well enough as you are, Will. I'm sorry our time here has been so short.'

'At least you kept your promise to meet up with us this side of the border.'

'I owe you twice over for my life now. The score is totting up.'

'I'll make a gift of both lives as a way of honouring your saint and keeping myself out of the pit of hell. May Serapion keep you safe, Rodric –' he glanced self-consciously down at his hands – '"brother", I should say, I mean, no disrespect.'

'As if any would be taken. Not when I'm called Brother Rod in some quarters.' They both laughed. 'I'm not much of a friar but I know of no way to thank you enough other than by prayers.'

'Just don't let it happen again, you know what I mean.' He slit two fingers across his neck.

'I can't guarantee that. I only hope you'll be around for the third time if there is one.'

They clasped hands, formal and brimmed with emotion at the relentless power of Fortune's Wheel driving them down separate paths into the unknown.

'Where are we with Glyn Dwr?' Will asked before they finally parted. 'Can he bring Wales together? Can they hold out against the English?'

'According to Merlin's prophecy they'll do more than that. They'll rule the roost for a hundred years, Welsh kings and queens both, a dynasty known as the Tudors after the brothers from Anglesey who started it all. When they've had their day they'll give the Scots a chance.'

Will chuckled. 'So much for the Plantagenets. That I could live to see the day when they're gone for good!'

Accompanied by his new squire Aethelstan, named defiantly by his mother after the first great Saxon king of England, Chandler reluctantly made his farewells to Will, Fulke and Greenwood.

FIFTEEN

England

This time there were none of Henry's men marauding about in the woods and with several days of hard riding and brief stops along the way he and his esquire eventually approached the border town of Wrecsam close to where they would cross over into English territory again.

Athelstan had climbed up a small hill and shouted down to Chandler. 'I can see England from here! Come and have a look!'

He stood gazing out with a rapt expression across the next valley and the next, and the one after that until they merged, hill and valley, into a blue and lavender haze reaching the horizon.

He called down, 'It looks so peaceful from here.'

Chandler climbed up beside him. 'Be not deceived by appearances, young lad. That is a land given to war for its own sake, run as it is by Normans. Even though Henry might be the first Plantagenet to speak English as his native tongue, it doesn't stop him from turning his kinsfolk into enemies. And now he's turned his malevolent stare on Wales.'

When they scrambled down again and picked up the reins of their horses, Chandler asked, 'So what are you going to do when you get back to London?'

'That depends.'

'Everything will be changed, you know that, don't you?'

'As long as Ma and the little ones are safe. They won't be so little now, I'm thinking. I'll try to find a way of helping if I can. I didn't give a thought to how she would get by if I left, lacking what I earned.'

'Your mother sounds like a resourceful woman. I'm sure she's been able to make her way.'

He had given some thought himself to Aethelstan's reception when he returned home to London but had come to no firm idea. He would need work. Not the hand-to-mouth job of running errands in Westminster Yard as when they had first joined forces, but something with a future, something with permanence as one of its attributes, something to make use of his special skills.

He caught himself smiling. He was beginning to think like a father. And he knew why. His smile faded.

They had not travelled much farther when they learned to their horror how malevolent that stare of Henry's could be. News filtered in at the next stop.

It was a small market town with a name both of them found difficult to pronounce but they were fortunate to find an innkeeper who was half English and could mock their efforts in both languages.

'Go like this,' he instructed, making a sound that was not easy for them, but before they could make further attempts a man came racing into the yard in great physical distress. His garments were torn, his hair wild, and he was sweating abundantly after, he gasped, hammering his horse through miles of countryside with news from the distant abbey of Strata Florida.

Shouting to all and sundry, he stood in the middle of the yard and raised his fist. 'That arseling Henry! Do you know what he's done?'

His news came from a courier further back who had it from one escaping the abbey the previous day. The message was short and simple.

'They have set it afire! Henry and his losels have set fire to the monastery! Strata Florida is burned out of existence! The most holy of places, gone! They have burned it to the ground and with it all our ancient books, our history, our identity, our birthright!'

This outburst was corroborated by others coming in over the day and night. The abbey had been laid waste. There was no doubt as to its truth.

The monks, unarmed, had resisted but been unable to stop Henry's war dogs from doing whatever they wanted. Emerging fully armed from the deep woodland that surrounded the abbey they had stormed into the sacred precinct, knocking monks to the ground, grabbing everything of obvious value and forcing everyone out on to the garth.

'We thought we were to be put to the sword.' An old monk travelling in a cart arrived and told them what he had witnessed. 'One who resisted was run through and lay groaning and bleeding on the ground while the Englishmen stepped over him and jeered and threatened with their swords anyone who tried to go to succour him. We had to watch him die throughout all that long, terrible day.'

The *conversi* who had travelled with him took up the story. 'The monks tried to carry out as many books as they could save but they were beaten back by Henry's scum wielding their swords and hatchets. Against them and the heat of the raging flames no one could get near. Even we lay brothers were chased off into the woods. We could only watch as the beautiful monastery was looted, windows smashed, scriptorium set on fire, and the stones pulled down. Eventually the roof of the church caved in and it became an inferno. The trees round about were set aflame by a hail of sparks from the buildings. When the flames died down towards nightfall smoke thick as autumn fog lay over the whole valley. The monks were sobbing and wailing to God at the destruction of such priceless works of art, such scholarship never again to be seen, the work of centuries and skill destroyed. We are weeping now in our hearts, never to stop. We cry to heaven at the desecration of our ancestors' bequest to us. We are bereft. We are ended.'

The monk said, 'Our lives are over. Wales is finished.'

When calmer voices sounded they talked of revenge. But they were helpless. They knew it. What could a few small guerrilla bands do against the royal might of a usurping warrior king and his thousands of paid killers?

Grown men wept openly.

Chandler cringed with shame at the barbarity of this self-crowned King of England.

To show such disrespect for learning was the nadir of all that had ever redeemed man from his primal state of bestiality.

Now we live like beasts in the field, he thought. No learning. No books. No memories. Only the blind response of animals at feed. These are the End Days the prophets warned us against. It is happening now. Where is salvation to come from?

*　　*　　*

To Aethelstan he posed a question later. They were both subdued.
'Do you want to take your bowman's skills back into England
– or would you rather remain here and fight for the Welsh
and for truth and beauty?'

The lad's face seemed carved in wood. 'You know the answer
to that, brother, there is no discussion, but first I must go back to
see my mother and make all right with her.' He lifted his head. To
Chandler he seemed to have grown in years. 'I can't believe my
own countrymen could be so vile. He shames us.'

'Then let's not delay. Let's get on to Chester and see what we
can do there, then on to London. And onwards!'

SIXTEEN

Chester

They were travelling north along the border and were about one or two sleeps away from Chester by now. Aethelstan, although pleased to be that little bit nearer the eventual road to London and home, seemed more than ever burdened in his mind and Chandler did not want to probe too far. It seemed it was made worse by what they had heard of Strata Florida.

Meanwhile he listened to his chatter as one day's hard riding followed another, teased him, tried to raise his spirits and continued to teach him what little he knew that might be useful to him later, his letters, numbers, the names of weights and so on. One day he also condemned his inability to cook with uncalled-for sarcasm.

Afterwards he felt it appropriate to apologize.

'I have no room to criticize your attempts, Stan. That stuff – rabbit you called it? – was far less burned black than my offering yesterday. We have both failed to improve our cooking skills despite our practise.'

'I'm just trying to copy you, Rod. I thought we were meant to burn it black before we ate it.'

Chandler chased him down to the nearby stream for this sauciness and said he had a good mind to throw him in, clothes and all, and both of them teetered on the bank, unwilling to get wet, when Chandler asked, 'Do you remember when you joined the brotherhood of bowmen by catching some fish for us?'

Aethelstan stopped his fighting and nodded. 'I was pleased with that.'

'I should have been warned about two things,' Chandler continued. 'Your cooking which then also involved burning – and your skill in catching sleeping fish which was much admired. Do you think you could catch some now for us? It must be a fish day somewhere in Christendom.'

Aethelstan's eyes lit up. 'Your command, oh master,' and at once set about finding a stick he deemed suitable for the task. As he was doing so he said, 'I was sorry they were almost asleep when I caught them.'

'I remember you saying it didn't seem fair.'

They were both silent for a moment with the weight of the great unfairness – beyond words – that had now been committed against the Welsh. A crime against fish seemed light, almost kind by comparison.

When they were sitting side by side on the riverbank waiting for the fish to rise Chandler thought the lad might confess what else was deeply bothering him but nothing was said.

The fish, small it must be admitted, were duly caught, cooked, one offered in thanks to the God of Fish, then, being only slightly singed, eaten with exaggerated relish.

Afterwards they built a shelter for the night, both quite adept and working in unison by now, then settled down to listen to the owls hooting in protest at having their private domain invaded by human predators, before drifting towards slumber.

What had happened at Strata Florida was like a wound in the peaceful world of living creatures, a hole blasted through the fortifications that held the civilized world erect. Chandler could not handle it in any way that made sense.

He tossed and turned.

There was no prayer that seemed suitable, nothing that did not seem like mere words, empty of sense and power.

Why would Henry destroy books? Did he imagine he could destroy every book in the world that wasn't written in his praise? He had ordered his men to trawl through every scriptorium in the kingdom to wrench from the innocent pages of the chronicles any word that did not condemn his cousin Richard or praise himself. Whole pages were ripped out, those that could not be removed were defaced, the knives scraping the vellum so that the words were almost illegible.

Future readers would ask themselves, why do so many chronicles end before Richard's reign is over? What happened between the last recorded event and the lauded coronation of Henry three years later? What really happened in those missing years?

He changed position and put his head in his hands but it did not bring sleep. The flames seemed to rise up and envelop him. He opened his eyes and stared into the darkness.

When they had tied him to the stake at Westminster and built their brushwood round him, he had wondered whether Henry thought that by burning him alive he could wipe out opposition to his rule.

He must be mad to think it.

Chandler shut his eyes and changed position.

Didn't he understand that people were various and multi-faceted, he asked himself, that they could not be regulated like the toy soldiers of childhood?

We have our own thoughts, desires and intentions, he thought, and does he not know that? We all live as best we can despite taxes and laws and the failed expectations of those we care about. Does he imagine he is any different to us? Are we not all on the same journey? Do we not all finish in the same place, whatever our social status, our worldly wealth, our fame?

In visions the host of souls appeared as splinters of light in a rainbow, many coloured, making a glowing hue, each one merging into the next so that you could never tell where one ended and another began. It was a community of souls. Now this so-called king had torn a hole in it and darkness had flowed in.

He guessed Henry had never had a vision in his life. He remembered his own boyhood when he had felt able to talk to the angels, the golden beings who peopled his imagination at that time, and now he wondered how and when he had lost them or whether he had failed them in some way and they had with-drawn their kindness from him and gone elsewhere. These days he saw only the destruction men caused and felt a deepening hopelessness that thus it would ever be, whoever wore the crown and pretended to rule.

That restless night brought a drifting half-sleep which was shat-tered by Aethelstan, howling like a child, which of course he was, and when he came to himself and sat up, shamefaced and blubbering, he sobbed, 'It was the devil – he was dragging me down into a great pit of flames! He would not let go. He had a grip on me with his claws and teeth. I struggled and prayed but could not free myself!'

He sobbed unconsolably and Chandler crawled from under his blanket and went to fetch the bottle of watered ale from his saddlebag.

'Here, have a drink of this and while you're doing that let me stir up this fire and we'll sit by the light for a while. The devil won't come near light even if it is a fire. He's a great coward, only at home in the dark, trying to scare young lads and wake them from their well-earned sleep. We'll send him packing. Trust me.'

Still sobbing, Aethelstan took a few sips then put the flask to one side. 'I'm sorry I woke you up.'

'Don't worry about that. I wasn't asleep anyway. And too much sleep is bad for you.'

When they were crouching round the fire he asked, 'So tell me, why do you think he picked on you tonight?'

Their faces were lit up by the flickering light from the fire and Chandler could see the lad's expression clearly and the struggle there.

Eventually he managed to admit in a halting and frightened tone, 'It's because I've not been properly shriven. That's why.'

'So what do you think you've done that needs to be confessed and repented and punished?'

For a long while Aethelstan couldn't bring himself to speak. The flames danced their ruby light over his face. He scrubbed at the trail his tears had made until he admitted in a small voice, 'I've killed men, brother . . .'

The pause after this lengthened until he went on. 'And I'm worried about my immortal soul. I fear what might happen.'

He stared into the fire and something about his stare reminded Chandler of Jack Underwood and how he had stared and stared at the pictured anguish of his family, visible before him in the flames, seeing his own weakness and the sense of guilt at the enormous crime he was too frail, too single, to shift alone. In revenge he had killed men and even confession had been little help to Underwood at that time.

'Rod,' asked Aethelstan, making a large effort to recover his composure, 'will you hear me?'

Chandler thought about the rules, whether they really meant anything, and how far heresy erased good intentions, for surely if in error, one's intentions were as nil? Was it error to listen to a confession as the Church claimed, just because you didn't have one of their licences?

'The thing is, Stan, I cannot absolve you, officially. I am not a priest, but when we reach Dieulacres I'm sure we can find someone to hear you and absolve you if you are truly penitent, as you clearly are. Can you wait that long?'

'What about Chester?'

When he remembered how he had been riding alongside Chandler and how terrified he must have been feeling, it made sense now. He feared something would happen before he could confess. Again Chandler remembered Underwood and how, even though he was not licensed, just by listening to the terrible guilt that afflicted him he had been able to offer solace.

He asked, 'We can find a priest in Chester who will hear you. Meanwhile do you want to tell me about it, to make it easier later?'

'It's why I want even more to see my mother and my brothers and sisters and not to have to kill anyone.' He was struggling in the attempt to work things out. 'It's this, isn't it? We should not kill because maybe, like everybody, we all have the idea we're doing the right thing – because everybody believes they're doing the right thing, even fake King Henry, whether they are or not and anyway, how do we ever know when we're not? Some people must know they're not doing the right thing, like Henry's men-at-arms. I can't see what makes them think it's a good idea to kill somebody who's unarmed just because they're told to. Maybe I'm as wrong as they are?'

'I believe you were doing the right thing when you defended your comrades-in-arms and had to shoot at your attackers. Is that how it happened?'

Aethelstan nodded. 'Blood came into his mouth and he cried out. He didn't die straightaway. That was the thing. He kept shouting for his mother. When he was eventually still it was like something shining being cut in two. One second he was there, alive, and the next he was nothing, just a thing lying on the ground. Not a man. He had gone. Something had gone. I could not talk to him. I could not bring him back.'

'And is that where your doubts lie?'

'I'm not sure. Maybe I should have just laid down my bow?'

'And been shot yourself? That would not have done much good to anyone, would it?'

'I don't know. Maybe it would. I don't know. What shall I do?'

'It's simple. We can look at the Bible ourselves where it tells us – that's if we don't mind being branded heretic by reading the words ourselves – and we'll find that God puts it very simply. He says, "If ye love me, then keep my commandments." That's all you have to remember, Stan.'

'But I haven't kept them. I've broken one deliberately. I've killed. Deliberately. I know I was trying to defend people when they were being attacked but will God make allowances for that?'

'You will be forgiven. God's understanding is infinite.'

Chandler was shaken by Aethelstan's dilemma. Such questions had been left behind in the hysteria of theological discussion aroused by the Lollards in the days leading up to Henry's coup.

Old certainties were openly questioned. People wanted to know the truth and not be fobbed off like children with stories and threats of punishment. Only the superstitious believed at heart that everything the Church told them was true.

Others, more logically, asserted that if it were, the ecclesiastics themselves would behave differently, no more corruption, no more bought-and-sold preferments, no cash exactions for spiritual purchases, no cruelty in every sense. They would be exemplary and everyone would strive to follow them.

SEVENTEEN

To St Werbergh's

When they came within sight of Chester he was glad on the boy's behalf as they saw the city walls and had to line up with all the others waiting to get in through the gate.

He took Aethelstan straight to the abbey church and as soon as the horses were handed over he introduced him to the novice master, explained the situation while Aethelstan was carrying their bags to the guest dorter, and was confident that they would take care of him when he came down.

'Now then, young fellow,' began the master when he reappeared, 'I hear you've been in some dangerous situations through no fault of your own. I think you'd better come with me and we'll see what we can sort out with God and his angels. What do you say?'

Aethelstan dropped to his knees. 'Most merciful brother, I have dire need of confession.'

'Then come and let's sort out this matter of you doing your duty to your comrades and see what can be made of it.'

Meanwhile, Chandler decided on his next move. There were choices. First he must secretly contact Pearce to find out what had happened in the months of his absence. If nothing had changed he would go to see Willoughby as if nothing had occurred in the interval between now and their last meeting. Now, for a little while, he could remain as a guest with the Benedictines and carry out a few enquiries of his own without having to account to anyone.

While he thought things over he went into the cloister and sat down to wait for his esquire to emerge from the church.

A message must be sent to Pearce, he decided while he waited. Maybe he had already tracked down the stranger in the red capuchon, maybe the mystery was solved, maybe everything was as close to normal as it was before Evelyn's untimely death. After all, he reasoned, it had been summer when he was here last and now it was well past Martinmas.

He went to the porter's lodge and asked him to send a message to a horse-master at the house of Master Willoughby. The request duly made he went back into the cloister and sat down to wait for Aethelstan again. His confession was taking some time.

When the young ruffian reappeared he seemed taller, stronger and, if it was not too fanciful, glowing with light. His eyes shone when they met Chandler's anxious gaze.

'It's settled, brother. I am shriven. I have a penance owed and I am truly contrite. He said I could not have done otherwise.'

He would say no more. But the glow of being back in the fold did not leave him.

What would the Lollards say to this? Chandler wondered now. They wanted to throw out all the frippery as they called it of confession, repentance and exactions and he agreed with them in spirit. But guilt must be forgiven if love and compassion are to mean much. Everything, he declared to himself with finality, is made of glass. Nothing lasts. All things pass.

Pearce appeared around the time the bell for Compline started. It would be nothing remarkable to be seen entering the parish church at such a time. He noticed Chandler at once but went straight inside without acknowledging him.

Chandler got up and followed. He crossed the garth and entered the church just as the priest was making his entrance with his acolytes swinging their censers and filling the air with smoke. Pearce was crouched over near the back wall with his head in his hands.

Chandler approached and knelt down beside him. 'Any change?'

Pearce didn't lift his head. 'No sign of him. He's lying low – or changed the colour of his capuchon.'

'That's a possibility. But Maud said he was quite distinctive looking, fair-haired, athletic, smiling.'

'Quite a few fellows about town would fit that description.'

Chandler glanced at Pearce. He would fit it himself, if it came to it. 'Any ideas about what to do next?'

'Brick wall.' He shrugged. 'It's not right.'

'What will happen if I show my face at Willoughby's?'

'Nothing much. Why should it? He sits in his solar drinking ale.'

'Is that usual?'

He paused. 'I admit, he usually finds something useful to do. It's not like him to sit about, idle.'

'Grieving?'

Pearce gave a wry smile. 'I doubt it. After these months? You know where he bought her, don't you?'

'Bought?'

'How else would he find a suitable wife? He went to the summoner who runs a neat little line in the procurement of girls. For a price, of course.' He paused then added with some cynicism, 'I can't see love emerging from a transaction like that, can you? No love, no grief.'

Chandler considered this. 'It had not entered my head that he would have to use a marriage-broker. I would have thought his status –' by which he meant wealth – 'would have ensured a plentiful choice of willing young women to—'

'He would deem it a waste of time to organize it himself, like being his own drover, or his own housekeeper, or his own cook! He went to the summoner for everything in that line.'

'Wealthy men,' murmured Chandler, and left it at that. He got up and facing east crossed himself like everyone else then made to go. 'I may stay at St Werbergh's for a day or two and then, perhaps you might mention that you've seen me in the town and if Willoughby is so inclined he may invite me as his guest once again. But by then,' he added, pulling up his hood, 'we may not need such a devious way to help me establish my reason for returning to the scene of the crime. Our enquiries may have yielded the result we want.'

After hearing what Pearce had just said, his mind was teeming with fresh suppositions.

Leaving him in a disgruntled frame of mind he set himself to wait in patience for a lead to emerge.

Pearce's words could be seen to lay Evelyn's murder on

Willoughby himself. He might, thought Chandler, want rid of someone who had proved unfaithful, making him a laughing stock, as horned and pathetic as any old man with a pretty young wife. He couldn't see Willoughby liking that idea at all.

Another thing Pearce seemed to suggest was that Willoughby wouldn't commit such an act himself, just as he would not dream of doing his own household chores. He would employ someone else to do the job for him.

It made sense.

It made even more sense when he remembered how Willoughby had hinted that Evelyn was passing on information about him to the sheriff, hence his performance of outraged innocence when they went to see him.

This fellow Maud had been attacked by certainly existed. Who was he? And the question remained, could he be in the pay of Willoughby himself?

Next day he took a walk along the riverbank by way of the cabbage strips and the line of cottages where he had spent a few brief hours of the night last summer.

In daylight he was unsure which one had afforded him shelter. They all looked much the same. An old fellow was mending the sole of a boot on a last fixed to a small trestle outside his door. He lifted his head when Chandler appeared and they exchanged a few words.

Chandler's previous visit lay unacknowledged between them. The rest of the cottages looked empty.

He walked on along the narrow path snaking through the long grass as far as the boundary with Willoughby's property, then looked about. The jetty lay just ahead. A boat was tied to one of the struts. He recalled the fellow he had seen early on sculling away downriver. Then he had not thought anything about him. It was just a man in a boat. Now he wondered if it had been the same fellow who was proving to be so elusive and only glimpsed now and then about the place. It might, he thought, be a good idea to find out more, like where he might have been heading downriver.

According to Maud, her abductor intended to dump her body out at sea. But she had been terrified and it was the worst she could imagine. Maybe it was the first thing she blurted out of fear.

What if, instead, he had a house on the riverbank? What if he was going to take her there? He didn't speculate on the reason for doing such a thing at this point but merely wondered what sort of place would such a fellow choose as his dwelling place. All supposition, he told himself. The fellow in the boat might be someone else entirely, a guest at the wake, going about his own lawful business.

At least he could take a look.

He found the old boatman in his shack, sleeping his life away and considered borrowing his replaced boat before he woke up. Then he imagined the hue and cry that would follow when he found it missing. He gave a cough.

The man opened one eye. He had probably known he was there all along.

Rooting around in his scrip Chandler drew out a few coins. 'Your boat? You know me.'

'I do.' He took the coins and stuffed them in a secret place inside the sleeve of his woollen cotte. 'You know where it is.' He closed his eyes again.

Chandler was about to walk on. Before doing so he asked, 'So who else borrows it?'

The old fellow feigned sleep, thought better of it, and opened one eye again. 'Who wants to know?'

'I do.'

'Like a fly round shit,' he murmured then thought better of his insult and sat up. 'No disrespect, young fellow, but folks nowadays is always wanting to borrow my boat. I say, do so, don't hole her, and bring her back.'

'I would do that without the added insult,' Chandler remarked.

'You'll see who borrows it if you go on far enough.'

Chandler walked away.

As he plied the oars the winter sun came out. A sense of peace at being on the water descended on him. The river here was wide and running languidly between banks of reeds and willows. The boat needed little effort to keep it drifting downstream.

Houses on both sides were sparse the further he went. The opposite bank was so distant the houses hardly seemed to matter. To get to them would mean crossing the strong mid-river current and then making a strenuous effort to reach the far bank. He decided it made more sense to keep to the town side of the water and row with the flow.

Beyond the walls and the watergate were meadows, sheep as expected, horses, a small cottage or two, nothing to attract his attention, and then drifting round a bend he saw a splendid house of grey stone with what looked like a parterre and a wall lower down to keep out the cattle.

Reeds grew thickly in the shallows at the foot of the bank and he drove the prow of the boat into them being at once partly concealed while he looked about.

It was quite a place, a merchant's house, maybe, owned by someone who liked fancy buildings, who had enough money to indulge his whim, a town elder, maybe, close enough to keep an eye on city matters but distant enough to preserve his own privacy.

There was no one around to ask.

He pushed the boat off and continued downriver but it was open country here and he saw only a few wildfowlers going about their business and in the distance the misty line that must be the gateway to the open sea. Eventually he turned with the tide to make his return easier and to give him another look at the grey house with its ornamental garden.

This time he was in luck. A couple of fellows were preparing to drop a line into the water. The one with the rod glanced up as the boat drifted up. Neither of them, observed Chandler, wore a red capuchon.

'Hail!' he called. 'Any luck?'

As with the brotherhood of fishermen a common language exists and although fishing bored him except when it was done out of necessity as on the journey back from Wales, he humoured the two fellows and slowed the boat enough to talk awhile across the water.

They were affable types, not, he would have laid a wager on it, the sort of men to abduct young maids from their neighbour's household nor, for that matter, push their neighbour's wives off roofs.

'We're poaching,' the man with the rod announced with a chuckle in the manner of one who would as soon have a poacher up before the justices as be on the wrong side of the law himself. 'Somebody's got to keep the fish down and it might as well be us!'

'It's a grand house,' Chandler remarked, nodding towards the edifice displayed at the top of the bank. 'Who's the lucky owner?'

'Not me, alas, my rights only extend as far as the fish. It belongs to Lord Oliphant,' the fisherman announced, a name that meant nothing to Chandler. 'Away on the road to Jerusalem with his lady wife this past year.'

'So who's in charge now?'

'Only his no-good grandson and yon steward Madeley. You a stranger then?'

'Just passing through,' replied Chandler. He took up the oars again. Plenty of taverns around where he might find out more without arousing suspicion. 'Good fishing to you, sirs!'

The man waved a nonchalant hand and his servant, as Chandler now guessed the second man to be, also lifted a hand and then stood watching him through narrowed eyes as he rowed away.

He left the guest precinct after making sure Aethelstan was comfortable for the evening with a group of servants about his own age in the retinue of another guest and made his way past the porter and on to the main thoroughfare.

A few streets away was what he considered to be the edge of the stews with a row of rowdy taverns vying for custom along the narrow street. He chose the most likely one and went inside.

It was the usual sort of place and before long he found he was in conversation with a cordwainer and his mates. They confirmed his guess about the proximity of the stews and even suggested he come with them when they'd supped up and made their move for the evening. The mugs were filled to foaming again.

Eventually an opportunity came to ask about the grand house downriver. He learned all about the merchant on pilgrimage with his wife and then he heard about the grandson and his steward, Madeley.

He repeated what he'd been told. 'I hear he's got a reputation of some kind.'

They roared with laughter. 'Get on the wrong side of him, brother, and you'll be walking on sticks for the rest of your life!'

'That is – if you're walking at all!' another quipped.

'So what's his trade?'

'Flesh,' said one succinctly.

'Male or female?'

'Any kind you like. Human or animal.'

'Is this the fellow you're giving your hard-earned cash to this eve?' Chandler adopted an appropriate expression.

'He deals in the best. It's a monopoly. Supplies all the wealthy merchants with whatever their hearts' desire.'

'Heart, you call it?' His crony interrupted with a gesture to indicate his breeches. 'I thought the heart was a bit higher than that.'

They all roared as at a great witticism and Chandler tentatively joined in.

He wanted to see this master of the stews as he could not ask outright what he looked like. Could he be Maud's abductor?

He didn't get much time to think about it because as if on cue the group rose to their feet and with one on each side to make sure he didn't renege they hauled him off with them down a network of narrow alleys lined with girls of all ages and prices until they came to a house with an overhanging upper floor, its windows open, and girls calling down to the cordwainer and his friends by name, chiding them for being late and for other failings too lewd to recount. They were delighted to find a new customer with them and promised all kinds of favours for being so considerate.

Chandler was speedily invited into a small chamber not much bigger than a cupboard but wide enough for a bed piled with hay-filled cushions where his rope girdle was quickly unknotted and his robes slipped from him with professional efficiency by a pleasant-looking dark-haired woman who would have looked at home in a baker's shop.

Fearing that she would be equally brisk when she thought she'd given him his money's worth he decided that as there were questions to ask they had better be asked now so, gasping somewhat he sank on to the haysack without resistance and cringing at himself asked, 'So how did you get into this game, a pretty girl like you—'

His words broke off as he gave a shuddering gasp that shook him from head to foot and for a moment he forgot where he was and could only fight for breath and the great languor that for a moment felled him.

'You monastics,' she said kindly, 'I could tell the minute I clapped eyes on you what you were . . . you go too long and then it's more pain than pleasure. Am I right?'

He nodded. 'Don't you get sick of us?'

'I like variety and that's what you get in this game.' She settled beside him, her hands fluttering over him. 'Great body,' she murmured. 'I might ask you the same,' she eventually continued. 'All that praying and abstinence. It's no good for a man. Where does it get you?'

'Even so,' he managed, avoiding the conventional answer, 'don't we do some good?'

Surprised he could still speak he tried to get back on track and remember what it was he wanted to know, but she replied, 'One or two of you might do some good, but not the high-ups. In it for the money no different to us, pretending they're so great.'

'So you have a good master?'

'He keeps me as I like to be kept, with only a fair sum going to him for looking after me and the hire of the chamber. I'm saving for a house outside the walls so I can live like a lady in my old age.'

'I saw a house today,' he managed to mutter. 'Downriver. Almost a palace.'

'That's his,' she confirmed, off-hand, getting off the bed and reaching for something to wipe herself with. Her eyes narrowed suspiciously. 'Did you know that when you came here?'

'No idea. I'm surprised.' he lied. 'Some lads in the Star dragged me along. They thought like you, too long without. Abstinence the great crime.'

'You,' she said, flicking a cloth at him. 'You're all the same. Do you want another go?'

It was clear she had no inclination to tell him more about her master. Not even his name.

He would find out later.

EIGHTEEN

The summoner

I t was quite a bit later when they all fell out of the brothel
into the street. He had never had a night like this since –
when? – since his rebellious boyhood before he decided to
take life seriously.

Feeling something was expected of him before they left, he
raised both arms as if about to offer a benediction from his Order.
'God save the man whose house this is,' he declaimed, slurring
his words a bit for effect.

A couple of thickset men in hauberks were lounging on
either side of the doorway and one of them said, 'I'll convey
your compliments to the master, brother. Bring the rest of your
cloister men with you next time. We can accommodate all types
here. Freedom hall! We can even save Emma for you when you
wish to come back. Make it soon.'

Everyone was in a good mood, pushing and joshing each other
but he had to know so he asked straight out, 'Who is he then,
our noble benefactor? All hail to him!'

'Get along, you drunk. It's Sir Edwin Oliphant as you must
know unless you live under a stone.'

'He lives in a cloister,' one of the gang jibed, 'same thing!'

Chandler decided it was time to reel off down the street before
any other questions could come to mind. And he would need
time before he would be able to present himself with any cred-
ibility at the gatehouse of the Benedictines.

It was shortly after making his farewells to his new friends
with the endless back-slapping and rash promises of enduring
friendship it entailed that he became aware of someone following
him down the alley pointed out by his new friends as leading straight
back to the abbey gates.

A footpad was his immediate thought. Noticing a drunk,
thinking, easy game.

He slowed his pace and slipped his knife from its sheath under his sleeve to use as a threat.

The footsteps caught up with him. He half-turned.

The grinning face of the summoner loomed at shoulder level, somehow more unnerving because of that than if it had been someone on a level with his own height.

'I never forget a face.' The summoner peered up from beneath his hood. 'What a delight it is to have you back with us, brother. I'm glad to see my warning was not taken to heart. I feel it my duty to warn off anyone I believe is here only to further their own interests rather than mine own. But I see you enjoy the delights of our city as much as any other man.'

He appeared to be unarmed but, puzzled why he should have been accosted, Chandler kept his hand on the concealed knife and gave him a stare. 'Do I know you, master?'

'But I'm the summoner here, brother. I believe you were the fellow way back in the summer who was asking questions about poor, dear Mistress Willoughby and her unfortunate accident?'

'Was I?' Marvelling at the lies he had told this evening Chandler could only screw up his face in puzzlement as if he had no idea what this was all about.

'We're a small community here,' the fellow explained. 'We all know each other. We were children together. We have our hierarchy. We have our roles. I am but a cog in a larger machine. What you must understand is that we have each other's interests at heart. And anyone who disturbs our arrangements is immediately punished. I hope you understand how things are?'

'It seems like a well-regulated procedure, master. I trust I have not transgressed in any way? The lady who gave me such entertainment tonight was paid to her satisfaction, I believe?'

'Indeed she was, and most content, I hear.'

'That pleases me greatly. I certainly have no complaints.'

'And are you merely passing through again?' He quirked an eyebrow, visible in a grotesque play of light from the flames within a cresset fixed to a nearby wall.

'Indeed,' replied Chandler. 'On my way elsewhere.'

'To . . .?'

'Only to a distant abbey somewhere up in the midlands, a place of little fame.'

'Then I trust you will have fair weather for the journey. As the snows are not predicted until St Lucy's Day it should be easy travelling to this abbey if you leave soon.'

'That's good to hear.'

'You know who she is, I'm sure. St Lucy? Terrible punishment she suffered. Blinded for her beliefs. Such a tragedy, but then, that's why we revere her as a saint, isn't that so? She saw too much and suffered the consequences. I bid you good night, brother, and fair weather for your departure. Try not to delay. Remember the snow.'

As swiftly as a shadow he went to join the other shadows in what, Chandler now fully understood, was a city of shadows.

'You were out late last night, brother Rod. The porter came to me to find out if I'd seen you and whether he could lock the gates.'

'I was busy.'

Aethelstan, not one to be fobbed off with ambiguities, smiled knowingly across the refectory table strewn with pots and jugs and platters of fresh bread.

'I'm going to see Master Pearce now.' Chandler frowned to deter any questions. 'Want to come with me?'

He needed no second asking. 'I hope this place belonging to your Master Willoughby lives up to expectations,' was all he said as he scrambled to finish his pottage and hand the scraped bowl to the serving man.

'I've something to do first. Won't take long. Wait here.' Chandler got up and went out.

As he crossed over to the church he had a glimpse of the busy street outside the gates. That glimpse showed a city looking innocent in the innocence of daylight. How could anyone arriving from the countryside and walking its streets believe that underneath its shining surface levels of corruption seethed?

It was the devil's cauldron, thought Chandler, and soon it would boil over. Henry's appointed sheriff might believe he ran the place but in fact, as he must soon surely learn, it was down to the Church in the shape of the summoner and his allies, among them the grandson from the big house, making money from transgressors while his grandfather purged his soul by dint of an expensive and time-consuming pilgrimage.

He had no doubt now that a red capuchon was worn by a fair-haired handsome and privileged young fellow living in the house downriver. He would have been drawn to Willoughby by the wool merchant's useful wealth with the allure of his young wife as a bonus. What their argument had been about – for sure there must have been a difference of opinion – was something he might never find out but he vowed he would nail the murderer by any means he could. And for sure, Pearce was aware of the name of his powerful rival. The town was too small to hold on to such a secret for long.

Still Lollard as he was, Chandler took himself into the church and sought a confessor in order to absolve himself of his previous night of sin. He did not exempt himself from the corruption of the world and the teachings of his youth were strong when it came to hope of salvation.

When he reappeared and beckoned to Aethelstan who was sitting on a wall in the garth waiting for him, they left for Willoughby's at once, the boy pointedly silent.

They found Pearce along with half a dozen other men in the large wool barn. It was being thoroughly swept out by Willoughby's servants and Pearce himself sat on a bale of hay near the door, picking at his fingernails.

Chandler did not return his greeting.

He simply said, 'I brought the boy with me. He's come from Wales. He's on his way back home to London. The rumour this morning is that Henry is billeting five hundred troops here.' His expression did not soften. He sat down beside Pearce, forcing him to move over to sit uncomfortably on the edge.

'You know why I've come, I suppose?'

Pearce lifted his head. 'Want to tell me or leave me to guess?'

'It's up to you.'

'All right, I can see you're aggrieved. I should have said more. You don't know what it's like. I could get my throat slit any time in some back alley if I step out of line. Do you blame me for treading carefully? Do you blame me for holding back his name . . . that is what this is about, I suppose?'

'I don't blame you. In fact I understand you very well. I would

want to tread carefully knowing what you know and how
dangerous my knowledge could be to someone. On the other
hand,' he continued, 'once I'd set out on the trail of the man
who had most likely murdered my lover I would want to make
sure I found him and made him pay.'

Pearce sank his head even lower and glared fiercely at his
hands, the palms open, as if he could read his fate in them.

Chandler continued, 'When did you first guess who this fellow
in the capuchon was, or have you always known?'

'I suspected almost straightaway,' he muttered. 'I prayed it
wasn't. I tried to convince myself that it was Willoughby. But I
knew . . . We all knew. Even little Maud knew. She was terrified
out of her wits by it. At least she's safe now . . . He's wealthy
enough from his grandsire's money to run everything the way
he wants it . . . Even the new sheriff eats out of his hand . . . I
didn't know what to do about him . . . he's untouchable . . .'

After a further struggle he gave Chandler a stricken glance
and asked angrily, 'What am I supposed to do? Take a knife to
him myself and risk his henchmen's vengeance? . . . I don't have
that sort of courage.'

'I know. It would be foolish. You're no sotwit, Pearce. I know.'

'How did you find out?'

'A small town. The summoner's vanity. Deduction. There could
only be one man powerful enough.'

He saw Pearce jerk his head up in a fit of nerves to ask, 'You
think I'm doing the right thing, lying low – allowing him to get
away with it?'

'What would change the situation?'

'If I could get him alone and if he didn't know who I was . . .
I'd give him something to think about. What he deserves.'

Chandler considered this. 'Rough justice,' he murmured.

Pearce leaned closer. 'How did you really find out?'

'I've told you – and you've just confirmed what I suspected,
that's all. But tell me, this grandsire who owns the house—'

'He knows nothing. A man on the level as they say. A donor
of alms. A supporter of the destitute. A founder of houses where
the afflicted can find refuge. I've nothing to say against the man.'

'Can justice not be left to him when he returns?'

'When he returns everything will have changed from the way it was when he left. King Richard was on the throne then, now it's his cousin. Nothing is the same. He will learn how different it is if he tries to cut through the new alliances that have sprung up. As he's an old man, waiting to enter the gates of heaven, he'll no doubt leave things as they are and spend his remaining time on earth looking at the river and praising God for the gift of another new day.'

'Meanwhile . . .?'

'Meanwhile she is dead. Forever.'

Chandler could only punch him gently on the shoulder. 'Very well. I'll get him for you.'

As he walked away, with Aethelstan trailing thoughtfully after him, he wondered what it was that had put Evelyn on the wrong side of the grandson. What had he wanted from her? If what Pearce said was true, she had been obtained for Willoughby and presumably the transaction had been concluded. Was she placed in the merchant's house to inform on him – and had she failed to keep her side of the arrangement? He wondered if Pearce knew what it was this Oliphant had wanted, or if, indeed, it mattered now.

He made himself known at the door and Willoughby came out of his solar and greeted him with amazement and a warmth that in anyone not so adept at putting on a show, would have convinced Chandler of his sincerity at once. He had seen his performance in the sheriff's office, however, and covered his scepticism with an equal show of his own.

Then he introduced Aethelstan and the three of them stood in the winter sunshine with their cloaks flapping in a light breeze like three good fellows with nothing happening beneath the surface of their banter that a child could not have smiled at.

When it was time to broach his question Chandler first murmured condolences for Willoughby's continuing grief, and reminded him that time is the great healer and all things pass and to brace up and think of the future as he knew he would.

'If you mean shall I look for another wife the answer's no. Not now I've got another little chap to consider. My thoughts and love are all stolen by my new grandson.' He chuckled. 'She insists on calling him Edward after being talked out of Dickon for safety's sake. A compromise as I'm sure you realize.'

'Very wise. And how is the sheriff these days?'

'Consolidating his power. He is not the master he thinks he is. Henry is about to impose a garrison here that will not be obedient to any law but their own.'

'Take care.'

'I do. I will. Easier now than . . .' He shrugged and showed he knew he said too much.

'And your housekeeper?'

'She's well.'

They exchanged glances.

Chandler could not tell whether Willoughby furthered her game or merely suffered it. Come to that, he didn't know for sure that what he suspected about her was true. He had already noticed several new faces among the young maids about the place and wondered when they would be moving on to a different kind of work. And how much of this Willoughby knew.

He judged that like Maud the girls were brought in from the country. Unlike Maud who had been saved from drowning and a life in the stews, they might not be so fortunate in their future occupation.

Willoughby, he thought, the web you weave, God save your soul.

Aethelstan ran alongside him as he strode along the high street towards the tavern quarter. 'Wait on, brother, why the hurry? Are you angry?'

'Of course I'm angry. Aren't you? Isn't that why you joined those bowmen and fought on the side of the Welsh?'

'It was the only right thing to do. You wouldn't expect me to fight for a king-killer, would you?' He kept pace, running at twice the speed to keep up with Chandler. 'You're still not telling me why you're angry now.'

'I'm angry because I'm helpless against evil and it offends me to the soul. But I'm also hurrying because I want to send a message to someone and then when the business is done I want us to get out of this benighted town and ride for a place of grace and sanctity called the abbey of Dieulacres. I'm tired of towns, aren't you?'

'Not of London, I'm not.'

Chandler made no reply. What was there to say?

NINETEEN

Blood for blood

At the Star he noticed that the same fellow was on the taps as on the previous night and went straight over to him. 'Good ale last night, master. That was very welcome. Will you send a message to Sir Oliphant's steward from me?'

'If it's not going to get me into trouble.'

'Surely not. A message to tell him that I have some information for him. To meet me in Willoughby's yard before I leave tomorrow morning, as close to Prime as he can make it?'

'You won't get him out that early.'

'Then the message must be sent at once to give him time.'

He grunted an assent as Chandler was leaving.

By the time he reached the door he heard him calling through into the back for one of the lads who haunted the place to stop fetching and carrying and run along to the sheriff's office where he'd likely find Master Madeley, Sir Oliphant's steward, and to give him a message he was going to drum word for word into his thick skull before he left. And to be quick about it.

While Chandler took part in the routine of the abbey and attended the canonical hours, Aethelstan spent the rest of the day at the butts and returned to St Werbergh's with a bulging pouch of small coins which he threw down beside Chandler with a smirk of satisfaction.

'Now I can pay my way like a man,' he remarked.

'Did I ask you to? You owe me nothing. I hope you got that by fair means?'

He patted his bow. 'The porter here thinks it's a sort of toy, more fool him. He nearly took it off me when we arrived, to keep it safe. "No weapons of any sort within the precinct," he said. I gave him a look. "Master porter," said I, "do you imagine this is a serious weapon of war?" He shrugged and muttered about new toys and how he couldn't keep up with them and then let me keep it.'

'You'll have to confess your lie at some time. Of course it's a weapon of war, especially the way you handle it.'

'I'll take that as another compliment, brother. I've had plenty today. I'll be getting above myself.'

'As if you're not already. But I mean it, Spindleshanks. You're back and forth to that confessor like a – what's that thing you were playing with the other day, that thing on a string?'

Aethelstan raised his eyebrows in disdain. 'Old man,' he said, 'I know what you mean but I may as well amass a few sins together and make one confession of it. And I certainly hope I can confess elsewhere? It'd be a disaster if he separated me from my bow when I'm most likely to need it.'

Chandler gave him a sharp glance. 'What makes you think that?'

'I'm no sot wit, brother. Don't you know that yet?'

'You're not getting involved. You're my responsibility and I forbid it.'

He might have been talking to the wall, he thought, when he saw Aethelstan eyeing up the meeting place early next morning with a professional look on his face.

'It's no good searching out a suitable perch here. I'm going to have him brought down to the riverbank. We're using the boatman's cabin.'

'He won't let you.'

'He already knows. He's gone off to see his sister and won't be back till tomorrow. That's where we'll do our talking.'

'Plenty of trees down there. I might go down now and have a look round then if that's your idea.'

A thick mist lay over everything. Hoar frost fringed each separate blade of grass. Winter was sinking to its nadir. The river seemed sluggish as if the water had grown heavier in the night.

When Pearce appeared he was muffled up with only his eyes visible. He was given his instructions and now Chandler repeated them.

Oliphant's steward turned up. To Chandler he said, 'Was it you sent that message?'

'It was, Master Madeley. Do you want to talk?'

'Not me. Him. He's waiting outside.'
'Fetch him.'
'I will.'

When Oliphant arrived as Chandler knew he would, he left his horse in the street with his steward and strolled across the yard as if he owned the place, as, in some ways, he did.

Fortunately Willoughby was still a-bed and only the gatekeeper saw him and, knowing him, let him straight through without asking questions. Two henchmen shadowed him. Chandler, standing in the doorway of the wool shed, came out and beckoned.

'I'm honoured you could attend me, my lord. Come, let's go inside out of this biting wind. It's enough to freeze the . . .' He checked himself in an exaggerated fashion and had the satisfaction of hearing Oliphant chuckle.

He was as Maud had described, fair-haired, handsome, full of animal energy and zest that, with no knowledge of his purpose in life, anyone might have found attractive.

'I hope this is worth getting me out of bed for, brother.'

'I hope so too. It's always good for the soul to get things settled.'

They went inside the barn. It was full of labourers, for some reason noisily busying themselves with a team of horses and Chandler appeared to be looking round without success for somewhere to seat his guest so they could talk.

Just then, however, the doors at the far end opened and a herd of cows lumbered inside, bellowing at their treatment, udders full and swinging, and obviously ready for milking and making loud complaint about it. They brought in the foetid stink typical of such beasts and Chandler curled his nose with exaggerated disdain.

He turned to his guest. 'Does this stench offend you, my lord?'

'I'm not used to getting so close to them.'

Chandler gave an audible sigh. 'This is no good. Let's saunter down to the riverside where the air is fresh. No doubt we'll be able to find some privacy there.'

The two henchmen were about to follow when Chandler suggested they might as well go across to the kitchen and sit in the warmth while they tried some of the new ale and, as if they

had agreed already, he turned, noticing out of the corners of his
eyes both men eager to accept his invitation. He led his guest
on to the path beside the shed and set off down the meadow at
once. After hesitating, Oliphant followed.

Leaving no time for conversation, Chandler headed straight to
the riverbank close to where the boatman's wooden cabin stood.
Shivering and pulling his cloak round himself he rapped on the
door and poked his head inside.

Turning to beckon to Oliphant, he said, 'I expect you know the
old fellow who keeps the boat? He's got a touch of the ague and
is sleeping off a potion I made up for him. He's as deaf as a post
and won't bother us even if he wakes up. At least he has a good
fire stoked. Come inside out of this blasted cold.'

Smiling, Oliphant did so.

As soon as he heard the door slammed shut he jerked round
in some surprise but Chandler, smiling affably, was leaning with
his back against it and put a warning finger to his lips, indicating
the sleeping boatman in his bunk beside the fire.

'Please, be seated. You can probably listen more carefully
sitting down.'

'Let's get to the point then,' replied Oliphant in irritation,
flinging himself on to a barrel obviously used as a bench and
stretching out his legs. 'What's this information you have? Is it
about Willoughby?'

'No, you misunderstand me. It is I who want information from
you.'

'Look here, I understood you had something to tell me about
Willoughby among others—'

'Willoughby? You mean our good wool merchant? I don't
know what he's got to do with it. He doesn't even know you're
here. In fact, to be honest, who does know you're here? Nobody.
Your two men? How much to buy their discretion?'

Oliphant sprang to his feet. He was wearing a sword. Chandler
felt that the elaborate scene about to be enacted could have been
avoided because he could easily have reached out and disarmed
the strutting young fellow with no trouble. It was a temptation to
resist. The plan had been laid. And there were other issues at stake.

'Perhaps I should tell you a little about myself and my need
for information? . . . Please, do sit down again. You probably

know that Lancaster employed me as an interrogator at the Tower? . . . You know, the Tower in London where King Richard so wisely handed over the crown? I worked for the Duke of Lancaster, old Gaunt, for many years – there are, sadly, always knaves working against great men as you'll know.'

Obviously Oliphant hadn't suspected the nature of Chandler's previous work because his pale eyelashes fluttered a couple of times before settling and allowing him to fix a glassy stare on a spot on the wall beside Chandler's head.

'Yes, we friars do get about a bit, I must admit,' Chandler continued. 'I can tell you something else about me that you may not know. It's this. I hate being lied to! In fact, I hate lies of any kind. They annoy me. Don't ask me why. They're the coinage with which the world pays its way. But it angers me. I don't like them. I feel they demean us. It makes us less than angels, don't you agree? And the thing is, I feel I've been lied to and really I've been told a pack of nonsense which I find most demeaning. So, sir, now's our chance to set the record straight, just to put my mind at rest and make me right with my lord?'

'I know nothing you'd want to know about.'

'I wouldn't be too sure. You see, what I want to know is, what led you to place Mistress Evelyn in Willoughby's household?'

'Is that all?' He began to smile. 'I won't lie about that. It's simple. You can work it out yourself. I know a fellow in the town, the summoner as it happens, who has a line in finding girls. Willoughby wanted a wife. I procured one for him.'

'And that's it?'

Oliphant nodded.

'You see, I'm not sure that is all.' Chandler frowned, looking perplexed. 'I think you might have expected something more than a single payment, you know? It struck me that you might be hoping she would be able to supply some bits of gossip about Willoughby, about his allegiance, for instance, about who came to the house, what they talked about, you know . . . that sort of thing?'

'And you were with Lancaster, old John of Gaunt, were you? All right. I understand what you're getting at.'

As if not to be deflected Chandler said, 'Even gossip can mean a lot in the right quarters –' he rubbed his thumb over his palm – 'or it can mean nothing at all.'

'That might have come into it. Yes, she liked gossip. It's always useful to know what people are getting up to. Especially in these times. So what?'

'And did she deliver?'

'Not as much as I'd hoped,' he rashly admitted.

'Ah . . .' Chandler considered this and eventually he asked, 'And how did that make you feel?'

'I didn't feel I was getting my money's worth, if that's what you want to know. No, to be honest I didn't feel I was, I felt, this isn't playing the game, is it? She's making a mockery of me.'

'We have a lot in common, we two, don't we? I'm angered by lies. You're angered by not getting your money's worth. Two angry men.'

'Look here, would you mind moving away from that door and letting me out? It's hot in here with that fire roaring in the grate. And look, I don't like having my time wasted either. I'm a busy man. If you've got something to offer, make your pitch. If you're connected to Evelyn in some way then tell me what you want. You must have known what she was up to. Now, if you don't mind, I'd like you to move out of my way!'

'In a moment. Be patient with me. Now, the young wife failed to fulfil her part of the bargain. You felt that she was not telling you all you wanted to know. It made you angry. You felt short-changed. So – you came to visit her at the house when you knew Willoughby was away seeing to his wool. You came into the house, knowing your way around after previous visits, and you went up to find her, knowing, perhaps, that she would be in her little haven on the roof. By the way, it has some wonderful views over the town, doesn't it?'

'What are you getting at?'

'I simply want to know what happened next. I can't work it out. Have patience with me. You came here to the house when her husband was away in order to have it out with her? Is that it?'

'I did. So?'

'You went up to the roof, calling, Lyn, I believe that's your pet name for her? And you stepped out on to the roof and—?'

'And nothing.'

'Come, come, don't try my patience. What did you say?'

'What do you think I said?'

'I have no idea. You tell me. You stepped out and—'

'I remonstrated with her.'

'And what was the lady's response?'

'She was belligerent. She said she'd had enough.'

'Enough of spying on her husband? . . . Yes, it can be tedious sometimes. Trying to find out what other people are intent on hiding from us. It's not right. It's enough to try the patience of a saint – and of course, none of us are saints, are we? So?'

'So I told her that she would have to deliver or—'

'Or . . .?'

'Or she'd be in trouble.'

'I expect that displeased her?'

'She came at me!'

'What, that young woman, she came at you?' Chandler looked askance. 'Was she armed?'

'It was beyond a joke. She had a pair of little sewing scissors in her hand. I took hold of her by the wrist to make her drop them. I gave her a good shaking and reminded her who I was—'

'Slapped her about a bit, maybe?'

'Not much. Not as much as she deserved.'

The old boatman in his corner gave a groan and turned over but Oliphant was not interested. He moved closer to Chandler. 'I don't know what this has to do with you. Why don't you mind your own business? But now you know what happened will you step aside and let me out before I have to—'

'Draw your sword?' Chandler asked mildly. 'We wouldn't want that, would we? But first tell me again, you told her she would have to deliver, and she told you she didn't want to, and then you shook her, and then . . .?' When he didn't answer Chandler said, 'Let me guess. You gave her a good push, she slipped, lost her footing and – over she went!' He clapped his hands once. 'It was as quick as that?'

'That's about it. It was the woman's own fault. Now let me go.' He put one hand ostentatiously on the hilt of his sword.

'Certainly.' Chandler stepped to one side.

Slightly surprised that his bluster had paid off so easily, Oliphant went to the door and Chandler opened it for him. He stepped outside.

At once the sound of a large bird whizzing overhead was

followed by a thump as something hit the side of the cabin and Oliphant gave a shout.

He tried to retreat and get back inside the cabin for safety but for some reason could not move. Something held him fixed to the timber.

Chandler silently thanked Jack Underwood for giving him the idea.

Oliphant glanced down and saw it was an arrow pinning him to the cabin wall and when he glanced wildly round to discover its source another one thumped into his other arm, pinning him on both sides with his arms out like a pair of wings.

The old boatman threw off his covers and strode to the door. When he saw his adversary pinned by both arms to the timbers his eyes above the cloth that covered his lower face were dancing with malicious joy.

Aethelstan jumped down from the tree, exclaiming, 'Easier than shooting fish in a barrel!'

The silent fellow, Ham, who had escorted Chandler to the abbey of Dieulacres through the woods with Pearce appeared from the bushes and strode over to the cabin.

Oliphant was unable to resist when Ham drew the sword from his scabbard and began to inspect the blade.

Chandler said to Pearce, 'Did you hear enough?'

'I'll get him to tell us it all again. One more time. We'd like that.'

'He's all yours.'

As he and Aethelstan began to leave the scene they heard Pearce in an official voice saying, 'As constables of the city of Chester, my lord, and as no one is above the law, we have reason to believe by your own confession just heard that you were instrumental in causing the death of young Mistress Willoughby by pushing her from her roof garden to her death at the premises of . . .'

As his voice faded all that could be heard was the flowing waters of the river as it swirled by at the foot of the embankment.

TWENTY

Resolution

'I thought you thought it was Master Willoughby who pushed his wife off the roof because she was too free with her favours,' Aethelstan remarked when they were back at St Werbergh's.

'It just shows how wrong you can be.' Chandler relented. 'Actually you're right. For a very short time I thought so too. It was only the way other things began to stack up that made me think otherwise. For one thing, everyone seemed to have a good word for Willoughby. He had the reputation for fairness in his business dealings and I thought that would be reflected in his personal life too. He could act as well as any mummer, sure enough, it was nearly his downfall. You should have seen him performing for the new sheriff, but that was to save his skin. He wasn't acting when he spoke to his daughter and his son-in-law. And more recently when he mentioned his little grandson, Edward, he was as glowing with virtue as you were after you unburdened yourself to your confessor.'

'No need to mention that,' muttered Aethelstan.

'Now things are settled here, we shall leave. I don't want to be around when Henry's troops come surging in. Tomorrow, we go to Dieulacres! We'll find out how young Dickon and Maud are faring after escaping this Devil's cauldron, and if all's well with them, we'll be straight back on the road to London. Suit you?'

'You bet. I'll be glad to get back to civilization.' He gave Chandler a sudden worried glance. 'But what about you? Won't they still be on the lookout for you? Aren't you still outlawed?'

Chandler nodded. 'I'm not going to stay long. There are one or two things I need to check out first. Then it'll be the open road for me.'

'You don't look pleased about it.'

*   *   *

Before they left next morning Pearce came to him. 'When you reach the woods you'll have safe passage. They've been told you're going through. They'll look out for you. Have no fear.' He nearly smiled. 'Willoughby pays them well.'

For all his swagger Aethelstan was wary of Pearce but even so he chipped in, 'He won't fear anything now he's got a bowman like me beside him.' After he left he asked, 'Is he really a constable?'

'I know nothing about that. We ask no questions about Master Pearce.'

'And what did he mean about Willoughby and them outlaws? . . . Does he really control them? . . . And why the gift of two horses?'

Chandler had been amazed when Pearce handed them over with a message from Willoughby to 'travel safely'.

He also handed him a letter. Chandler opened it and read:

> Horses excess to needs. I am to be a corrodion at St Werbergh's in order to spend more time with my grandson. My wool business is being sold. I am now a happy man and content in my dotage.

Dotage was a joke, but this was the safest choice Willoughby could make in the circumstances. Chandler was pleased for him and no doubt his business with the homeless folk living in the woods would continue to thrive.

His contentment must have been emphasized by the scandal that broke just as the two smartly mounted travellers were leaving. It caused some delay at the city gates.

What had happened concerned a body found in the river at first light that very morning. Rumoured to be a man, although it was said to be difficult to be sure as the body was so disfigured, the body was garbed in torn but costly garments but could not be identified by guesswork alone as it was so mutilated, either by prolonged immersion in a river full of predatory fish or by human beings in some macabre ritual before being thrown into the water. Black magic was mentioned but could not be confirmed.

By the time the corpse was being carried through the streets to the coroner's house to have some facts established, the disappearance of young Sir Edwin Oliphant had been noted, but by the time the gates were finally opened the town gossips had moved on to the upheaval caused by Henry's troops who were already pouring in from Worcester. Their insatiable appetite for food, ale and women which they expected the townsfolk to supply without stint was already leading to trouble.

The two horsemen managed to leave before any violence broke out and by the time the full five hundred fighting men had made camp and sorted their priorities, Chandler and his esquire were long gone on the road to Dieulacres.

After shaking the dust of the city from their feet with mutual relief they made good time along the drove road. They experienced no threat from any of the outlaws said to swarm the woods since Henry had cried havoc on Cheshire. Riding hastily across a land subsequently depleted of crops and with little sign of the inhabitants who had once lived here in peace, they were mostly silent. Even Aethelstan could find nothing to say to lighten their mood.

And then, at long last, the abbey lay like a golden city of spires and pent roofs before their gaze.

The first thing Chandler did after introducing Aethelstan to the guest master was to go in to see the abbot and already taking from his glove the letter Glyn Dwr had entrusted to him.

He dropped to one knee to make his obeisance and with a sense of relief handed it over. Now his work was done.

When Brother Senlac stepped into the light he was smiling. 'And in exchange, brother, one for you. It arrived some time ago. I trust the matter is not urgent?'

In a corner of the cloister Chandler slit open Archer's letter in some haste and scanned it.

News from London: all was well, Archer himself was well, Brother Martin was well and the master of all plants, Brother Daniel, was well, even Adam Pinkhurst, now a member of the Guild of Stationers, was well too.

That was all. It ended abruptly in Chandler's opinion.

Frowning, he folded the letter and was about to place it in his scrip when on the back in very small writing he saw a paragraph he had missed. It was partly scrubbed out. The sort of lax manner untypical of Archer the ex-coroner.

He scanned it eagerly. But it only concerned Galfrido. He was well too.

Stoically he gazed along the empty cloister for some time. That was that then.

They were all well. Mostly all. He was glad about Galfrido.

He took out the scrubbed vellum and held it up to the light and noticed that by holding it so, more lines that had been scrubbed out became legible.

Archer was glad Galfrido was safe but sorry he was so frail. 'Surprised he is back in England but understand his declared wish to see his son and daughter and their children.' The usual desires of an old man whose life is all but done. 'I cannot imagine him not writing his –' The word was erased. 'He will be happy to know Pinkhurst's copy is now safe.'

More words like the trail of an insect continued. 'Let's hope Thomas takes care to –' Chandler peered at what it said but the letters, almost scraped out, were again not entirely legible.

He could imagine Archer scraping at the vellum until the frail letters were only visible if you held it to the light and saying, That should tell him enough, if the losel has any sense in his head.

So Galfrido was staying with Thomas, was he? Is that what he meant? He knew Thomas held property somewhere near Warwick. He hoped it meant Chaucer had been safely smuggled back into England and was secretly living out his old age in his son's house. The rumour that he had been taken to Saltwood and died there after being tortured was maybe nothing but that, a rumour with no foundation in fact.

Feeling that he would have welcomed even more of Archer's penmanship but refusing to let her name enter his head, he sat for some time with his thoughts, then later went along to search out Aethelstan. They would leave as soon as they could.

He found him in the cloister answering Dickon's hundred questions about archery, how he could hit a target what – the child demanded – even when it was moving? And how did he know what feathers to use for fletching, and how did you fletch an arrow anyway, and which tree gave the best arrows and how did you fix the head, poisoned or not, to the shaft, and what about the bow, how big did you have to make it, did it have to be as tall as a man, what if you were really small? – and a million other questions besides.

A shadow passed over Aethelstan's face when he mentioned his instructors. 'Only the very best bowmen are engaged by Glyn Dwr's army,' he said with pride. 'Mine were a Cheshireman, a Londoner like me, and a famous Yorkshire bowman called Greenwood.'

Dickon wanted to know the names of the others and Chandler, seeing that all was as well as it could be, went in search of Maud. He found her giggling with some other girls of her own age in the laundry, making mock of the monks' undergarments.

They tried to straighten their faces when Chandler looked in but Maud ran to him. 'They say I can stay if I want to and my ma agrees. She couldn't believe her ears, she said, that one of her own flesh and blood should become a lady in an abbey.'

So all's well that ends well, thought Chandler. He went into the church, knelt, prayed, felt a little better, refused with an effort to let her name enter his head, then went in search of supper.

When Aethelstan appeared, hungry as usual, he asked, 'So were you looking for me earlier, Rod? What's that about?'

'I wanted you to know that I've completed my errand here and we can start back to London on the morrow.'

'I shall be sorry when you've gone.' Dickon slipped his hand in Chandler's but his words were aimed at Aethelstan. 'I hope you'll come back one day when I'm bigger and have had some practise at the butts and then I'll wager you a mountain of silver I can beat you.'

Aethelstan, fourteen himself, not much more than a child with similar fantasies which only his growing maturity made him keep to himself, smiled. 'I'm quaking already, Dickon.'

When the time came for them to leave and they could not put it off any longer Dickon held the arrow Aethelstan had specially fletched for him and stood a little way away from the group of girls who had turned up too.

They stood waving goodbye under the gatehouse arch for as long as the two horsemen were visible on the winding track leading to the king's highway, to the distant place called London where the kings and queens of England came from.

TWENTY-ONE

London

Westminster Yard did not seem to have changed. The only thing Chandler could remark on was Aethelstan himself.

He looked him up and down. 'You're taller by a head at least since you left here. Will your mother know it's you or try to throw you out?'

Aethelstan looked both worried and proud at the same time. 'If she throws me out I'm going straight back to Wales.'

Chandler considered the likelihood of Aethelstan being one child too many for the widow and said, 'I tell you what, I've got to sit here on this wall out of sight for a while to see who's who and all that. Also I'm old as you keep telling me and I need to rest awhile after that long ride. Why don't you go back to your mother's and if all's well, run back to let me know before I go on to Brother Daniel's in Hackney?'

Looking less anxious Aethelstan agreed and before he ran off he warned, 'Keep that scarf up over your face, Rod. I don't want to be running back for nothing.'

Nobody either came or went at Chaucer's house across the yard. He remembered last time when he had been able to come back without being recognized because of the beard and some women had told him that the scribe who sometimes worked there had left and gone to establish himself on Paternoster Row with the other scribes and newsmongers.

Trusting now to his disguise as a mendicant, the beard as thick as ever, he thought he might wend his way along the back streets as soon as Aethelstan returned. See Pinkhurst if he must. Then get out to Hackney.

He did not have long to wait for the beaming boy, transformed into a child for the moment, to come hurtling back into the yard. He held a large piece of pie in one hand with a bite taken out of it and another in his other hand, intact.

A string of children trailed along behind him like followers in the retinue of a saint.

Pushing the unbitten piece of pie into Chandler's hands he announced, 'She says she would never have believed it if she hadn't seen me with her own two eyes. And she says why don't you come and stay with us? She's making out well, busy as always, and something good cooking by the smell of it. You'll be more than welcome, she says.'

'Tell her I'm full of gratitude and that later, when I've finished my business in the City, I will certainly come and pay my respects in a day or two.'

'Brother Rod, I'm going to miss you.'

Aethelstan's face suddenly reddened and began to crumple and, feeling close to tears himself at the end of things, Chandler said brusquely, 'We're both tired and travel-worn and now you're home you can get yourself fed properly and have a proper night's sleep in a proper bed and do nothing except help your mother and . . .' His voice broke. 'Do nothing, that's what I'm telling you. Rest. That's an order. For a few days anyway. Get your strength back, Spindleshanks. Then decide if you want to go back to Wales. I'll come by and . . .' He waved one arm.

He was remembering the day when the lad had rowed him downriver, following Matilda to the safe house belonging to the Earl of Oxford with Chaucer's *Book of the Lion* lying like a viper in her basket before he had the courage to throw it far out into the river – and the lad had rowed her back to Westminster and they had all come together to break him out of the situation he had got himself into – and there was no way he could ever repay them.

And now it was over.

He snarled somewhat, 'I have to take care I'm not recognized so go on, curse you, you grinning ape. Get along. And thank your mother for the pie.' He waved what was left of it and turned away.

Then he was jolted to a stop. His breath left his body. There on the other side of the yard was Adam Pinkhurst, his fair hair clearly visible over the heads of the crowds that surged between them. Sitting astride his shoulders was a child with black hair and a very straight back as it sat aloft the scrivener's shoulders as if riding a horse. Pinkhurst was strolling out of Chaucer's old house at that very moment.

He stared. It was like a mirage.

Aethelstan must have noticed something had shocked him because he felt his grubby little paw grip his sleeve.

They stood watching for a long moment as Adam, oblivious to the fact that he was being observed, went up to an oyster-seller to buy a cone of scraps. The child, holding on to his hair, was trying to gee him up like a horse.

And then, even more shocking, there *she* was, walking alongside them, smiling . . .

There, he thought.

She.

Her long red-gold hair was mostly hidden in its coif, unchanged.

It could not be.

He felt Aethelstan shake his arm.

He heard the boy say, 'Are you just going to stand there like a post?'

He watched Adam hand up a little morsel to the child on his shoulders.

EPILOGUE

Aethelstan says something else and he is aware that he is following his glance and then he knows he notices Matilda too because without saying anything, he releases his grip. They both stand without speaking.

Eventually Aethelstan says, 'It *is* her, isn't it?'

Chandler comes to his senses, turns, and begins to walk away, randomly, without answering.

'Wait on, is that it? All this way . . .?' The boy runs after him. Chandler keeps on walking.

Aethelstan catches up with Chandler and hangs on to his sleeve. 'I cannot believe my eyes! Is that it? Are you just giving up?'

When he doesn't answer but keeps on walking the lad runs rapidly away across the yard with his entourage at his heels to where Matilda is reaching up to tickle the child and when he calls her name and she turns, he says something and gestures wildly across the yard with one arm to where Chandler is hurrying away.

She glances across.

Aethelstan says something else. He begins to drag her by the arm. She allows him to lead her like a sleepwalker towards Chandler who by now has reached the top of the steps leading down to the ferryboat.

Aethelstan shouts his private name for Chandler. 'Rod! . . . Rod!'

Chandler halts at the steps and turns his head. He stares, first at the boy then to the young woman. He cannot speak.

Aethelstan leaves them and runs back to the oyster-stall where the man with the child is loitering while Matilda drifts towards the quayside.

When she reaches a pace or two in front of Chandler they both stare at each other without speaking. They are unable to say anything because of the weight of time and events that have pulled them apart.

Matilda is the one to manage first. 'You look terrible!'

Chandler fingers the scar on his neck from the rope caused months earlier in the woods at Valle Crucis. He cannot say anything.

Matilda allows a tear to slide down her cheek.

Chandler reaches out with one hand. He does not touch her. 'I-I had to leave.'

'I know. I saw you. It would have been foolish to stay – with the fire and those armed guards . . . and all . . .'

Silence falls.

Chandler tries to begin again but cannot think how to start.

Matilda says, 'I know what's been happening. Archer told Adam about—'

Chandler forces himself to speak. 'You and Pinkhurst – are you . . .?'

'He comes over once a week to the Vintry where I'm living . . . in the master's old house . . . he takes little Rodric and me out in a boat when he has time . . . he loves the water – it sends him wild – Roddy I mean, not . . .' She looks flustered.

Chandler smiles tenderly. 'Roddy? . . . He looks like . . .' He shrugs, still struggling for words.

'He looks like you,' she says hurriedly. 'Imagine how people stare when he and Adam are out together! They can't work it out. Is this the father? Is this—' She laughs wildly and breaks off.

'Maybe I can – maybe I can show them he has a father of his own . . .?'

Her laughter turns to sudden tears. 'Would you ever want to?' A sob shakes through her. She doesn't seem to notice. She stares at him, ignoring her falling tears.

He nods.

'A quiet life?' She wipes her tears away with the back of one hand.

He nods again.

'What about St Serapion?'

He spreads his arms and shrugs.

She says, 'We'd have to leave London. Go to a place where they wouldn't know you . . .'

He smiles and reaches out with both arms and takes her into

an embrace. She does not resist. He holds her without moving, breathing in her essence, her being, her love. He presses his face into her hair as her coif slips back.

Placing one arm round her waist he turns her towards the group standing with the child, his son, with Roddy.

Aethelstan is smiling. His little entourage of brothers and sisters clap their hands, aware that something good is happening.

When Chandler is close enough, Roddy reaches out to him and hoots with joy at being lifted on to this other man's shoulders. He is as light as a feather and grips Chandler's thick, black hair in both fists.

Chandler reaches up to hold the boy safely with one hand while with the other he draws his love close beside him. He tells her that after all that has happened they will never ever be parted, not even for a day.

AUTHOR NOTE

Historical records are often confusing, and a single prejudiced remark can become enshrined as fact and repeated endlessly down the centuries until it seems true. When skulduggery is involved – as it might be when you decide to grab a crown you have no right to, and murder the anointed owner – these so-called 'facts' are often a deliberate attempt to conceal the truth.

To find out more about the real historical facts behind the events of this book, I can suggest nothing better than a book called *Who Murdered Chaucer?* by the late, great Terry Jones, a maverick medievalist as well as a much-loved Python, the title of which explains much.

Next, you might look at Christopher de Hamel's *Meetings with Remarkable Manuscripts*, where he mentions Dr Linne Mooney. She's a medieval handwriting expert who seems to have identified Adam Pinkhurst, the scribe who saved the only contemporary version of Chaucer's *Canterbury Tales*. This is the one now in the Welsh National Library. (How did it get there? It's a good question . . .)

Similarly, the chronicle of Dieulacres Abbey, one that escaped the censors, can be seen today at Gray's Inn. It is an alternative account of the facts around King Richard's final days and how so-called King Henry IV was so unpopular he had to impose his diabolical repression on England and Walesto maintain his grasp on the crown. You can read more on my website: www.cassandraclark.co.uk

Finally, a big thank you to my publishers, Severn House. I'd like to thank the team for all their support with the series, in particular Rachel Slatter, Tina Pietron and Shayna Holmes in editorial, Martin Brown in marketing, Michelle Duff in sales, Piers Tilbury and Jem Butcher in design.